MW01119183

Before her death in July 1997, beloved lesbian-feminist author Chris Anne Wolfe published two Amazon adventure novels – *Shadows of Aggar* and *Fires of Aggar*. But these two volumes are only the first half of the four-part Aggar cycle. Chris Anne also published two stand-alone novels – a time-bending romance, *Annabel and I,* and a retelling of Beauty and the Beast, *Roses and Thorns.*

As her publisher and friend, I was honored to inherit the manuscripts of Chris Anne's remaining novels, short stories, poetry and songs. These hand-written volumes include both remaining Aggar books – *Sands of Aggar* and *Oceans of Aggar* – and more than a dozen retold fairy tales, and original fantasy and contemporary novels. Only Blue Forge Press has the right to publish Chris Anne's work and we take great pride in that mission.

Jennifer DiMarco
Publisher
Blue Forge Press

TALISMANS & TEMPTATIONS

Aggar and Beyond

Chris Anne Wolfe

Blue Forge Press
Port Orchard * Washington

Talismans & Temptations: Aggar and Beyond
Copyright 2013 by Blue Forge Press

First Print Edition November 2013
Second Print Edition January 2023

ISBN 978-1-59092-936-0

Artwork by Skye Montague.

Also available as an ebook exclusively at Amazon.com.

All rights reserved, including the right to reproduce this book or portions thereof in any form whatsoever, except in the case of short excerpts for use in reviews of the book.

For information about film, reprint or other subsidiary rights, contact: blueforgegroup@gmail.com

This is a work of fiction. Names, characters, locations, and all other story elements are the product of the authors' imaginations and are used fictitiously. Any resemblance to actual persons, living or dead, or other elements in real life, is purely coincidental.

Blue Forge Press is the print division of the volunteer-run, federal 501 (c)3 nonprofit company, Blue Forge Group, founded in 1989 and dedicated to bringing light to the shadows and voice to the silence. We strive to empower storytellers across all walks of life with our four divisions: Blue Forge Press, Blue Forge Films, Blue Forge Gaming, and Blue Forge Records. Find out more at www.BlueForgeGroup.org

Blue Forge Press
7419 Ebbert Drive Southeast
Port Orchard, Washington 98367
blueforgepress@gmail.com
360-550-2071 ph.txt

Table of Contents

All sections open with introductions and reflections by Jennifer DiMarco

Dragon Dreams

Chris Anne and I met when I was touring with my dystopian novel, Escape to the Wind. *Before the book hit bestseller's lists and launched two national book tours, Chris Anne was one of the first to review it. While some readers might think that Chris Anne was only a fantasy writer, look closer. There are science fiction elements in almost all of Chris Anne's work. But more than anything, she disliked the idea of "genres". Of being stuck in any one box. She was always looking for a good story, first and foremost.*

That being said, she always admitted her guilty pleasure was Disney movies. She loved Disney villains, Disney heroes, and especially Disney princesses. When much of the lesbian community was still frowning at long hair and make up, Chris Anne was more than willing to admire a well-placed tiara. And it wasn't because Chris Anne herself was particularly feminine. She was slender, tall, and wore her silver hair short; in some ways, she looked a lot like Diana in "Shadows of Aggar." It was simply that Chris Anne loved all adventurous women – all shapes, sizes, and attitudes. And Disney princesses? From having their voices stolen by sea witches to proving a beast isn't a beast, those young ladies have some pretty grand adventures.

"Dragon Dreams" was the opening section for a novel Chris Anne left me the outline for. Her special twist on "Sleeping Beauty," tells the story from the point of view of Princess Charming – a dashing rogue named Camey. Instead of talking animals, as common in Disney films, Chris Anne's world is populated with talking dragons... and sleeping dragons, too.

Drenched, exhausted and near sick from the cloying marsh stench, Camey gratefully dragged herself out of the slimy water. Her small bundle of pack and sword fell with a thump, relief aching through her neck and sword arm. It seemed like a century since she'd waded into the muck with her gear balanced so precariously on top of her head. It was a miracle that the dogs hadn't gotten her before she'd made the swamps, and she knew all too well that it was thin luck that had kept her clear of quicksands, carnivores, and drowning. As it was, she doubted she was going to survive the night.

She shoved hard and managed to lever herself up as far as her hands and knees. Panting hard, she tried to get an idea of where she was. The peninsula was a tiny one, barely ten feet across. An arm's length from her, the tangled mass of jungles grew too thick to see how far it extended or if it connected to more solid ground somewhere. The weepy tree beside her seemed a lot like her, she decided... bedraggled and soggy. Only instead of wearing black silks and leathers, it was covered in knotted vines and orange, diseased moss.

Well, at least her dark copper hair wasn't quite that hideous shade of alarm... she would have attracted every predator in the area, if she'd been so brightly marked. And given the damp droopiness to that moss, she figured she should be glad, too, that her hair was short and curly enough to resist matting into such snarls.

Her breathing finally steadied some, and she sat back on her knees. It registered then that her feet and actually, the whole lower half of her wasn't wet at all, merely thoroughly chilled. Somewhat surprised, she looked down at those thick, skin-sleek leathers and then vaguely remembered they weren't really leather. The scaly hide had come from the dragon kill two years ago, and of course the things were waterproof – after all the fires, sword swipes and blizzards she'd endured in them, she should have guessed they'd be watertight, too.

Which meant she should've stripped down to her vest and trousers before wading into the mud. Nice thought, if she'd had the time!

She held out her arms in disgust, surveying the dripping mess that had once been a very fine, bloused shirt of silk. And then she screamed.

She was on her feet, spinning about frantically – pawing off the shirt and vest. Sweat broke and hands shook as the stuff peeled away.

She was covered with them!   Dark, squishy – abominable leeches!   Nothing like the tame little thing the physicians used... that she never let them use near her! Nothing tame or sane or – dear gods!

Camey felt her sanity slipping as the panic swelled. She gritted her teeth and stared upwards, blinking at tears and shaking her hands loose to keep from clawing at those nightmarish things. But it was almost too much. After the last week of hounding, after word of her father's death – after getting lost in this gods' forsaken place of all places... she almost broke.

But she didn't. Her fists clenched tight. Her eyes squeezed shut.

Salt! She had a little. Maybe it would be enough. Gods grant so. She couldn't see any way to start a fire in this dankness, and she couldn't cut them off with her knife... that would only leave those horrid little heads in under her skin. And in this wet?! She didn't even want to think about the infected sorts of horrors she could get from this hell hole!

With sheer willpower she forced her eyes open. A few of the awful things wiggled, and her stomach went queasy with its own wiggling.

In the name of Thunder, Gale – and Death herself! – what had she ever done to warrant this journey?!!

:If you hold very still, I'll help you.:

Her back stiffened. She sent the skies and Anyone who was listening, a prayer of thanks.

:But keep moving like that, and I'll end up burning you instead of them.:

Camey found her voice choked tight, so she nodded a bit and went still. The woman's low voice held an authority that gave Camey's tattered courage the wherewithal to finally repress the shivers.

A soft whoosh with a very, very faint flick hit her shoulder. She swallowed her relief at the tiny plop as the dead leech hit the mud. Another fell. Her nerves grew steadier with each demise.

:Smart to wear the lizard skins on the bottom. Tight-waisted enough, too. If you'd done the same on top, you wouldn't have picked up any at all.:

In other words, Camey thought – it could have been worse. She nearly groaned.

:Turn around and let me do your front.:

She did, then froze. It wasn't a woman she faced. Quite suddenly her stomach uncurled. Terror died beneath the simple, unalterable fact that there was absolutely nothing she could do. Standing there bare handed... bare breasted, she was completely defenseless. It would either kill her... or it wouldn't.

The huge, lizard-like head was as broad as Camey's shoulder span. Its soft scaled hide was dappled with greens on beige, and everything behind its head was hidden in the denser foliage.

Inconsequentially, a piece of Camey's mind wondered how anything so big could have come through that undergrowth without any noise.

It tipped one of its great, round eyes forward, considering a leech. Camey found herself staring at a starry six-point pupil amidst an iris of swirling silver. There was no white.

Delicately the blunt muzzled lips formed a small 'oh' and a thin tongue of pale lavender appeared. The forked tendrils centered on the leech as the tongue rolled to create a narrow trench. Fire sprouted quickly, tumbling down that slender trail to its target. The singed remains dropped away. Camey glanced down in amazement as the process was repeated.

:You have very little faith,: the creature remarked between leeches. Its tongue flickered with an almost inaudible hiss.

Camey shifted an incredulous gaze back to the star-eyed thing. She realized the voice had come from somewhere inside of her ears, not exactly from outside.

:Are all humans so mistrusting?:

The last of the leeches burned away, and Camey dully realized there'd been a question put to her. She moved her head senselessly, managing neither a nod or a shake.

:Do you speak or merely screech? I understand some humans don't speak, but I'd thought those couldn't scream either.:

Camey got her mouth open, but no further.

The head craned down and sideways, bringing the other great eye around to study her. So close to Camey, it didn't seem to be able to see her clearly with both eyes; they were set too broadly apart, although they seemed to be far enough forward to provide some binocular vision.

:Perhaps you simply can't hear me?   Or don't you understand me? Hmpf, that would be interesting. I've never met a species that couldn't understand me. Except, naturally, for those with too little intelligence to understand anything.: The star in that eye seemed to go rather squat, as if in speculation. :Humans aren't suppose to be that sort of stupid.:

Camey jerked up a bit. She scowled, a perplexed awareness dawning that this creature wasn't apparently interested in eating her. Hands went to her hips and her stance widened as she suddenly demanded, "What the hell are you?!"

The creature blinked, head rearing back slightly in surprise. It ignored the rude tenor of the question and answered peaceably enough. :A dragon, of course.:

The hazel of Camey's eyes went an angry green, and all the authority of her heritage resounded in her commanding glare. "Fire breather you may be, but a dragon certainly not."

Again the creature looked startled. From a higher angle, it slanted its head again to point that silver eye at her. The thin tongue slithered out as an astonished tone asked, : When have you ever met a dragon to know otherwise?:

"I've met several," Camey returned flatly. "I wear their hides, as a matter of fact."

That head bobbed down a bit as it looked at the sleek black trousers and boots. The tongue flicked forward once more. :Oh, you confuse dragon with lizard. Not a very flattering error, mind you. But I'll admit a grudging respect nonetheless. It's no small deed to take on a black, winged lizard. They may be dim-witted, but they do have nasty tempers.:

Camey's frown deepened.

:A dragon is neither black nor winged. We also tend to avoid humanity rather than devour you. The Black Lizards will never be more than fire-breathing reptiles. Scarcely anything for brains and certainly no talent for magic. But then, they are reptiles, and as such there are limits to their nature.:

"Whereas you're not, I suppose?" Camey drawled.

:Not what?:

"A reptile... a wingless lizard?"

That brought its head up with obvious indignation. :I am a DRAGON.:

"What's the difference?" She wasn't giving an inch. If she'd stopped to think about it, maybe she would have. Most folk certainly would have considered diplomacy to be more prudent in the face of anything that large and fire-breathing. But Camey was her father's daughter, and neither she nor King Stephan had ever been easily intimidated. They'd also been extremely straightforward about asking what they needed to know, and Camey frequently unbalanced challengers with that rare style of determined honesty.

This so-called dragon was no exception, it seemed. It sidled back a step, half lifting a four-taloned claw in confusion.

"I asked, what's the difference?"

It blinked down at her from the height of two men, head arched high on a supple neck. Camey noticed it seemed to have changed colors somewhat, a mistier white shimmering beneath the greenish dapples.

:I'm a dragon,: it repeated, bewilderment plain in its voice. :Lizards are... well, they're cold-blooded, dry-scaled and basically instinctual. I think... read... write! And I'm as warm-blooded as any furnace fire!!:

That swirling silver stuff whirled around in the iris, reflecting annoyance as explicitly as Camey's own stance. The head swung forward and that immense star-eye stared her full in the face. That lavender tongue hissed loud and long. :I am not – I repeat NOT – a lizard!:

"Warm blooded makes you a mammal, then." Camey pressed it mercilessly. She felt a belly-deep satisfaction in confronting this patronizing, flame-spitting bully! After days of running, it felt so good to finally stand and fight!

But the creature withdrew, taking a moment to assess the woman before her. Slight breasts heaved in breathing. Damp red curls clung to neck and face. Fists clenched knuckle-white, no longer resting against hips but forward now, ready to lift as if she would take on this huge monster with teeth and hands alone. The blunt nose drifted a fraction higher as the creature looked beyond to see the sodden gear. A sword hilt of cracked ivory poked out of the pack. The bag itself was suspiciously deflated, suggesting little if any edible food was left within it. Again she turned to the woman. Haggard bruises beneath those glaring eyes spoke of nights without sleep. The pale skin was scattered thickly with ruddy freckles, but there were bruises and cuts evident as well as chilled goose bumps. Very slowly then, the dragon lowered her great head to a point just below Camey's eye level.

Taken aback, Camey faltered and fists opened.

:I am a dragon,: the voice said kindly... gently. :I am neither mammal nor reptile, bird nor fish. I am merely dragon. My sort have been upon this earth since the days of the greater reptiles, before your forbearers were ever even imagined. I am a magical beast, a dragon. And my name is Jewel.:

Camey stood there, drowning in the mists of silver and feeling the shame wash through her. The unfairness of her attack suddenly made her heartsick. Then the fleeing and the aching and the sheer despair of her endless nightmare flooded her. Tears came, wetting her cheeks with grimy trails even as she stood tall. She did not care that she cried; she was only sorrowed that she'd been so vile-tempered to one who'd offered only help.

:What may I know of you, warrior?:

"That I am a knight." Camey bowed stiffly. "And I admit my poor manners are befitting neither the title nor your courtesy. I apologize. You were in no way deserving of my ire."

:A knight? I've heard of knights on dragon-slaying quests.: The dragon seemed more curious than disconcerted. : Did you think to find a Black Lizard here instead of me?:

"No, I was on such an errand in the north. When finished, I was summoned home. Since then the journey... has been a difficult one." She leveled her chin and dredged up a semblance of a smile. "Some call me Camey."

The dragon closed her silver eye once, slowly – like a cat, pleased and approving. :I am honored to meet you, Camey.:

* * *

Phoenix Rising

A complete short story, Chris Anne wrote "Phoenix Rising" after immersing herself in every lesbian science fiction novel she could find at her local gay bookstore. Sadly, back in 1993, there weren't that many of them. She wanted to find science fiction like she read as a teen – like Asimov or Card – but written by and for lesbian readers.

That was a driving force for Chris Anne. She wanted to read books with her in them – with strong-willed, opinionated, open-minded lesbians who loved romance and adventure and each other. She wanted to write these books and give voice and life to characters no one else was creating at the time. No main stream publishers were embracing lesbian characters and even lesbian presses would have one or two token science fiction titles among their dozens of formulaic romances and mysteries. In a time before out lesbian had talk shows and gay characters were kissing on prime time television, Chris Anne was writing lyrical tomes with rich worlds and fully realized lesbian heroes.

I know she would be very proud to see how far the world has come.

I wait below, feeling the icy winds tear through my body and watching the frozen crystals swirl in dances above. The vibrant forces of the winds fill me with fresh wholeness, nurturing my pale shimmering into a rich flush, and I fairly hum in expectation. But then the moon has waxed and waned innumerable times since I've seen you. My impatience is not some heightened sensitivity spawned by this maelstrom. It is from knowing that you're coming... that somewhere, above in this mire of whirling frosts, you are descending to me.

The first glimpse of you, as always, both elates and terrifies me. To have you finally appear is an exquisite end to anticipation, but to endure watching your descent is a thing my nerves have barely mastered. That thin veil of cloth seems too thin to endure my world's hailstones for long, and the slender wires with which you guide the fabric down are too slender to save you, should you miss my welcome and find yourself thrown into the glassy crags around me. Orange flares at your back, a packet sending up hot gasses into that net of cloth and slowing your approach. It melts some of the wind-born ice about you, too, and for a brief moment you hover as you find your bearings.

I think of you, concentrating, and turn a bright crimson... a flare in the endless whiteness. My own bright self becomes your guide and with a sudden spin, you have rounded and caught the gusting eddy. Your booted feet turn their soles flat as your knees bend in preparation, and abruptly you have landed, rolling across our narrow pier top as the winds drag you for that sheer edge. I clench inside myself, helpless to halt your tumbling and despairing that you will not loosen the edge of the billowing cloth, but you do... you always do. I feel the laughter of release as you climb to your feet in a blur of strange, bundled garments and fluttering fabric with strings. You give me a jaunty salute from the edge... such a familiar yet odd gesture, one of many I treasure. Only you have such audacity. Only you have ever had such courage to make that descent more than once, to endure the isolation from your own kind which being ambassador to my people demands... only you of all those your world has ever sent, have I understood so well.

Your things are wrapped together and stuffed into a silver bag. I watch as you pause to lift the translucent top to the storage hut and toss in the equipment. I remember carving that shelter from the mountain's glassy stone for those before your coming. They had called the refuge primitive, but they had always preferred it to our homes which lay deeper within these beds of crystal mountains. They had always found this world eerie and inhospitable in some way, and we in turn had come to believe that they must be a little insane to so fanatically avoid all contacts with the environment. It had taken you to explain how the winds destroyed rather than nourished your flesh... and how temperature was not merely a sensation but a survival factor.

Now as I watch your approach I become a ripple of patternless colors, a disconcerted essence waiting for you to define my being. And yes, I do wait... precious moments evolving, time moving us forward to our inevitable joining of soul and heart... to the inevitable awakening of sheer being!

You pause, covered from face to toe in thick, bulky protection against our winds, and only your eyes are visible to me. I hope you like what you see of me; it has seemed so long and always I am afraid that you will find you've come to prefer your own kind in the course of our separations. The deep, brown darkness of your irises enthrall me as you study me... the alien hue so shocked me the first time we met; you are still the only one ever to bring that color to my world.

You tug off a glove and bare your hand, despite the colds and winds. I concentrate carefully to contain myself as you reach forward with a single finger, stroking the fine aura of my edge. I resist responding; I do not want to inadvertently flicker across your sleeve and dissolve it... or harm you within. Again I remember, you were the first to venture touching with us – your courage rising from the ashes of those disastrous mistakes from the beginnings. After those frightening, uncontrollable flash fires, the others believed contact was lethal. We could not make them understand, it was only the clothing we could not safely touch... because that stuff was so unlike the transparent compositions of our world and because it was not made of living tissues.

Then the corners of your eyes crinkle in the way they do when you smile, and I know you have indeed come back to me. I am glad you have not found another in those worlds beyond my star.

You cover your hand again, pressing the fabric of that heavy glove down between your fingers. It is hard to resist enveloping you here and now... it is hard to witness the cloaking of that tender flesh again, but you are right. The temperatures are dropping and I know you need to be below. I move aside from the steps and allow you to precede me into the tunnels; again I am aware of the fatality an accident could cause if you inadvertently slipped and I was below you. How can your people be so fragile... and so reliant on materials which are even more frail than yourselves?... yet still be explorers? Or perhaps more of your people have your courage than I think.

Below we move through the endless tunnels of my community like ghosts through an emptied hive. None would threaten you with their presence yet, and there will certainly be time enough later for more cordial greetings. It is understood that first you must shed those infernal garments and recover from your long journey. This time of arrival is solely ours; I feel my auras glowing. Ahead, you are shedding your hood and gloves, but I dare not move to face you – not yet. I do not know if I am strong enough to keep my sense of safety if you turn that smile of yours on me... your steps are quickening and I realize you have thought the same.

Together...at a distance from one another we pause. The chamber is my own, and there is no
escape now; there is only the passage which brought us in. I remain in the entry, waiting... watching.

You move slowly, in a sequence I have memorized and yet always find new. Your back to me, you slip from the outer layers of your things. You stand there with your head tipped to the side a little, staring at that great pulsing wall of crystal. You are entranced by the flowing, molten liquids beyond. The steamy breath of our air condenses upon that see-through stone and creates rivulets of water which pool in the hollow at the chamber's edge. Your chin tucks as you almost look back, glimpsing me only from the corner of your eye, and we both remember the last time I interrupted your bathing. The steam begins to touch the darkness of your hair with its moisture, your skin starts to glisten in the heat, and still you refuse to look at me. Instead, you begin to remove the last of your clothing.

The sleekness of your shoulder bares and I flutter, wanting you. The roundness of your hip stretches as you bend. Your foot catches in the fabric and you turn further away from me, struggling not to slip. You regain your balance, and I find myself spellbound; you remain bent to sort and stack your garments... or is it to stay so open, so visible to me? So that I may see the moistness which dampens the thatch of hair you have tucked there... and the way your wetness has touched the under-curl of your buttocks? I want you.

You smile at me quickly, but move away even as you do so. The stone box where you leave your things is the only structure in this room aside from those glowing walls. I feel myself growing fuller... richer, and I wonder how I ever thought the box was ugly. It is a treasured thing now that marks the permanence you have taken on in my life.

Then you have stepped back into the middle of our room. The churning swirls of the liquid rock beyond the wall frame you with motion and color, and I remember why I wait for you... why I think you beautiful. I begin to draw near, and you begin a smile. Such a small shift in your facial features and I come to feel the winds outside have just swept through me again. It astounds me that you command so much from me with so little... astounds and delights me. I pause for a moment, just beyond the limits of your reach. Your smile deepens, then breaks as you take a deep breath of air and shake your wrists to loosen muscles. You shift your footing to a more comfortable balance. I wait, knowing we share both anticipation and nervousness; it is always this way after a time of separation. But it reminds me to be gentle, at least for now ... until our bodies become accustomed to one another again – until we become more limber.

You grow still, finally, and your eyes return to me. There is no smile this time. There is wanting instead. I don't know which expression I cherish more. I thin and spread before you, and your eyes narrow in suspicion. I begin to reach around you, still avoiding any touch and you say nothing. It is my turn to make you wait – to heighten your senses by watching me. You could hurry me. We both know it. You have only to touch me, to smile again at me... to move in any way, and I will not deny you. But you watch me in the slowness of this approach and do not demand.

I complete the circle around you, holding you in the very center without contact. My colors twirl and reflect the streaming flow of the room's. I warm the air, holding very still as your skin prickles and grows slicker. Your head falls back as you breathe so very deeply. The thrust of your breasts tempt me even as my shimmer tempts them. Sweat begins to run in tiny rivulets, so much like the thin trails on the wall behind us. I grow hungry for the pool I know grows between your thighs. And then your stance widens as if you've heard my murmur and you want to tell me you'll deny me nothing... and there is nothing I want to make you wait for.

You arch in my grasp as I take you, lifting you to the

balls of your feet and stretching you to feel every slender crevice – every sleek curve of your beauty. Your softness eclipses my senses... betraying our differences in our joining. My invasion of you... the way you open your mouth to gasp and find me filling your lungs with the very air I allow you to breathe... is all encompassing, all demanding and I claim all of you. You keep nothing from me... not the darkened tight places, not the lush damp depths, not even the folds of your clenched fists. And in my turn, I am lost in surrounding you. The softness... the utter softness of skin – I feel your body... the taste of your mouth, the shudder of your muscles as I stroke your senses with my sheer being. Your body – your flesh... I have never known touch from the inside out. I have never known physical drawing forth emotion... never until you.

You climax, falling, and I catch you. I take you to the floor gently, remembering you bruise so very easily sometimes. I withdraw to slacken the whirling of your senses – to let you breathe more easily, but I do not release you. I remain deep within you, cherishing the moistness and fullness. Wrapped about you, I find the peace you cherish as ours. I keep you warm – and fascinated, feel the lingering trail the sweating droplets leave upon our skin. You smile and your stretch of muscle flutters in me. You laugh faintly; you'd almost forgotten how your movements create swirls and eddies within me, which in turn touch you again, even in those intimate places... or especially in those most intimate places.

"I am back," you say, eyes still closed. Then you smile again at the way the vibrations of your speech ripple and press within us. "I finally convinced them to give your planet a name, Love – to recognize yours as a true folk and not as mere energy bits.

"Do you remember the legends I told you of my people's hopes?"

You have told me many tales. I have remembered them all, but my favorite has always been the one which recalled our own precious beginnings. Yes, I know the story you mean – the one of life and hope that rose from the ashes of fire.

"You do remember." You sigh, feeling the precious touch of our oneness again. "I chose a word – a name from your favored.... I thought of how our peoples had struggled so against fears, at the start. I remembered the angers, the pain... the death we shared, yet fought to surmount. And then I thought of what you and I share – together."

So very much we do share, I who am Soul and you who are Heart... we who become so complete and alive when together.

"Yes.... I thought of us together, when I claimed a name for your world of life... of hope. It was the nearest thing for such joyous transformation that I could ever conceive of finding. I chose for you – for us."

I hold you more tightly, almost daring you to struggle to be let go... yet I know you won't go. You're staying now. You'll not need to leave again.

"Oh Love, they'll know this world as Phoenix."

* * *

Risk & Reward

Though Chris Anne is certainly known best for her Amazons and Shadows, the planet Aggar was not her own fantasy world. She loved to play in variations on the theme, adding knights or dragons or mysterious tribunals. The idea of a ruling council overseeing young people always reminded me of her trials and tribulations with the dissertation board when she was earning her Ph.D. Leave it to Chris Anne to turn the mundane into the fantastic.

In "Risk & Reward," Chris Anne is exploring another of those fantasy settings, this one a tad more classic fantasy than Aggar that always dabbled in science fiction. She jumps right into the action here because she was still stinging from a review that called the Aggar books "dense".

Personally, I don't think "dense" is a bad thing. "Dense" could just as well be "rich" or "lyrical" or "thoroughly realized" or "complex". But with this short story, Chris Anne showed that her writing could also be action-packed and fast-paced... while still delivery a world that readers can fall into, and characters we can fall in love with.

Chris Anne was as far from a one-trick pony as someone can be. She was a chameleon, she was a shapeshifter. She set her sights on a goal and obtained it. She envisioned a world, then created it. No one will ever say that all Chris Anne ever did was write variation of Aggar. She may be most-loved for Aggar, but she was so much more.

"No!" Her body snapped rigid as the knight made to move near. From the corner of her eye, Alys glimpsed the jeweled long knife she'd struck the dragon with. With a lunge she was across the room, crouching with the blade held outward.

The black knight went immobile, sword point still to the floor.

"I'll not go!"

Very calmly and very distinctly, the knight explained again, "We will die if we stay, mi'Lady. We must go."

"Then I will die," Alys allowed grimly, and she reversed the blade to press it below her breastbone. "Only worse awaits me above. I'll not rejoin the living!"

For the first time, the knight looked carefully at their surroundings. The small parcel and cloak tucked in hiding was spied. It lay between the ornate, carved claws that were supporting an ancestor's stone box. A stunned, still moment followed, then a ragged whisper came, filled with amazement. "You were going to risk the beast and tombs for freedom?!"

Alys nodded, a stiff jerk of her head.

"But why? Why mi'Lady?! Your courage – your quickness against the beast... I could not have slayed this demon but for your help! Any noble house would be honored to shelter you!"

Grimness tightened her pale lips. Alys shook her head in absolute negation. "The price is too high."

"Price?"

"I am – was the King's Ward. First, as His Lady's House Steward, then as his. But now–! I refuse to become my foster brother's play thing!"

"Then leave. Flee as you sought to in the beginning–"

"Not above!" Alys hissed, and her bitterness grew scathing. "Where in this kingdom could I go?! The Crown Prince becomes King. He owns me! If he knows I am alive, he will hunt me! To save face, if nothing else. I am better dead. Here!"

"No–!" the black knight pressed forward, then stopped, hastily stepping back at the threat of that long blade angled towards the lady's heart. For a moment the ebony figure wavered, an empty leather fist closing – grasping... reaching for something unattainable. Then quite suddenly, the knight dropped to one knee and bowed the helmed head. "Then I beg you, mi'Lady, come with me to my own realm"

"I take no pity!"

"And I offer none."

That startled Alys. Warily she straightened from her crouching stance. "Explain yourself."

"I have seen your courage at close hand. I witness your pride and honor in your desperate wish now. Your forethought to provision for your escape attests to intelligence. All are qualities to be cherished, mi'Lady. I ask now only that you consider another alternative."

"That I come with you. At what price?"

"Honorable handfasting, mi'Lady... Mistress of my own – our own – estates."

Alys balked, her fingers growing cold about the hilt of her knife. The black-clad knight noticed her distress and rose swiftly but made no move to close the space between them.

"Mi'Lady?"

"Your offer is most generous," Alys whispered, but the blankness in her eyes and the stillness in her body belied the words. She found herself struggling with a lifetime of convictions and assumptions, questioning her courage and the cost of her dreams when pitted against sheer life.

"Mi'Lady?" Urgency pleaded speed in her answer.

"I am sorry," Alys managed through stiffened lips. "It is just – I had always imagined myself paired with a woman."

Gloved fingers fumbled with the helm's fastenings, and with a duck of the head, the steel mask was torn away. Bright hazel eyes captured Alys. "Will I do, mi'Lady?"

Speechless, Alys took in the pale flushed skin and the dampened tendrils of dark copper hair. Disbelief warred with hope and produced a tremulous smile. "Yes, my good knight, I think you will."

A sour stink and a grayish, thin wisp of smoke edged beneath the low arch of the descending tunnel. The knight glanced above at that warning sign and gestured to Alys to hurry. "Our time's done, mi'Lady. Bring your things."

Alys moved quickly, fetching her cloak and knotted cloth parcel. She left the jeweled knife on the King's chest without remorse. In the end, surprising as it seemed, his arms had saved her from his sons above.

The smell of the dragon's poison lingered in Alys' nostrils even as they left the smoke and King's chamber behind. It spurred her forward, nearly running, as the black-clad knight followed closely. The bulk of armor and sword made her feel dwarfed in comparison, but it was a welcomed feeling of reassurance to have that between her and the swirling poisons behind.

They emerged into the tombs of lesser personages as a

great ebony steed reared, screaming its shrill greeting. Alys cringed, drawing back, but the knight was behind her and the beast came down to all fours on command.

"Up now," the knight guided her swiftly to the side of the war horse. Heart in her throat, Alys let herself be bundled behind the saddle's proper seat amongst the packs. Without thought to vanity, she gathered the hems of skirt and shift into her lap as the knight shoved her things in a saddle bag. Then the knight was mounted, and with a gasp, Alys' chin hit the black steel of back and breast plates as the great horse lunged. She clutched to the leather-clad waist and hugged tight.

The broadsword was sheathed as they rode. The black helm was donned again, and ducking through the last archway, they burst into the sunlight.

The stallion wheeled and curt orders were flung with an outstretched hand. The attendants rushed to seal the brass doors, and with their thud, a cheer rose from the crowds below in the courtyard.

Alys couldn't help grinning at the waving hands and laughing faces which reflected such joyous relief. That the dragon was dead, they had all known from the echoing wail and that initial outpouring of vile, black smoke. But to have the hero emerge unscathed with a maiden in tow was nothing short of a miracle.

The solemn countenances of the four princes who strode forth to greet the black knight were tinged with arrogant embarrassment at a deed so well done by one who was not themselves. But the roar of the crowd held even William's displeasure in careful check. By the King's Final Decree, the reward due this dragon's slayer was dauntingly generous. And – he was acutely aware of the fact that if this knight wished to receive the crown in payment, the crowd might create a very bloody scene at the Prince's denial. William knew that he and his brothers were more feared than worshiped by these commoners.

"My honored guest and good knight," the crowd hushed and William deemed a formal bow was necessary. He offered one stiltedly. He rose, extending a more gracious wave towards the crypts. "Your hand has struck the witch's curse and sent the hell beast back to the nether-reaches where it belongs. Our gratitude – is yours."

The black horse stomped, its white teeth impatiently chaffing at the bit. The knight said nothing.

"As decreed by the King's last words, we grant royal favors to a dragon's slayer!" William's back stiffened. He resented the other's mounted position and the haughty silence. But mindful again of the crowd, his words rang out with a sweeter charm. "Name your wish, Black Knight. And if it be within my power as Heir and Regent, I will see it done!"

"The maid."

For the first time, William took note of who was sitting behind that armored figure.

"I claim the King's Ward as my own."

He could hardly believe his good fortune. William burst out laughing, arms spreading wide – "Done!"

William heard his brothers chuckling behind him, equally satisfied – the tart was certainly a cheap enough favor. And to the people–! Their cheers were testament of their approval.

With a regal wave, he gestured to the castle doors and his voice boomed across the crowd's heads. "Come join us for celebration and feasting! My father would have been proud to know his wake and this victory go hand-in-hand."

"Your offer is most kind–"

The helmed head tipped in a courteous fashion. But William felt his hackles rise at the faint thread of amusement in the low pitch of that voice.

"Unfortunately, I must decline as I have pleasanter tasks to attend."

The attendants and younger princes held their breaths at the audacity of the taunt. William's eyes narrowed, darting to Alys' half-hidden form almost accusingly. Then suddenly, a gleam lit in his soulless eyes, and his laughter shouted across the courtyard. He pointed his brothers towards Alys, and they too finally saw his joke.

Alys blushed. A lump rose in her throat to choke her, and she almost wondered what sort of brigand she had pledged herself to when her ears caught a muffled "witless toad...!" from within the black helm. She bit her lip hard to keep from breaking into laughter and pressed her face into the cool steel of the shoulder before her. She did wonder, then, if her fair knight had even noticed the innuendo those words could spawn.

"Then away with you, Good Knight!" William lifted a hand in merry salute. "May your riding be – oh so sweet!"

Alys caught another muttered "imbecile" and then felt the hard clamp of angry heels send them off. The stallion took care to pick its way down the stone steps, then with neck arched and tail high, the steed cantered across the court and beyond. They crossed the drawbridge as another wave of cheers rose in farewells.

Alys held more tightly as the stallion snorted a disgusted 'good riddance' to the stone and wood footing. His muscles bunched and then sprang. In full gallop, they topped the hill crest, and without pause Alys left her old life behind.

The other shrugged and looked off into the gathering gloom. She nodded to where her stallion was grazing on the hillside. "Bastion there will tell us if it's anything different."

"Is he good at scenting ghosts?"

The woman's eyes came back to Alys.

"These plains are supposed to be haunted," Alys explained quietly. She nibbled at her cheese, wondering how inane she was sounding.

"Well–" the woman straightened a stiff leg, "they'll just have to haunt elsewhere tonight. Heraldic rules clearly state that knights and damsels shall not be disturbed by meddlesome spirits, until a proper respite has been allowed after dragon slaying."

Alys stared at her in astonishment, then suddenly hid a smile to answer in kind, "And what is defined as a 'proper respite,' may I ask?"

"Ahh now!" A conspiratorial grin rose. "That has been left rather vague. But I'd chance to guess, we're due at least a good night's sleep."

Regardless of the heraldic rules' ambiguity, their banter left her feeling much better, and Alys returned to the rest of her meal. As she finished, she found to her surprise that her companion was still watching her.

"More drink?"

Alys shook her head. Her last taste of the spirit-laced water was still stinging her throat.

"I should thank you."

Puzzled, Alys asked, "Whatever for?"

"The dried fruit – and fresh bread. My usual trail fare of wafers and cheese can grow rather tiresome."

"But it's very good cheese."

"Good enough. I shouldn't complain – I've certainly had times when I had far less." A charming, self-conscious sort of shrug was offered. "But it does become rather ripe after a few days."

"Do we have far to go, then?" It was a quiet question, but one that sent Alys' heart racing. It was the first time she had ventured to ask anything about their future.

"No, not far."

Alys chanced to look up as the knight rose and walked around the side of their fire ring. She pointed beyond Alys into the darkness. "We go about half a day in that direction."

She thought very hard, but Alys could not remember any mention of a fief in this region.

"Then we meet a stone ruin with an arch. It's a passage of sorts."

Alys set her bowl down and drew her cloak around her more tightly to hide a tremor. She had never stopped to question the origins of this knight. Too late, she reminded herself of the silver web-light that had edged that black sword.

"Does the idea of magics frightened you?"

"I'm not sure," Alys countered truthfully. "Should it?"

"I am quite mortal," the woman murmured slowly. "The magic is used only to allow me to fight the dragons."

"Does it... protect you from them?"

"Some." A single shoulder lifted faintly. "Less than I could hope."

"You fight a lot of them then?"

A lingering nod came. "Too many."

The woman turned abruptly to face the fire. She squatted down and fed another stick or two into the flames. With a flat tone, she added, "I am called the Dragons' Bane. I hold allegiance to the Witch White Tower. Fighting dragons is what I do."

"You're a sorceress?"

"No–" She seemed rather startled at the idea. "No, Elsbeth is the witch." A crooked smile appeared. "She's a little cantankerous, but that's mostly because she worries too much."

Alys' thoughts went to the fiery beast they had stood against that morning. "I can see why she might worry. Dragons are not very pleasant creatures."

"No.... I guess they're not."

Curiously, Alys leaned forward in order to better see the woman's face. "Do they frighten you?"

"They do."

"Then why–?"

Lips pursed and silence enfolded them as the question was considered. Thoughtfully the knight shifted to sit and then with honesty admitted, "Sometimes I don't know how I could not fight them. They're such terrible beasts reeking such havoc and pain. I don't know how I could simply stand by and not at least try to stop them.

"Once, years before I came to the White Tower tournaments and won my title, I saw half a country wiped out by dragonfire. Then a tyrant rode in on the heels of that destruction and used the disaster for his own gain. He stripped the pride and the prosperity from the kingdom, banishing the regents. He turned justice into – a personal whim. Chaos turned bitter, into famine and plague. The people suffered tenfold beyond the dragon deeds... but so often the ambitious descend after the dragons.

"And it is always the people who suffer. Even when it's a sorcerer or a witch seeking some personal revenge – when the winged lizards are released, it's the farmers and merchants and commoners that are hurt most... not bishops nor kings.

"I was raised to protect the folk in my trust. Now with Elsbeth, I protect all folk – or at least, as many as I can – from the dragonfires."

Silence came as the story ended, and slowly Alys turned the words over in her mind. She realized the country half-eclipsed by the dragonfires must have been this woman's home. No, she amended – it had been her own family that was banished by the invaders... it had been her people who had fallen before the dragonfires and who had been crushed beneath the tyrant's heel. But being what she was – protector by birthright and by conscience – the battling would never be done. Although Alys saw too, the woman's passion did not rise from bitterness nor guilt, only from truth – dragonfire brought destruction to the innocent and the knights able to defeat the beasts were far too few in number. There was no choice for this woman save one – the fight. It was not a matter of courage or honor or laurels. It was simply a matter of necessity – people needed protection, so she would give her life to provide it.

Alys understood that position. She had stood between the King in his illness and his son's assassination attempts. She had taken the first lashings across her own shoulders when intervening between the soldiers' drunken tempers and her house staff. She had defied ignorant clerics with her granny's witchery to heal fevers and breathe life back into drowned children.

She looked again to the silent woman, respecting the quiet aloofness and the haunted solemnness now that she saw them for what they were. The pain that had been witnessed, the failures endured... the fatigue brought by victories – those were stories best left for more trusting times. But Alys had no doubts now that such trusts would come to grow between them.

She smiled faintly as the knight glanced back at her. Their gazes caught, and with a quizzical tip of her head, the woman waited.

Alys blushed faintly, chagrined at a belated thought. "Do you have a christened name? Or do they always call you Dragons' Bane?"

That brought a grin and the melancholy air about the woman lifted completely. "Nicol."

"Nicol? Nicol of–?"

"Knight of the Witch White Tower... or less illustriously, the Black Knight."

"Well... I can't see why!" Alys protested teasingly, and they laughed together. Her voice softened then, "I think I prefer Nicol, though."

"So do I."

"And I am Alys."

"Alys? Maid of good cheer – that's nice. Lady Alys... it's pretty. Almost as pretty as its bearer."

Alys gave her a wry, tolerant sort of look and ignored the comment. She had never thought of herself as anything other than pleasantly plain. "It seems rather odd, doesn't it? That we're just exchanging names now."

"No stranger than being engaged to someone you know nothing about except for their name. At least you knew I fight well, and I knew of your courage."

"Yet...," Alys wet her lips hesitantly, "I forced you into this—"

"You did not." It was said quietly, evenly... without a hint of annoyance. "If I had not desired a partner, I would not have asked for your hand. I would simply have disarmed you and taken you above without your consent."

Of course she could have.... Alys had suspected it all along. Her conscience pressed again. She should still challenge... but did she really want to invite the consequences? Did she actually want to know that this alliance was based only on chivalry – or worse, on pity?!

Would it change her own pledge, if she knew? No, she had given her word. It bound her as tightly as the King's once had. But Nicol... might she want to withdraw the proposal if...?

Quite suddenly – guiltily, Alys realized she didn't want anything to change.

The wind crept in, teasing her fears with its chilly fingers.

"You grow cold," Nicol murmured and rose.

Alys watched as the handsome young woman went to retrieve a blanket from their travel goods. She came back with a gentle smile that oddly didn't seem at all out of place with the sword and leather lacings. She draped a broad, fleecy cover about Alys' shoulders and sat down close, an arm slipping around Alys to hold her for warmth.

There were words other than pity, Alys remembered as she straightened to offer Nicol a soft smile of her own. Words like compassion....

She opened the blanket and Nicol slid near to share it. The fire crackled as they turned to watch it, and above the stars began to appear. Cocooned in the snug warmth, safe within the crook of Nicol's arm... Alys felt the whisper of contentment rise around her.

"You were right," Alys murmured.

"About—?"

"The ghosts have left us for the night."

"Yes," Nicol's arm tightened, hugging her strongly. "I'd noticed too."

* * *

The Sultan's Daughter

Chris Anne was a unique woman who backed her ever belief with an articulate discussion of physiology and psychology. She supported polyamorous relationships and believed a race of muses walked among us. She wished for a matriarchal society to save young men from war and felt science should be responsible for procreation, not sex.

As a writer, Chris Anne was perhaps even more unique. About half the time, she wrote detailed outlines. It was because of these 10,000-word outlines, I think, that Chris Anne felt so comfortable willing me her unfinished works; in my own writing, I always write from an extensive outline. Plus, because I had helped her as she wrote "Fires of Aggar" – creating or reworking long sections when she was too ill -- she knew I could emulate her style well enough that her editors and readers could not pick out "my" sections.

But outlines aren't what set Chris Anne apart from most writers. It's what she does next. Chris Anne then jumps into the writing process... not at the beginning. She writes scenes and even entire chapters out of sequence, nonlinear, driven by inspiration. An "unfinished novel" by Chris Anne, might very well have chapters one through four, then chapters twenty-two, thirty-four and forty. In this way, Chris Anne married two writing approaches – planned and spontaneous.

And that special process resulted in "The Sultan's Daughter" being a fragment of a novel with an Arabian Nights feel. Once again, Amazons Unite hopes to one day bring the rest of this manuscript to light from the sheaves of hand-written notes, stand-alone scenes and pages of outline.

I

Some would think that growing up as a daughter of the Harem meant that Isela was a sheltered, naïve girl who was innocent in virtue and ignorant of reality's unpleasantness. This was undoubtedly the Sultan's assumption, if he ever gave thought to the existence of this youngest daughter of his Favorite. Then again, perhaps only those of the Harem ever really understood how thoroughly reality did intrude into Palace life. Indeed, the Harem had taught Isela lessons that some sultans are lucky enough to escape all of their lives.

It was true that she had never known hunger or thirst... or gone through a sandstorm afoot. But by the time Isela was nineteen she'd been through sandstorms, both actual and figurative. At four, she rode a midnight ride of terror, clinging to the saddle, held tight by a eunuch as the Sultan's household fled the Insurrectionists. At seven, she watched as an intruder to the gardens – a male – was beheaded along with his lover, a concubine of the Harem. When she was nine, her mother, Sultan's Favorite and Ruler of the Harem, began to instruct Isela on the intrigues of the Court; in that year she learned of the poisons of both gossip and food as the Favorite assassinated a young sheik who had publicly challenged the Sultan's authority once too often. By twelve, Isela could recite the Secrets of Royal Lovers and knew explicitly what each passage meant, although by virtue of her rank as the Youngest of the Favorite she had escaped the duties of entertaining the Sultan's honored guests... while by virtue of her mother's guile and her own ability to keep out of sight, she had also avoided the Sultan's more amorous attentions. Precipitous hiding, however, did not spare everyone, and Isela had witnessed beatings and rape – suicide before she'd ever been aware of poisons. She'd seen women loving women and shuddered at women hating women. Abortions – by choice and by decree, murder – outright and accidental, petty jealousies, and somber plottings... all these made Isela much older than her mere age.

And when she was thirteen, she danced the Dance of Daggers at her elder brother's Feast. It was the first time she danced for any of the male family, and as her brother was the Heir, it was a great honor – as well as a great responsibility. She danced it well. The assassin died from her blade, his own falling into the Sultan's lap as his body tumbled across the Heir. Her brother took the credit for the kill, as Harem code maintained was correct; it was testimony to Isela's skills that he could. Yet the Sultan's son had been impressed and later summoned her, granting Isela a wish. Her plea had been not to marry young, but to train as a Veiled Sword. Given the number of older daughters the Sultan had to dispose of at the time and the advantages of adding obvious talent to the Harem's less auspicious guardians, her brother had found it an easy matter to arrange. So she had become one of the few women of the Harem to train with the eunuchs as a warrior.

No, by the time Isela was nineteen, she was anything by naïve. She was deadly.

>>> <<<

"Hmmm – you look menacing, my dear. Who are you off to challenge today with your ruthless genies?"

"Thank you, Mother," Isela bowed with an amused glint to her eye. "I don't know, actually. They only told me to dress for dark and stealth."

The Favorite sighed indulgently, content with her daughter's black garb of sashed tunic and trousers. A turban scarf hung over one shoulder and the sickle sword was worn with obvious comfort; this daughter would never be a threat to the Favorite's place in their Sultan's eye. She shifted a bit on her pillows, careful not to spill the wine from the chalice in hand. "When will you return?"

"No specific time has been mentioned," Isela answered cautiously. "Have you something in mind for later, Mother?"

A rather sarcastic smile marred the olive beauty of the Favorite's countenance. "Not I, my love. But the Omnipotent One has summoned me for discussion, and it will concern you as his daughter."

For a moment, Isela considered that, then as bracelets jangled with her mother's impatience she forced a pleasant tone and response. "Should I attend the audience or await your return here?"

The tension visibly melted from her mother's curvaceous figure, and a genuine smile surfaced. In a voice almost gentle, the Favorite suggested, "Attendance might be more suitable."

"Then I shall be there."

"However, you do have plenty of time for your sword work this morning. He's not expecting us until after his mid-day rest."

Isela bowed again, hand atop the hilt of that sickle sword. The weapon had a smooth, cool feel to it, and it helped to steady her nerves as she departed. That there were no teasing comments or tittering giggles as she passed through the inner court today was not noticed. The almost stone-hard cast to her features deterred the women's jesting. Dark eyes that normally sparkled with amusement and tolerance glared at an unnamable foe and obliterated any softness the round beauty of her face might have offered. Today, no one of the inner court or the outer gardens dared to interrupt that swift stride, and many hurried to step aside from it.

She entered the small orchard and from habit, secured the brown waves of her hair beneath the turban. She was intent only on gaining the privacy of the training field beyond the fruit trees. Inside, she was torn between anger and exasperation. Her father's sudden interest in her obviously meant a marriage contract was under negotiation. Her mother would not have termed this afternoon's summons as a "discussion" if the Sultan's interest had been of a more personal nature. It was somewhat understandable; at this time, she was the only unwed princess by his Favorite, youngest full sister to the Heir, and she was still a virgin. Bundle that all together and she suddenly made a very appealing prize, even if she was a bit old by most marital standards.

Damn him! She'd almost gotten to be too old! Another year or two and she would have been safely, acceptably spinstered among the Veiled Swords. A valuable commodity in that role as the Heir perceived it, she'd have retained a home even after the Sultan's eventual death. But the Sultan himself probably had forgotten all about her training!

At that last thought Isela nearly laughed. Admit her prowess with swords and knives to her father now?! She'd do best not to even remind him of any training at this point. It would make her unmarriageable in the eyes of many, and the Sultan was not one to tolerate anyone spoiling his grand plans. She fancied neither torture nor death from his wrath... although depending on his choice of suitors, she realized she might be facing something very akin to either.

II

"Someone should do the fighting for you. You're no good at it – as I tell you time and again."

"Ouch!"

"Hold still. I have to clean this before I bandage it. You know that."

The woman ground her teeth shut and tried not to flinch as the doctor dabbed at her shoulder again. The shaggy, shoulder length of her hair was still damp from the rains outside, but the braziers glared bright in the marble hall, and there was no wind to sweep drafts in through the open portico. He finished with his pat-patting and set to bandaging. Her grey eyes went flint-hard as she sucked in the air. She was ignored; his touch wasn't any gentler.

"Replace your captain! Then I won't have to do this anymore."

"Liar–" she muttered.

"What's that?" He peered over her bruised and skinned shoulder, his round spectacles perched high on his nose.

"I called you a liar." She hissed suddenly from the pain, jerking forward uncontrollably. "You patched me up even when the Hun guarded me."

A scoffing grunt ended his ministrations and he folded his things away as he shook his head. "When are you going to listen, Keyesh? You're a magician, a sorceress beyond repute. I won't contest it. But it's sheer folly to touch a blade. You barely have the fundamentals in grasp. You don't have the time, woman! You can't study sword and sorcery. There aren't enough hours in a day to be proficient at both."

"And I don't pretend to be proficient in swordplay, my friend." She gingerly shrugged back into the loose wrapped tunic of white. "Furthermore, I have never wanted to be. I don't want to be. I'm never going to be."

"Then why do you persist in–"

"Blazes, Aidam! I can't help it sometimes!"

"So find a decent captain for your guard!"

"I have a decent captain. What I need is a companion. So when I go flying off to some harebrained disaster I can take a harebrained adventurer with me and leave the captain here to take care of this place!!" Which is getting harder by the season, Keyesh admitted to herself. The valley was prospering so well that the neighboring folk, eastern Mongols and western Celts alike, were beginning to get notions. Her own reputation among magicians wasn't helping either; every up-and-coming egotist was hoping to outwit her and willing to press their attack even to her doorstep, if she'd allow it.

She should have settled down with the goat herder's daughter when she'd had the chance. Obscurity had its advantages.

"Keyesh?" A warm hand tenderly squeezed her good shoulder. "At least give yourself a good night's sleep." The silken swirls on his quilted jacket sparkled in the light as Aidam came around to face her, tipping her chin up with a crooked finger. "You know, sometimes you remind me of a little granddaughter. Such puzzled grey eyes, such guileless pale beauty... I forget you have seen so much of life. But please, Keyesh, find someone to ride that great white beast with you? For all our sakes."

"I've had friends searching, Aidam. I won't call them off just yet, aye?"

His deep chuckle brought the smile back to his face, his head shaking in dismay again. The old man shouldered his bag of medical tricks and tucked his box of bandages beneath an elbow. But he couldn't resist a last reminder. "Try to be gentle with that shoulder for a few days. Even with your remarkable healing powers, it will be stiff after the tissues have mended. Don't lift a sword! Merely for a few days... a few days isn't so much to ask, is it?"

She fought it, but her mouth quirked up into a rueful smile anyway. "All right, Aidam. I promise. I'll be a good little magician and practice my spells... and only my spells."

>>> <<<

Normally the sandy pit of the Bed was opened to the night breezes, but with the sheeting rain the huge wall-doors had been rolled shut tonight. The slant-roofed structure towered over the neighboring stables and dwarfed the slopes of the pastures behind it. Keyesh slipped in through the single door of human-size and...

FRAGMENT 1 ENDS

Panicked shrieks filled the air as Zahm alighted on the garden patio, her massive talons barely making a scratch upon the marble. Smoke billowed above with her roar to create a foggy ceiling. The screams of the women were absorbed into oblivion. At the outer edges of the gardens, in the upper rooms of the Palace... no soul beyond the Harem heard anything amiss. And on the outer edges of that smoke, any who might carelessly glance towards the Harem's Garden would see only illusions of greenery and sunlit, polished tile.

But beneath that nebulous cloud, the fleeing concubines were soon replaced by flowering eunuchs with shining swords.

Zahm raised a clawed forehand and bellowed skyward as someone threatened to come too close. Her great white wings spread high, blocking out the sunlight for a terrifying instant. The mightier warriors managed to stand their ground as the others cowered and edged back. Yet to due them all credit, none ran from the patio.

With a flourish Keyesh removed her white furred cloak, still astride her dragon. The gold of her filigree sash and tasseled boots glittered against the whiteness of her silks even as the dark ash of her eyes glittered through the half-slit of her turban scarf. The deadliness of that gaze challenged those at the front of the guarding line.

The Captain stepped forward. His arms folded solemnly. Broad bladed scimitars arched upwards from each hand. His expression was a stoic mask of defiance.

None of it seemed to impress the Magician. A leg swung over the scaly neck, and from the height of two men, Keyesh dropped. Her knees bent to absorb the impact and she ended comfortably in a crouch, eyes never leaving the Captain's face. His weight shifted from one foot to another, though he made no move forward. But then Keyesh was still harbored beneath the arch of that great beast's head and behind its foreclaw.

Uncertainly, the Captain glanced to his sides. It was only somewhat encouraging to find his warriors still present. He set his jaw squarely and had almost decided it was going to be his duty to die today, when Keyesh reached up and tore the masking cloth from her face. The Captain blinked in astonishment and felt giddy as the blood drained his swarthy skin pale.

Zahm screeched to the smokey skies, tail lashing through the pool in challenge as Keyesh slowly rose to stand. Her tousled, short mane of black hair framed the ivory of high-cheek bones and a beardless chin; her gender was undeniable even as it seemed impossible. Her voice rang out commandingly, "Law of the Harem says no man save the King-Sultan shall enter here and live! I claim right of entry as a woman – and as a guest of the Royal Household."

His swords crossed before his breast as the Captain's head came down in a formal bow. Steel sang as the others slashed in quick imitation, and as one his warriors fell to bended knees.

Keyesh approached the Captain warily, surveying the entire company with a measuring coldness. Each and every eunuch felt the chill pass the bared nape of his neck; it felt as if an executioner's axe was taking aim and lifting. The Captain braved her eyes once again as she stopped beside him. Her grimness froze his very soul.

"Take heed of my warning." Her words were barely a harsh whisper, yet each heard her as clearly as if they'd been there in the Captain's own shoes. "My right for passage is as a woman. My right for discretion is as a Royal Guest. My curse for any lax in that discretion will be as Magician. No One is to know of my visit. My business is with the Favorite. It is of no concern to any other."

The Captain fought to withhold the words of immediate assent. Her grey gaze imprisoned him with immobility, and frantically his mind raced through the oaths and loyalties he'd promised. But he was no fool. The Captain knew the Sultan's wrath as well as the kingdom's need for this Magician's powers – and there were no specific pledges her demand would force him to break.

"Silence...!" Keyesh hissed. "Yours and theirs. Agreed?"

His tongue was released just enough for his speech. "Agreed, Amir."

She turned on her heel and strode past them all into the coolness of the Palace interior. The Captain gulped for air, the suffocating powers finally slackening with her departure. Then Zahm's thunderous rasp suddenly reminded them all of her beastly presence. Her head swung down, fanged teeth the length of arms – hot breath the scorching of desert sands. The Captain swallowed his prayers and cringed as that great tail snaked out and behind his warriors, blocking all from Palace entry. He waved to the others, signaling them into a protective crouch, and turned back to the dragon. She withdrew towards the clouds a bit, and he cautiously settled himself down for the wait; obviously, no one would be following the Magician-woman inside.

FRAGMENT 2 ENDS

* * *

The Story of the Kiwi

Retelling myths was a hobby for Chris Anne... no, to be honest, it was more than that. Retelling myths was Chris Anne's addiction – pretty much her only one! She loved to tweak common or uncommon mythological stories into contemporary tales or weave brave lesbian characters into them. She didn't so much turn tradition on its head as smooth and mold the primal clay into something with the same substance and intention but a different shape. She wanted to keep the heart of a myth while changing the trappings.

Another delight of Chris Anne's was her love of a challenge. Sometimes, she received her challenges from friends or fans. Other times, she perceived challenges in the words of her reviewers or critics. She never dwelled in a negative sense, nor did she ever rest on her laurels. She always sought to make herself a better writer by proving – if only to herself – that she could write anything she set her mind to.

"The Story of the Kiwi" is a complete retelling... in less than seven hundred words. Brevity does not exclude creativity and Chris Anne enjoyed writing both four-hundred page novels and tiny haikus... and stories somewhere in-between.

L et me tell you a story," the Wise Woman began. "It is the story of a bird, a Kiwi bird."

The Kiwi was a small creature of long, fine feathers and a long, thin beak. The Kiwi had eyes that were round and bright. The Kiwi had legs that were strong and quick.

The Kiwi lived in a good land. There was fresh water to drink. There was grassland with food and warm sun. There were cool places beneath the trees for when the sun got too hot.

It was a good life that the Kiwi lived. Certainly, there were burrows to keep clean and rocks to turn. Sometimes, there were dangers to flee. But there were also many things to take pleasure in, like quiet friends to be with and safe nest to rest in. The Kiwi was quite happy.

One day the Kiwi was nestled in the cool ferns, enjoying the shade. The Kiwi looked up into the forest and saw a shadow flying by. The shadow did not fly far but came very near. As it came to rest on an old log beside the Kiwi, the Kiwi saw that it was a Wren-Warbler.

The Kiwi was shy but piped a "Good-day" to the Warbler, because the Kiwi was a polite bird. Being a friendly bird, the Warbler sang a song for the Kiwi. The Kiwi listened, amazed at the beautiful sounds the sparrow made. When the Warbler finished, the Kiwi asked, "How do you sing so wonderfully?"

The Warbler said simply, "I am a bird."

Then the Warbler sang another song for the Kiwi. This time the Warbler sang it in the air while flying. The Warbler dipped and sailed and sang. The Kiwi thought it was all very, very wondrous. When the Warbler finished and fluttered good-bye from the sky, the Kiwi sighed.

That evening the Kiwi stood beside the lake and looked at the mirrored reflections. "I have fine feathers but no wings, so I cannot fly. I have a fine, slender beak but cannot warble. What kind of sad bird does this make me?"

The Gentle Wind blew across the water. The melancholy of the small Kiwi made the Gentle Wind want to answer. "What kind of bird do you think you are, Friend Kiwi?"

"A poor, earthbound bird," the Kiwi said sadly. "Flying and singing are beyond me."

"Are they?" the Gentle Wind asked. "When you listen, do you not appreciate the beauty in the songs? When you watch do you not marvel at the wonder of flying?"

"Yes, I do," the Kiwi answered.

"Does the spirit inside you not rejoice and sing with the Warbler, when the Warbler sings? Inside you–did it not feel as if it were you flying, when the Warbler soared?"

"Yes, I felt that way," the Kiwi said. "I felt great joy. I felt free. But I am earthbound. Without wings and without beautiful songs, I can only watch and listen."

"You are earthbound now, my Friend Kiwi. Someday your spirit will not be, and you will soar free. Think on that when you become sad." Then the Gentle Wind blew past.

The Kiwi thought very hard for the next few days. The

Kiwi thought of that inner spirit's joy. The Kiwi thought also of the earthbound joys like the warm grasses to play in and the cool shade to hide in. The Kiwi decided it was very special to be a spirit inside, but that it was also very special to be living on the earth. So, the Kiwi became content.

Time went on and the Kiwi lived happily in that good land. Until there came a day, when the Kiwi could not live there anymore.

On that day, the earthbound Kiwi died. And the Gentle Wind came to greet the Kiwi's spirit. The Kiwi Spirit said goodbye to the earthbound, because the Kiwi was a polite bird.

Then the Gentle Wind blew and the Kiwi lifted from the earth. The sun was shining warm. The clouds were cool and shady.

And the Kiwi flew up into the great beauty of the sky, singing a wondrous song of joy.

* * *

Poetry

These thirty-two poems were culled from three and a half inch diskettes, scrawled in the margins of journals, penned in love letters, and even woven into sketches on the back of photos and postcards. Written between 1979 and 1993, some are universal and others are intensely personal.

I waited a long time – actually writing all the other introductions prior to this one – before writing these words to open the poetry section. I kept asking myself: What can I say about these poems? What is too much? What is too little? Many of these poems were written before Chris Anne and I met and became friends and companions. Others were written during our time together in California; driving across the country (she taught me how to drive a stick shift); living on a farm in tiny Radnor, Ohio, or after our lives had parted ways. In the end, I've decided to share this:

Chris Anne had a single tattoo. It was on her thigh. A hummingbird. The creature was sketched in color and seemed to be drenched in soft feathers, the colors shimmering like a live hummingbird. It was a symbol for Chris Anne, both of sensuality and mysticism; she believed that hummingbirds were like fey, tiny beings that drink from flowers and seem to defy gravity with their swift movement and incredible hovering.

But more than all that, hummingbirds lived life at a furious speed, the racing counterparts to the blooms they fed upon. Chris Anne was an incredibly prolific writer, moving from beautiful idea to beautiful idea, feeding on myths and images of wonder to create remarkable feats of inspiration.

So while I know the poem "A Hummingbird Upon the Hand" is more erotic than a reader might first suspect, I like to think of it, instead, as a meditation on all of Chris Anne's creative life and her courting of many a muse.

Recipe for Home

Mix   1 part common sense,
       1 part honesty with
       2 parts patience and listening.

Stir with trust, add a pinch of salt
and a dash of humor. Bake in a pan
greased with agreement-to-disagree.
       Serve with love.

12/92

Once More

to drown in eyes like yours
is to sail on winds through
bluest skies and hail
none but you, my love
whose gaze yet flings
my heart above
And then I think,
drowning and soaring are,
alternately, grand things.

6/93

Love's Bright Wings

Weary moments,
flowing–running
Time by slow.

Haunting memory
of loss–broken
Trust and more.

Then gentled words
rise–floating
Calm in mind.

Peaceful intent,
tantalizing
brush...Soothing.

Eyes pledge to truth,
with such kindness
comes the Gift.

Embrace light hope,
transcend...assured,
soaring pair.

7/93

For Your Wedding–

Candlelight to show the way,
a plate for sharing bread
and sure arms to hold you dear
are finer things than those
of gold or gilted edged.

These, then, are the magic things
that bind true dreams with life.
The glow of hope, the very
warmth of nurturing hearts...
Behold the joy–
        the courage that greets each dawn!

4/89

For You I Am

For you of misty eyes and hair of rich softness,
For you of lips of tender sweetness,
For you I feel...
                    I know...
                              I love....

                                        11/84

Water and Sun

Smile, my love, and allow the stars of night
     to nestle brightly within your gaze.
Laugh, my dearest, squeekily as the maple branch
     bends in its dance with the joyous wind.
And touch me,
     I beg of you.
Touch me and let me be you for the instant–
     the mixing of water and sun, we are.
     Different, Incompatible, forever Separate
     and yet look!
             –Rainbows of colors.

                7/93

Her Eyes

Touch?
        felt and true,
        but blending has meshed those
                skins beyond mindless words.

So smile–
        slow, subtle with true joy.
Growing–
        easily, upwards with steadiness.
Lightened–
        brightness caught fast and briefly held
        explodes with piercing shards of scatter'd stars.

Touch?
        meager thought,
        far past such mortal bounds,
                far lost in timeless depths.

                                        7/93

For You

Soft and gentle, quiet, true,
these, my love, I feel for you.

Should time call and pass us by,
matters not to you or I.

My heart I give all, yet few,
'til you–feel love that is new.

Fresh and clean, warm, whole,
these, my love, come from my soul...

                              for you.

                                        7/93

Echoes

Opened doors, straining hinge.
    Brittle, crackling silence.
Dim lit dust, covered pasts,
    tender, empty place.
Laughter muted, touches struck,
    teary choking wound.
Love ensnared, precious boxed,
    tucked so deeply away.
Rusted closed. Memories held,
    softened tread of leaving.

9/84

Be Safe

Tired, lost, weary soul
strayed from loving grasp.
Whirl, press, running
                         thoughts
questioned hearth beyond.
Traded pain for empty nest,
traded warmth for bleakened
                         hope.
Wander on, protected coat,
search again for innocence.

1981

Weary

The failures of men come in assorted sizes
and vary with which they're received as surprises.
Failures in tasks bring frustrated sighs,
the failures of love cause bitter crying.
But with the failures of dreams–
        numb shock begins, and an emptiness sets in.

1981

Growing Pains

The shallow voices murmured in fear;
      the Dark One struck a flame.
Angry curses blew knowingly in vain;
      the candles tore a hole.
A silence fell within the lone soul;
      the ancient rite was done.
The threatening riddles were fully shunned;
      Black Cassock retained high throne.
Yet the flickering light no longer shone;
      it was quenched by a tear.

1980

Through Time

A sailing cloud,
a loving phrase,
a way of sharing
                quiet things.

A snowy man,
a mittened hand,
a way of making
                memories.

A moment's pause,
a simple kiss,
a night's fun
                has begun,
and lovers' time'
                has come.

1981

Her Work

What the poet does whisper,
my body has sung.
As in the black night,
we have made love.

While her verse is yet fashioned,
together we clung.
Her odd written word
joined us as one.

With mute strokes she shares freely,
our secrets of night.
Twilight comes to find
          us sleeping entwined,
while she writes on.

1984

Concerto in Love

The sweet joyous song that
      fills me from within,
A singing of my body
      with the happiness of no end.
The sound of your quiet words
      give my formless timing rhythm.
As the loving, soften'd gaze
      molds this inner melody.

The smell and feel of winding strands,
      give my hungry silence lyrics.
And my mind is filled with astoundment
      at this endless playing.
As play your hands lightly do,
      granting me such harmony.

A harmony of prose and poetry
      that my body has never known,
Of singing joyous serenity
      that this love within has sown.

9/93

Innsbruck's Greetings

Loving greetings are elusive things
when time is bound by mountain scenes,
        whose misty cloaks forbid
            a coming spring.

        But love itself is not so tied,
        by mountain peaks with
            timeless pride.

So hear the breeze of mountains sigh—
        and feel my love inside.

                                        1979

A Hummingbird Upon the Hand

surprise, delight
approach then flight.
beneath so many rippling leaves,
does the trust come near or go?

alight, then lift,
shiver or tremor?
fleeting sweeps to hidden lutes,
does stay mean touch or no?

surprise, delight
approach not flight,
whisper'd sighs do sooth the fear,
so stay means gentled slow....

1993

Young Amazon

The Amazon
      has touched thee with
      her praise and yet
      casts her eye upon thee
          with her strength you step
          with her courage you stand
          with her quickness you grasp
          with her heart you choose.
The Earth
      has blessed thee with
      her praise and yet
      cushions thy way upon her
          with her clay you formed
          with her wind you breath
          with her expanse you abandon
          with her order you calm.
               In Eons gone, the Two
                   passed life through
                   the pale nostrils of Diana,
                   and in mind did
                   the goddess rise.
               Again, the Two
                   mold and touch
                   their lips to new lips
                   their fingers to new breasts,
                   and in flesh now
                   a maiden lives.
Known by the tresses of Diana,
      those waxened strands of moon's touch;
Known by the gait of Them,
      the light, free pace of denied drudge;
Known by too few
      in her precious being–
          the fools know not how time must pass
          before the Two raise such a wommon again.

                                  1993

Hers
(Quiet Depths)

Quiet, soft, and warm
does scented breeze come 'cross my cheek
and stir memories fleeting yet bold
of satin'd skin and tighten'd hold.

Night of quiet depth
did wrap the shadows thicken'd here
(in guard of senseless, tainted faces)
broken by the gasp of two in life.

Senses softened then
as if awaken'd from the womb
and new so did press to meet with lips,
last does explode such sweetened agony.

In warmth two embrace,
the coursing waves had calm ensured,
and the settled throb of oneness glowed.
air of sweetened taste, of love
touched the sweated bodies...

                    and cooled...

                        and slept.

                              1981

Welcome

Soft... sparkle–shimmering light,
languid...lingering–loving caress.
Catch...careful–coloring blush
blueness...bold–bewitching stare,
soften...sheltering–sharing lair.

7/93

Begin Again

Young Muse
Young Love
Seems simple...just two.

But no,
Each plead!   Subtler,
Accuse mistrust!   new Muse
        emerges then.
Each beg–
Entreat!   Gentler,
Poor time's the score.   new Love
        steps light, yet near.
With shame,
Shameless   Respect.
Vye they for note.   Admire...
        Encourage craft.
Discord!
Ascend   Patience.
To sheer torment!   Cherish...
        Balanced new dance.
Honor
only   Behold–
lays forgotten.   How rich
        Blending makes both!

        True Muse,
        Deep Love–
        Binds Your Life Whole.

8/93

Cry!

Cry! As the dust of stars dissolves to dawn,
Loose the melody of lonely song.
Weaving the twilight, name the wrong.
Emptied shadows yield and show—
   my sweet lover's gone.

7/93

Soft Denim Blue

Blue.
So blue.
Silken shadows of your blouse reflecting.

Soft.
So soft.
Gentle glimpses of your soul reflecting.

Blue.
So Blue.
Subtle secrets, your desire reflecting.

Soft.
So soft.
Gazes joining, your heart's joy reflecting.

Blue.
So soft.
Brushed denim blue, your eyes–your eyes so blue.

9/93

To Touch In Trust

ignite
ascend
blend
soul to soul of heart to heart
unite
and ... remain.

9/93

Bound...

Muse belov'd so,
Hearts entrusted.
Passions unfurl'd~
in wind touched Fire!
Behold them bold.
Bless'd of Goddess
Light, Moon kiss'd Souls,
Such are those found...
                by the Firebird!

9/93

Please

Into your sacred dew bring me,
      cup of holy chalice.
Baptize this tasteless rue of err,
      and cleanse ill tongue of crimes.
Restore our hallowed trust again...
      In Gift–exquisite wine.

10/93

Discover

Across the breezes of the night
the scent–the brush...solely new...
comes velvet touch to linger,
Spoiling dreams of fantasy
in sultry tease of waking...

To eyes of star-reflected light,
to fond curved bow of welcome–
to kiss and pledge abandon...
Then leap! In fire–stunned. Eclipsed!

Intoxicating blue descends,
claims and fully takes the whole.
Yet heed–! More than all is won.

11/93

For The Woman I Love~

You hold my world
in your hand,
so easily—so safely.

The pearly glow
of my tears—
stem from wonder ...
                at your love.

11/93

Alight?! No!

Amidst the stars and snowy land about,
come ride with me on dreams and love,
come ride with me into the night–
into tomorrow–
      into the magics of sheer Life!

                                  12/93

A Wedding Wish

Exquisite dreams in dark arise,
yet often fade as dawns arrive.
May you two be within the few
whose morning's dew sparkles silver.

12/92

Wedding Invitation (one)

Come Near! Rejoice! As trusts are bound–
As lives entwine. The dance of two
Is bless'd by One. Let hearts sing–
Rejoice! And Come!

3/94

Wedding Invitation (two)

Heed the day!
Herald with song!
Grace descends
Blessing vows.
Join the dance!
Joy begs–come!

3/94

* * *

Songs

Chris Anne was not just a prolific writer but also an eclectic one. Just like she jumped genres, she jumped between mediums. Songs were little stories for her, not far removed from novels and almost indistinguishable from poetry. She crafted notes and words together at the same time, her mind creating a tune while her hand jotted down the lyrics. She played the guitar and would add the music like making a final pass to flesh out a manuscript.

One of the greatest losses I've had to face as a publisher was the melodies, the music to all but one of Chris Anne's songs. She never learned to write music but, during the last month of her life, two of her caretakers at the beautiful hospice where she lived, offered to take a cassette tape of her singing and playing her songs and write all the music down for her. Unfortunately, though the cassette of the songs did indeed disappear from her possessions, no family or friends were ever contacted by the two caretakers and Chris Anne never mentioned their names.

The only song that still exists in its entirety is "Lazy Day." Chiding me for being a workaholic, Chris Anne would sit and sing "Lazy Day" to me until I couldn't help but shut down my computer or close my ledger book.

Through the Pain

There are windows set in the wall at the end of the hall
With a box seat nestled in pillows of calico red.
And the cat in the sun lays curled asleep on her bed.
(But) the window is clos'd and the world there outside just
hurries on by.___

Refrain
Through the pain I find,___
yes, the sun still shines____
and the sky is still blue ___ even without you.

But your hands___
And your voice___
And your smile___
Still reach___ out to me.____

Through all the tears and the jeers my heart does not yield.
With the anger and hurt my mind screams to me, "Now
Leave___"
But the quiet time comes and calm whispers to me.
(And) I know that there's more to this life that we share than
these scenes.

Refrain

Through the years and the fears, the clouds will pass by.
With stumbling steps and graying strands, we'll survive.
Peace might descend or torrents of madness may fly,___
(But) together we'll sit in the sun at the end of the hall.___

And long past the pain,___
we'll see the sun come out again,___
and the sky will be blue ___ even with you____
with you.

Let Love Descend

Hush my Darling and dry your tears.
Take our hands, Dear, calm your fears.
The darkness shall not hide,___
the joy we have inside!___
Peace shall come, let love descend.

Corner'd and hidden without light,
fears grow stronger, hatred spawns flight.
But darkness shall not hide, ___
the joy we have inside!
Peace shall come, let love descend.

Alone the well is icy and harsh,
freezing the soul and chilling the heart.
But empty hearths can warm again.___
Our fire has no end!
(All) come gather near! let love descend.

Hush my Darling and dry your tears.
Take our hands, Dear, calm your fears.
The darkness shall not hide,___
the joy we have inside!___
Peace shall come, let love descend.
Peace shall come, let love descend.
Peace shall come, let love descend.

Journeys' End

Turning, reaching, finding truth.___
Turning, changing, face of love.
Bitter wines, sorrow'd times,
Havens found yet moorings unbound.
Winds that guide may falsehood hide.
But journeys' ends are coming now.
Journeys' ends are coming.

Turning, reaching, finding truth,
turning, changing, wrapped in love.
Colors fold in rhymes untold.
Forgotten words of trust and true.
Careful touch, uncertain of foe.
But journeys' ends are coming now.
Journeys' ends are coming.

Turning, reaching, finding truth.
Turning, changing, warming love.
Friend to find, a patience kind.
Sharing comes as sweetly as slow.
Peace descends to heart and home.
For journeys' ends are coming now.
Journeys' ends are coming.

Turning, reaching, find truth.
Turning, changing, warming love.
Sweeten'd wines, biding time.
Haven found, strong moorings now bound.
Winds that guide have naught to hide,
as journeys' ends are coming now.
As journeys' ends are come.

Sweet, Luring Light

The skies are turning crimson now,___ coming is the day.
The stars are fading quietly away;
My gaze will seek the stirring form___ laying at my side.
In a moment. missed. the stars have come___ to rest in her waking eyes.___

Shine bright, oh luring light.___
Arms entwine, gone is the power of time!___

Leave me tarry a moment more,___ whispered is my plea.
Enchantment stays the climbing sun, I see.
Sweetly now I taste the brew,___ wetted are my lips.
Our kiss fulfills the timeless need...consumed by the light in her eyes.___

Lazy Day

Lazy day of misty raindrops___.
Holding hands and sipping chocolate___.
Smiling eyes of stormy shades
      pull my cloak away to find my soul___
      so fine___ a touch...
      so fine___.
The day is warmed by your song.
And love is bright in our home.
My heart is won by your quiet ways___
as your gentle kiss enchants___
      so fine___

Sharing bread of homemade recipes.
Dust the shelves and fill the teapot.
But waiting eyes of stormy shades
      pull my cloak away to find my soul___
      so fine___ a touch...
      so fine___.
And fire is lit within my breast.
Hands draw us near, one tender rest.
Let time drift by___ with our gentleness,
As the rain plays on the rooftop.

Lazy day of misty raindrops___.
Holding hands and sipping chocolate___.
Smiling eyes of stormy shades
      pull my cloak away to find my soul___
      so fine___ a touch...
      so fine___.
The day is warmed by your song.
And love is bright in our home.
My heart is won by your quiet ways___
as your gentle kiss enchants___
      so fine___ a touch.

A Proposal

Moonlight and stars,___
Wishes aplenty,
A daydream come true___
could I give to you!___

Glitter and diamonds,
romantic cruises,___
these would I gift to you!___

But posies and violets,
and long silent walking
are all I can offer anew.___

Fine timber lodgings,
a collie or two,
a view from Monaco___
would I share with you!___

But pennies aren't copper
and silver's yet rar'r.
Gold have I neith'r, 'tis true.

So posies and violets
and long silent walking
are all I can offer anew___

But posies and violets
and long silent walking,
these I do offer to you!

An Invitation to Waltz

Touch me, Stroke me, Feel___ My Love.
Holding soft in blanket of night.___
Trusting, warmly, guiding with hand.
Come, My Love, embrace my soul.___

Touch me___ Join me___ with loving hands.
Stroke me___ Hold me___ through climbing seas.
See me, Know me. Well, My Love?___
Come and dance with me tonight
        And the stars will blind in our light___ (rest)

Touch me, Stroke me, Feel___ My Love.
Holding soft in blanket of night.___
Touch me___ Stroke me___ Know me...____
        Perchance we'll the stars outshine, Love.
        Perchance we'll the stars outshine._____

I've gone through days of lonely chills ___
and nights of mellow blues.
I've had the sun rise up to see
the shades of dreams___ just___ flee.
I've ridden the roads alone,
and shared a year or two of hope.
I've sought so many times
to find the way ___ for heart ___ for soul ___ for love ___

(My) Life's been rich with giving freely ___
sharing and sheer being.
(My) Life's been full of precious ones,
sweet with friends ___ and fam-mily.
Yet moment came with clarity,
no doubts would cloud my mind ___
a sense of absent kin,
some soulmate undefined ___
for heart ___ for soul ___ for love ___

Behind the words of prose I'd write,
beyond the setting sun ___
Within the harvest glow of night
when autumn's Moon ___ rose full ___
I'd sometimes swear I saw
you there, beckoning with light ___
I'd hear your whisper in the wind, in song ___
for heart ___ for soul___ for love___

Now days of lonely chills have gone ___
and nights are passion hued.
The sun rises up and finds
two lives have joined ___ as one ___
Bring minstrels with their worlds of joys
Or ballads of poor times ___
All are met with strength and pride
with you near ___ my heart ___ my soul ___ near with love

Beneath the Candle's Light

Melt the shrouded darkness wrapped 'round my poor heart!
Catch the tattered threads of my life!
Spell bound I'll watch as you gently weave me ___
new breath ___ new life ___ beneath the candle's light ___
      Graze of eyes or smokey misting?
      Candlewick and flickering flame.
      Cat in hand and whispered chanting.
      Softest touch or breath? Am I sane ___?

Warmed by the touch of your lingering hands.
Assured by your radiant smile.
Caught in your arms as you lead me ___
in love ___ in trust ___ beneath the candle's light ___

Now bid I you to move in my grasp,
feel my stroking softness.
Blending and skin, numbing in sense ___
spiral of (em)passion'd___shadows and light!

Christmas Prayer

Candy canes, singing carols
Secrets held, bows a'tied,
Listen well, heed the time
as Christmas draws near.

Wishes and love ___ have brought us so far ___
Hand clasped to hand ___ now laughter not tears ___
Know this home warms ___ it's a special year ___

Packages small ___ and glittering lights ___
Sugar and dough ___ red wine and clove ___
Sharing this night ___ our blessings we know ___

Our treasures shared ___ from our hearts ___
gifts put aside ___ know our love ___
by the touch of my hand ___ by the glow in your eyes ___

Our treasures shared ___ from our hearts ___
gifts put aside ___ know our love ___
by the touch of my hand ___ by the glow in your eyes ___

To the Ends of Time

Tales of old log cabins ___ and fires burning bright___
The winter wind's a whistlin' ___ as I nestle close to your side
___

And I'm happy, oh so happy ___
with the melody in your eyes ___ of a love from deep inside ___

It's in the way the strength of your arms surround me,
holding me so close and yet ___ so light ___ I know...

You love me.___ As I love you ___
And we're destined ___ eternally ___ together ___
For my love I am yours ___ as you are mine ___
To the ends of time ___

Log cabins turn to houses ___ and fires may burn low ___
Outsiders may stare coldly ___ but our love ___ is still whole ___
It's reflected in the tender reverence of your kiss,
and the gentle touch of your hands ___ on me___ yes...

You show it in the words you speak of knowing care ___
your voice so low and kind, you could make me cry___ yes.

* * *

Under a Crimson Sun

Here lie the fertile seeds that grew to become "Sands of Aggar," the third book in the Aggar series. Filled with gypsies, war-mages, pixies, and polyamorous relationships, a blood feud drives the plots forward with an unrelenting speed.

Tweaking her own unique approach to writing, Chris Anne dove into "Under a Crimson Sun" without her usual outline. She originally set it on a totally new world; she didn't want any rules or pre-existing guidelines to hamper her creativity. But as she wrote – creating scenes out of order, writing in a nonlinear way – she couldn't escape the truth.

This world was Aggar. These characters were the descendents of Amazons, Shadows and even Aggar natives and Terrans. This is what came after "Fires of Aggar." The adventure was continuing. She stopped all writing and drafted a outline which she mailed to me, hand-written.

I don't know if Chris Anne knew she'd never be able to finish "Sands of Aggar." She often sent me hand-written outlines and stories without any explanation. But when we last spoke on the phone, her intentions were more than clear:

"We're good, aren't we, Jennifer?" she asked.

"Yes. I think so," I assured her, honestly.

"And you have the outlines and all the finished chapters. You can fill in the blanks and no one will be able to tell the difference." And then she laughed.

I never intended to try to "fool" anyone – readers or editors alike, and I don't think that's what Chris Anne really meant. She meant that the stories, the ideas, and many of the words, were hers... and even if I finished some of the chapters for her, they would remain hers. She didn't want me to ghost write; she wanted me to know, beyond a shadow of a doubt, that every word I put down would be the very ones she would choose.

With the grace of those muses that Chris Anne believed so strongly in, I hope, some day, that her "Sands of Aggar" will be in readers' hands. And yes, every single word will be her own.

The music was frenzied with tin rhythms of shaker bells and tambourine trim. The pipes, then the fiddles, were lost in the tempo. A quickening, dizzying, rushing tempo – it grew, driving the dancer faster and faster. Her hair swirled in long tangles of red fire. Muscles corded in calf and thigh, then arching back and into the springing leap. The pointing of a bare foot... the rippling of white, oiled flesh... impressions were lent of clothing, colored scraps – of beauty, as none of the body's stretch nor pull was hidden. In mid-leap – around and into a spin she went, knee bending for landing and her spinning never ceasing.

Torches whirled into a solid ring of light. Music became only tempo, only the madness of spinning with arms wide – then pull in at the elbows, faster.

Crowds faded with the fever burning, faces blurring – spinning. Spinning–

Darkness, then blackness eclipsed. The vision rose in the instant. A warrior woman, tall and silent... a silver shimmer from her helmless head to booted toe. The sword blade shimmered. Held high, it descended with a death blow.

Dancia's green eyes blinked – startled, and the present returned to her. Through her masses of red hair, she peered out. The crowd was applauding. There was laughter tinged with amazement. She was huddled over a knee, her arms flung back.

So – she had completed the dance then.

Whooping shadows leapt in over her head. Dancia pasted the sparkling smile to her face and without fully rising, back out of the dancing circle. The acrobats with their long knife splendors had arrived. Her part for the evening was done.

Kelsa greeted her with a thick blanket and pulled her further off to the side. After the sweating exertion of the dance, the night air was quick to grow icy; the scraps of ribbon and string that covered her breasts and hips were not worn to warm her.

"You danced a vision again, didn't you?" Kelsa pressed, rubbing her sister's arms through the blanket. Another of their wandering *vana* hurried past, handing a mug of brewed tea to Dancia with a quick grin.

Kelsa slanted a look at her sister; it was half teasing, half serious. Sometimes Dancia did not leave her visions behind when she left the dancing.

"I'm fine," elven-slim brows lifted with sudden mischief. "Since when have you such an interest in another's visions? Or did my feet lose the timing with my meanderings?"

Kelsa laughed and spun her sister to face the crowd. "Since I'm wondering if that one there has taken your fancy in the dancing? You seemed to be using him for your focal point. I wondered if you'd been seeing him and the stars for the coming night!"

"Not such a bad notion–" Dancia shrugged the blanket up onto her shoulders a little more. She noticed the clean jerkin and britches favorably. She noticed the heavy money purse at his hip even more favorably.

Then, the sandy haired fellow moved aside a step. His grin took on a knowing, good-natured quirk, and he nodded to direct his companion's attention towards the two sisters.

"I take it all back," Kelsa murmured impishly. "I should have know it wasn't him you were noticing at all."

The woman was lanky with a short cap of honey-blond hair. She met Dancia's bold stare and then blushed brightly, backing a step away and out of sight.

"She looks awfully young–" Kelsa mused warily. Her eyes, however, were still plainly glued to the fellow. "Sibs do you think? Or are we about to walk into something unpleasant?"

"She's not young," Dancia corrected absently. A very small, very pleased – slightly wicked, smile grew on her narrow chinned face.

Something in her sib's voice caught Kelsa's attention. She peered over Dancia's shoulder, looking more closely as the woman ventured back into view. This time the woman managed to withstand the sisters' scrutiny.

"You're right," Kelsa conceded slowly, appreciatively. "Not young at all. Merely that 'always do right and be a good little merchant' sort of girl."

"And they are sibs. Look at the set of those eyes – those straight noses." Dancia turned, sliding the blanket from her shoulders and dumping it back into Kelsa's hand. From Kelsa's own belt, she untied the flat folded pouch of soaps and herbs and common sense sort of things as an impish little gleam lit her eyes. "And I'll bet the whole family is the very 'good little merchant' type – the type that doesn't want to be good tonight!"

"Dani – you wouldn't! You didn't even notice him until I said something!"

She couldn't resist tormenting her sister with a baiting chuckle, but before Kelsa's fury could erupt, Dancia grabbed her in a hug. "Relax, dear Sib," she whispered against her ear, and kissed Kelsa's cheek in peace-offering. "She'd run frightened as a hare from a fox at the very mention of a threesome."

Relief and chagrin mixed in Kelsa's laugh. Then raising a mischievous brow herself, she challenged, "I wouldn't wager against her running, if she knew what you're up to anyway–"

"Up to? Me?" Dancia rumbled a deep throated purr and rounded, her gaze seeking the woman in question. Her fingers fastened the small pouch to her hip string-cloth. "Why – I'll not do a single thing she'll not want done.... And I shall tell Big Brother to watch for your coming dance."

"Tell him, it will be especially...," Kelsa drawled slow, smiling yet slower, "–for him."

Their laughter rang low, their green eyes sparkling with joy and promises as they parted.

The music played. The bells and pipes had claimed the fair. Dancia felt her pulse match the tempo again. Her feet, delicate and yet so strong, instinctively stepped into rhythm even as she walked. The night smelt clean to her. The air was crisp. The audience – these townfolk were happy, perhaps – just edging towards giddy recklessness.

Her smile curled into a delicious invitation. Her emerald eyes glittered with the silver of pixie dust, and the young woman turned to spy Dancia's approach.

The breath caught in the stranger's throat. Trepidation was flooded beneath the pounding rush of blood in her veins. But the music captured her in its rhythm – held her bound still in Dancia's unspoken vow... in the magic of the enchantress.

Dancia smiled, extending a slim-fingered hand. It was a beautiful night to love.

>>> <<<

"Who do I believe in, do you mean?" Briar uncrossed her legs and dangled an arm across an upraised knee, head tilted a bit to the side as she stared into the fire; it was an unconscious mime of Sana's pose. The gesture implied an intimacy that startled Dancia. She threw an almost accusing stare of emerald across the fire, but Sana said nothing. Calmly she rearranged her feet flat and hunched forward with her elbows on her knees. She raised a single brow of challenge at Dancia's continued scrutiny. The other relented quickly.

And still Briar had not answered. Her silence drew them both back to her. Her hazel eyes seemed almost copper bright in the blazing light of the campfire. The faintest of frowns spoke of concentration, and puzzled, Dancia scowled. The Goddess Mother of the woods witches was a fairly common character to the folk she'd visited in the last few years, and the nurturing comfort The Figure preached was a simple, straight-forward doctrine... at least, so Dancia had thought.

"If you had asked me last spring what I believe, I wouldn't have thought twice of my answer," Briar began at last, her words coming slowly. "Gentleness, mercy... balance of spring growth and winter death. The mysteries of the Goddess Mother are infinite, but the limits of my understanding were... bearable? I admit, I was content."

Sana watched her through the dancing curtain of flames as Briar went quiet once more. Lips pursed, then she prodded, "That was spring, it's autumn now."

"Yes, and beliefs change. I... changed."

Dancia heard pain in that admission. "You don't like what you've become?"

At that Briar abruptly looked to the elfkin, her hazel gaze intense and disconcerting. But her tone was low and unaccusing with, "I don't like what I must do. That is not the same as disliking myself."

"Then how do you reconcile it?" Dancia snapped, anxiety bringing the words our more harshly than she'd intended.

"With the teaching of the Goddess Mother?" Bleakly Briar's eyes went back to the fire. "Her balance between spring and winter has been broken. Left unchecked, these brothers..." her glance flickered briefly to Sana "...these brothers would indiscriminately destroy the innocent. She is Mother of all children... to all those of any good, and like a mother whose cubs are threatened, She can not sit idle and watch that destruction descend."

"So you were elected as some sort of Hand of God?"

"No," Briar gently countered Dancia's cynicism. "I hurt. I saw the others hurt. I could not deny what needed to be done. I could not live with the knowledge that there would be others... not and try nothing to stop the terror."

Sobered, Dancia nodded. Her voice softened, "I'm sorry. I meant no disrespect."

"I know," Briar smiled in reassurance. "Despite the healing of both your Moonborn and my Goddess Mother, the pain returns from time to time." She looked at Sana, including her in that acknowledge and not ever wanting her to be alone with that kind of cruel grief. But the Swordarm was staring at some nebulous point just above their campfire... grey eyes unblinking. With fingers steapled before her chin, much of her expression was hidden by her hands and the shadows.

Dancia felt the uneasiness stir—that vague tremor of her visions rose to remind her of how haunting she found Sana. Yet a fist seemed to close about her heart, squeezing with the sight of one so...so exquisitely, poignantly alone—a grey ghost of a figure. She felt tears prick at the backs of her eyes and she blinked as her throat tightened.

Then Briar's gentle voice reach out through the night. "What do you see, Sana?"

"Death." The soft reply mirrored no emotion, merely fact. "Unless we can stop them. It takes o magics to see that."

"And yourself?" Dancia breathed, almost too frightened to ask. "Why do you follow these men, Swordarm?"

Grey eyes—steel silver eyes—pierced her. "Because I am the Chosen Hand of the Star Strider." Sana rose then, leaving them with a murmur of "I'll claim first watch."

>>> <<<

It was miserably wet. Thunderstorms rumbled in the east, promising to turn the chilly spring drizzle into a torrential downpour before twilight completely faded. The cobbles were slick, and the steel shod hooves of the war mare chipped the stones with each heavy clop. But there was barely anyone to notice. The small town was shut tight against the rains. Timbers and gutters dripping, mortar sheeting wet, and mud running thick all made a stick and gravel sludge of swirling brown water that cautioned any traveler. Smoke was thicker, curling gray-blue as it was drafted down from chimney spouts to make a damp fog in alleys and dead air spaces. The place smelled of wood burning and sewage, but the rankness was muted by the wet cold; it would grow worse later beneath summer suns.

The blacksmith's doors were slanted open, the orange blazes dancing deep in the shadows. The ping-ping of the anvil's hammer echoed a strange sort of welcoming.

It was one Sana accepted. She ducked low and rode Dread straight through the smithy's door. The rain tarp cowled both her and the gear across Dread's flanks. For a moment, the hammer's song stilled. Then she loosed the throat string and slid out from beneath the oiled skin, stepping down from the saddle with a very mortal creak to the leather seat.

The hammer thunked against the stout floorboards, and the burly male picked up a towel to wipe the sweat from his hands. He passed the rag through the matted hair of his chest in an absent gesture, through damp fur that rivaled the growth on his face, then tossed it aside as Sana took a stance across the anvil from him. She was nearly as hidden as she had been beneath the tarp. The heavy silverish gray of her cloak covered her from calf to head. The hood was pulled forward and low, creating a dense shadow where her eyes should have been, and only the smoothness of her pale chin hinted at her sex.

"Cold day," the smithy noted. His hands curled into hammer-like fists on his hips.

"Cold enough," she returned levelly. Fingers gloved in grey, stitched leather underlined her resources as a gold bar the size of a thumb was extended to him. "She needs shoes, the padded sort to dull travel shock, but with sharp honed edges to the fore pair."

"Aye," he nodded and took the gold piece. "I've done the like for merchant guards and passing kings' men."

"And her tack needs a slow drying, not too near the fire.

Then a good cleaning and oiling."

"Have a girl apprenticed to me, she'll do it right. If you like, I've stalls for boarding too. Better'n the Red Griffin next door, although theirs aren't bad. Both are broad, fine boxes. But I've got tack shelf and saddle bar in each, for your animal to guard your pieces."

It went without saying that Dread was the sort of steed to have that training.

"An' the side door's always open. You can leave at your own pleasure, waken me or not."

"Fair enough."

He picked up an iron length, clanging the triangle hung above as Sana retrieved a smaller bag from beneath Dread's tarp. A squarely built youngster of fourteen appeared as a door whacked shut in the back. Sana noted the attentive glint in those hazel eyes and approved.

"You listen to these two," she murmured to Dread and her mare gave a snort, nodding consent. She turned to the smithy again. "Keep your movements slow. If she gets nervous, step back and keep your hands where she can see them. She'll calm down by herself, if she's satisfied."

"An' if she isn't, you're not goin' need worry 'bout it anymore," the man warned his apprentice. The girl nodded but didn't flinch.

Sana paused, watching as the apprentice came forward and led Dread away. The mare flicked her tail and tossed a chiding look back at Sana, as if to remind her rider that she too was capable of distinguishing between children and dubious spies. It made Sana smile. The youngster moved out of ear range, and Sana amended, "There is another thing."

The smithy paused, his hot bladed knife angled above the gold bar ready to cut her change.

"A less tangible need."

He laid the blade aside and consideringly weighed the money in his hand. His sharp eyes darted back towards the stable hall to be sure his girl wasn't near enough to hear something that might get her hurt later. He grunted, hefting the gold piece again. He tossed it into the leather bucket with others and nodded for her to continue.

"Who has passed through and what routes out did they

take?"

"How far back?"

There was a silence, until finally, "You tell me."

He gave a short sigh, then another nod. "War party, fresh looting."

"That's the one."

"They split by two roads. East and Southeast. Most of 'em went east, but the dangerous ones maybe went separate."

"How so?"

"They were ridin' the faster horses. Every one of 'em carried barbed spears 'long with side sabers. No archers that I could see. They were meanin' business. Took food an' the saddle packs they could carry, but they left the pack animals an' the finery with the others. Looked like scouts, the lot of 'em... travelin' so light."

Or a skirmish attack honed in on a target, Sana corrected.

"Another thing. One circled back in from the East Road group. He came with a merchant's band, a big one from the Nor'west Way. He's dressed fancier. Last time he kept his cloak on and his face mostly covered, but we recognized 'em. The tender of Red Griffin as well as myself. A big fella with black beard goin' gray in streaks. He's got a good smile to 'em, but it's the kind that don't reach his eyes. An' he don't look at you much when he's talkin'. Instead, he's busy watchin' the doors an' roads beyond the windows."

Her step-father's brother, Gryert... a battle weaned sergeant grown into a general's strategist who'd probably given her brothers every last trick in his arsenal of ploys. He was a mercenaries' delight; she was about to become his nightmare.

The smithy watched as she mutely picked up her bag and gave him a brief nod of thanks before stepping out into the rain. His eyes narrowed speculatively. He'd do best to keep the apprentice upstairs with his missus tonight. He'd take his hammer up as well. He never much liked looters, that more than the money had been his reason for talking to the stranger. But he wasn't a stupid man either, and he had to respect anyone wearing a sword the way that fellow in Red Griffin did. He hoped the woman knew what she was doing — for all their sakes.

She entered from the side, near hidden in the smoke and shadows of the long bar's end. It was a common enough place to come from, since it was the door nearest the smithy's front and in such weather any traveler needing their horse re-shod would have chosen the same. But instead of joining the warmth and hustle of the center room, Sana slipped further back into the corner to watch. Her hood pushed back some, enough to let the lack of whiskers and the angular caste of her features become clear, yet not enough to bring her whole face into view… and her silver cap of hair was still quite covered. She knew Gryert might not recognize her face after all the years she'd spent away schooling. He'd recognize that pewter hair, however. If not for herself, then for one like her in hunting him and the Triplets. And she held no fantasies about toying with him or learning anything of value from him. He was here for the sole purpose of identifying the hunters that would be sent after the nephews, and he was undoubtedly charmed against deceptive disguises. That arcane power would tie him to the boys as well, allowing him to pass on much of what he saw whenever he willed. The trick would be in catching him off-guard enough that he didn't send them her image.

Later, there would be time enough for her brothers to know she followed. For now, she would use the anonymity.

Yellow light streamed in through the thick tobacco haze, bringing smells of greasy fats roasting and caramel sweets browning. Behind the bar, the kitchen opened in a yawning wide gape above the ale kegs, and food passed out as dirty trays slid in. The clanging of metal pots and cooks curses mingled with the ruckus of the tavern customers. Lively betting on some card game vied with another table's rowdy celebration of a young soldier's merits. Ermine cuffed jackets and stained sheepskin vests rubbed shoulders here. It was a merchant traveler's lodge where the better swords and the traders' off-spring drank together even as they did on the journey roads, because the first were well paid and the second still too young to disdain.

Sana noted the variety in meats served as she exchanged coin for ale. Their selection was impressive for so small a town, so far from the rest of humanity. It was also probably the only inn around with private rooms. The liveries she had passed on the outskirts had been lined with barracks above to allow goods, stock and guards to stay near enough to one another, and they were more than likely a caravans' first choice for crew lodgings. That explained why Gryert was here. He would want his privacy to discourage the locals' questions and yet need the access to the travelers' news.

She knew then, he would certainly be here... somewhere.

Across the room she finally saw him. He was a sable clad man of older years who leaned to the side of his chair, a leg extended parallel to his table and his shoulder comfortably pressed against the stone wall. His back was mostly guarded by that wall. His fingers played with the jeweled hilt of the short sword at his hip. Above him, the upper stairs glowed brightly from lanterns in the stairwell, and the creak of the wood boards would have announced any's descent. Before him, laughing and filling their short cups with spirits, a pair of merchant sons revealed in some story he was encouraging from them. His grin showed white teeth through his smooth, thick beard as he chewed on a mint taper. He nodded at something the two said, eyes rounding through the crowd haphazardly.

He was becoming lax in his assumptions, Sana noted. The rains had begun to pour and the thunders lashed with lightnings outside. The weather was altogether too nasty for anybody of sense to be traveling in, and he was beginning to think he would be safely unhindered for at least another night.

She ordered a bowl of mushroom barley for dinner. She could afford to wait and let him grow assured.

He looked straight at her. But her face was not particularly hidden and her manner drew no attention. The bar was crowded with quieter locals towards her end, and her greyish cloak faded in with their drab browns and greens. She mimed the hunch of those about her well, their hoods bared just enough to invite a friend's conversation and hide enough to discourage a stranger's frivolity. Again his gaze swept past her.

Gryert had indeed become careless since the years she had known him. But then the boys' magics had undoubtedly given him less need for caution.

Or perhaps, she was under-rating how her own skills

had grown.

She watched, and as the night drew on his back inched further and further away from the wall. She ordered another ale and asked about rooms.

"Plenty, if you're willing to share?" the bar's tender prodded agreeably.

"The room yes, the bed no."

"Still got a few to choose from."

"Something with less noise would be best."

The jovial grin took on a somewhat more ironic twist. "You've got a choice 'tween kitchen clatter an' customer chatter."

A slow smile answered him, although he couldn't have said if it was being good-natured or sarcastic in return. "The kitchen's will do fine."

"Good enough then." He fished a great ring of keys out from beneath his apron and extracted a wooden one from the set. He held it out of her reach. "Money up front."

She slid a pair of small, but flawed jewels across the bar to him. "Instead of coin stick?"

"Acceptable." On a merchant's route, it wasn't such an unusual thing. He pointed at the stairs behind Gryert. "Top floor, back hall not front. You'll find space in the double, third room on the left. Fire's not lit, but your wood's included. So's breakfast porridge an' breads."

She nodded and stood, pausing for a last pull on the weak ale as she saw Gryert rearranging his chair. She put her stein down as he faced himself towards his table, drinking a parting toast with his companions. She moved along the bar, slipping between elbows and shoulders unnoticed. The merchant boys left to join the dicing games, and Gryert reached across the table to grab a half-emptied glass and drain it. The motion freed his sword's pommel knob, an octagonal gem bright in its bloody redness, and she recognized the talisman from her brothers.

He stretched again to retrieve the bottle. This time she closed in, the slender length of her short sword skritching as it left its sheath. He rounded at the sound, hearing it even in the tavern's noise. His hand went down, but too slow, and the scabbard belt sliced, his sword falling. She grabbed for his hair as he shoved the chair back hard into her belly. She missed and the table went over in his scramble.

They faced each other then, across the width of the suddenly silent room. His long knife was drawn. His dark eyes squinted, his confusion apparent as he tried to fathom why a lone swordarm would be attacking him; he'd anticipated a mercenary crew. She unfastened her cloak and let it fall aside, covering the red gem of the weapon at her feet. Her baggage dropped with it.

His stance widened as did his eyes, disbelief and fear mixing as he rasped, "Why?! It means the Order's outcasting for you!!"

"Kin blood!" she hissed.

He recognized her then for who she was and not merely what. "But you're dead?!"

A knife flew from her hand, his blade angled up to deflect it. The second he never saw coming, and it pinioned his arm into the wood beam above him as the knife fell from his fist. She slammed his freed hand against the wall as the point of her blade jabbed beneath his sternum, barely stayed by the chain mail beneath his sable vest.

"They said you were dead!"

"Not quite."

Silver-grey eyes stared into his fear, steady and unflinching, and the calmness he saw made him in an instant, certain of her three brothers' demise. All their plans, all their ambitions... there wasn't going to be enough blood in the world to succor the Triplets into powers to withstand her onslaught.

"Tell me who rides east and who southeast?"

He swallowed thickly, knowing what would come. In a whisper he said, "No."

"Aravin sith vin...." The slender steel of her blade slid through the chain mail, her magic turning it to less than butter.

The room's silence was deafening save for that last gurgle of breath, and then his head rolled to the side. Only then did Sana step back, letting his carcass fold down into a heap. She wiped the slender length of her sword clean on the silk of his blouse sleeve. Her blade returned to its sheath upon her right hip. Then she stood, shrugging as she did to resettle the heavier weight of the larger weapon strapped to her back. Most in the tavern had not even noticed she carried another sword before now, they'd all been too intent on the conflict itself. Sana bent once more, snatching a leather tag from Gryert's neck and snapping its thong with a deft twist.

She looked around the hushed crowd slowly. "Who travels west?"

An uncomfortable murmur ran through her audience, but quiet fell again as a dwarf stood and stepped away from his table. Another of his kind followed, placing himself at his friend's elbow. Their unruly long beards were tucked into wide belts, and both were armed with short, fat knives and heavy, two-bladed axes.

"We do, Warmage," the first one rumbled, thumbs tucking into his belt as his chin thrust forward. "We go all the way to your capital city."

He surprised her. This far from her country's borders, Sana had not expected to find any that knew of the Grey Exiles from the Order. She lifted the leather bit. "Will you take this with a message to the Tribunal?"

Her gentle tone was utterly surprising to the folks; she spoke clearly with question and gave no hint of command. The dwarf stalked forward, halting a pace from her outstretched hand to eye the tag cautiously. There was nothing more than the family seal embossed on it. He grunted and nodded. It made sense; she had cried for kin blood.

Sana gave it to him and gestured at Gryert's body. "He'll carry gold stick in his purse. Whatever he has, it's payment for the favor."

A rumble assent of sorts accepted her terms. Then he faced her more squarely and prompted, "You said a message too."

"Tell them, it has begun ." Their gazes met, and the dwarf understood. It would be the last thing her people ever heard from her; but it was a testimony more than a message. It meant at least some price had been extracted for the crimes, and her folk would not be forced to hire mercenaries to pursue the matter more.

He honored her with a waist deep bow, a thing almost unheard of with a dwarf's pride. She returned it in full.

He went to retrieve Gryert's purse as she rounded

towards the bar and the tavern's tender. She flipped a gold stick through the air before he could protest the dueling. He sized it in his palm, then her in her grey leathers. His fist closed about the money, and he turned towards the patrons.

"House pays for the ale! Set yourselves down'n we'll bring it right to you!"

The tender sent a pair to clear away the body, and Sana retrieved her things near the stairs. She took Gryert's sword too, careful to keep her cloak draped about it. But she wasn't concerned that someone might accuse her of theft. She was wary of the talisman gem. It was still a thing to be dealt with.

In the dim passage above she found her room quickly. It wasn't surprising that it was empty; the hour was still early. Although, given her display downstairs, the one who'd paid for the bed next to hers might think twice about claiming it. That, and it wasn't the sort of room that one would generally spend a lot of time in. The place was clean, but stark. A pair of cots with worn, but thick woven blankets and a small table with a single chair were its complete furnishings. There was also cut wood in a heavy ceramic pot next to the fireplace and a matching set of oil lamps suspended in sconces above the mantel. It was not a particularly comfortable place for entertaining. But it would serve Sana's needs.

She dumped her gear on the bed, carefully laying the cloaked sword beside it and lit one of the wall lamps. Turning to plank table next, she shoved it's shorter end up against the wall. She took a step back, decided there was too much light and dimmed the wick some. There was no reason to tell her brothers exactly where she was, if they should notice her use of their talisman. Although she wasn't certain they'd ward it against a stranger's use, because she suspected arrogance might have made them too sure of Gryert's skills to bother with such charms.

From her rolled pack, she extracted a bundle of thin, but sturdy hide tubes and chose one. The parchment map shook out and spread easily; she kept them well oiled so they'd be malleable and fairly waterproof. She hung the sheet over the table, tacking it into the wall with two small knives that had made a false buckle on her back sword's harness. Then she retrieved Gryert's weapon from the bed and beneath the cloak, unsheathed the blade. She drove the end into the table top with a thud and then cautiously moved away, holding her cloak up like a curtain behind the bespelled thing.

The red gem glittered atop the sword's hilt, bound by a little wire cage. With an unnatural splay of sparks, it spat and hissed for a moment. She waited patiently for it to settle into a steady, pink glow and then drew nearer again, still keeping the grey cloth high. A beacon-like stream of ruby-blood light began sweeping — rotating — in a full circle. Sana watched from over the edge of her cloak with a growing satisfaction; there had been no warding.

"Questions for thee," she rasped in a low, low voice that mimicked an elderly sage or a hoarse demon tone. The jewel responded, drawing its auras back into its center in readiness. "Three masters thy have, aside from the fool bearer. Fashioned were thee as the eye for the Triplet's. Now comes the time,these Three must thee find. The First is Eldest, Laik by name..."

The red light flashed out, singeing a brown smote on the map's line of the East Trader's route.

"... and the Second is Middle, both elder and younger. Gettival by name."

Again the light burned the map, the spot growing blacker as the same place was scorched.

"Then is the Third, the Youngest of Three... thy master Foxsen."

This time it lit a fainter mark on the Southeast Road. Sana smiled grimly. Fox was still magically the weaker of the three. In some ways the bullies had not changed much since she'd known them in their toddler skirts.

"Now Fire Eye, another query of thee. Show the place they will meet, to join again as Three."

Beyond the denser forests, the red glow shadowed a village-small town labeled Cont. It was less than she had hoped, the light left no singed flecking; their plans were tentative, at best. She tried a last question, knowing those distant masters were probably already sensing something wrong.

"There are targets to be struck, precious goods to reap — all will come before the Three meet. Point to these places thy masters ride for, point to the rape and the war."

Lightening struck out in scarlet bolts and left smoke curling about a ragged, charred hole. It pointed at nothing her maps knew. There wasn't even a nearby road's turn or a hunter's trail indicated in that forested landscape. But there was something on that Southeastern route...something so vitally important to the Three that their ambitions were completely united for it.

"Sleep now, thy rest is earned." Sana was almost haphazard in remembering to cover the talisman again.

It was a puzzle that remained, even as she bound the gemmed hilt with shredded blanket cloth and laid it in the hearth. With her uttered spell, fires engulfed both sword and talisman in cold, white flames of magic. She stood, watching that steel and ruby weapon evaporate into harmless nothingness, and then when it was gone, she struck a match to the other candle sconce, carefully packed the map away, and drew a small bowl from her things. She settled on the hard wood floor, ignoring the cold drafts and emptied a bit of powdered incense into the blue-black swirls of the ceramic piece; the center depths looked like the starry sky on a clear night. She sat herself down solemnly, feet flat against the floor on either side of the bowl and elbows on knees. She drew a breath and clasped her hands, head bowing, and a tiny blue-white flame leapt into life in the shrine bowl.

And she prayed, for the boy's soul Gryert had once held, for the waste of the man that had turned from gentler ways... for the potential of the life she had taken. Silent tears fell to sputter the flame, but it did not go out. She sent what she could of his soul to the Star Strider, what little good was left in the depths of his blackened heart, but she did it without reservations and the faint essence of what could-have-been crossed back into Her mercy at the plea.

Then the flame finally died. Sana blinked the scorched, salty tears from her vision and steadied her breathing. She rose to find her bed.

She never thought to pray for herself. She had been through Hellthorns and returned whole; the Star Strider must have seen some use in unsheathing Her Weapon. Sana had accepted the role without question, trusting that Her Need was great enough... even knowing that this was only the beginning

and that she might very well lose her way — and her soul before
the end.

>>> <<<

In its usual implacable constancy, day was fading into night.
Sana had been vaguely hoping, none-the-less, that this eve
would be different from those most recent; she'd hoped to
spend the night indoors and not on the trail again. But the
Southeast Road was not always the simple route her maps led
her to believe, and she'd begun to resign herself to accepting
her chart was yet again in error.

It grew chilly. The sky was a cloudy, grumpy gray. Dread
snorted with annoyance. It was time to find a patch of ground
less muddied than the road and make camp.

"Soon, my friend," Sana murmured. Her eyes narrowed,
head cocking as she used the corners of her vision. Far ahead of
them was something that moved along the road's edge, near
hidden in the haze and the overhang of the trees. "Hmmm —
are you mortal or demon I wonder?"

Her mare obligingly quickened into a trot. The figure
vanished into the woods at the echoing clip-plop of hooves, but
the prints in the mud were mortal enough to Sana's sense. She
whispered a word and watched the faint glow seep into the
track below. Reassuringly, nothing happened; whoever or
whatever it was held no pact with evils.

The signs suggested it was probably a human carrying
something, someone smallish in build. The scattered drop of
bark bits and fresh splinters added that the burden was most
likely cut wood.

The stranger did not reappear, and Sana drew Dread
back into a slower plodding as she scented the sweat of fear.
She frowned in the shadow of her hood. Trader roads were
usually well traveled with monied patrons. That meant
opportunities for local folk to sell everything from fresh baked
bread to lodging in barns, and all at good prices. Her own
arrival should have piqued more curiosity than fright.

Dread stopped, flicking an ear towards the woods. Sana
amended her earlier thought. Even without the barbed leather
bridle plate, a warrior's mare undeniably heralded caution.

Dread stomped a back hoof, switching her long tail at some irritating insect as Sana concentrated on those murky shadows. She pushed the cloak's hood back from her head. In the twilight her shaggy pewter hair lacked any of its brighter sheen and could have been a match for Dread's own mane.

She raised a dry grin and leaned forward, crossing her arms over the wide pommel of her saddle. "I suspect I look like some ghostly wraith in this gathering fog, wood carrier. But I'm only a woman. Quite mortal, I promise you."

The forest remained still, lending her no response at all.

Sana sighed and straightened. She pointed east along the road. "Ahead there, could you tell me how far it is to Drakewell? Is it near enough for sheltering tonight?"

There was a pause, then a rustle in the brush. A shape appeared, distrust marking every inch of approach until it gained the road. A woven basket of split logs was set down, and a strong hand curled over the axe shaft that was half hidden in the basket. The bearer wasn't all that old for her strength, however. The woman was about sixteen, with furry hide boots and vest adding an illusion of bulk to her lanky frame. Her gloves were fingerless. There was burlap patches on both of her sleeves and on the thigh of her britches. Her hands and face were grubby, but the brown hair was coiled up neatly enough, and her eyes were wary with intelligence. Her eyes were also drawn at the corners with that upward flair and the star-shaped pupil of the elfinkin.

Sana inclined her head in a slight bow, acknowledging the courtesy given in the other's courage to come forward.

"Drakewell you say?" The voice was a rough mixture of a human's low, cautious tone and an elf's curious lilt. It was not unpleasant.

"Aye."

"What do you want there?"

"A place to sleep. A chance to by some food for myself and my horse. I'll move on in the morning."

"You can pay with money, not labor?"

Sana eyed her calmly, but she was puzzled by the wood cutter. "I've some coin."

The girl eased her hand carefully away from the axe as she took in the slender sword at Sana's waist and the knife sheaths in both belt and boot. It was plain that Sana would outmatch any maneuver she might make. She glanced over the huge horse; Dread was taller at the shoulder than her head topped. The young woman chewed on her lip, assessing this pair with obvious uncertainty. Her experience was more suited to reading the quality of trees than fighters.

"Drakewell is close then?"

Starred eyes flew up, fear sparkling brighter. "You don't want to overnight there. Nobody does now."

The barest of frowns touched Sana's brow. "And why not?"

The woman hesitated again, gnawing away on the other side of her lip this time. Then abruptly she asked, "You're a mercenary?"

"No." Sana froze the woman's fidgeting with a level stare. "Perhaps someday, but not yet."

Rebellion, fierce and yet fearful, glared back at her. "And just what's that to mean?"

"It would be safer for you and your kin not to know. My enemies aren't nice people."

That made her unsure of her footing again. She shifted uncomfortably, turning towards that eastern road. "Are they in front of you? Or behind?"

"My enemies?" This time Sana did frown.

The other gave a nod and looked down into her wood basket. It was clear that she was wanting to reach for that axe handle, and equally as clear that she had the sense not to.

"Ahead."

A heavy sigh answered Sana. The young woman's shoulders slumped wearily as if she'd known that fact all along... as if there was a burden in that knowing which held some measure of hopelessness. She shrugged into the wood basket's harness and started off with, "Best come with me. Da will give you a seat at the hearth. There's none left in Drakewell to do it."

Sana spurred Dread ahead of the woman and spun about, blocking the other in her tracks. "I warn you, Wood Cutter — I do not forgive betrayal."

"Us?" A sad, dead sort of smile twisted the woman's lips as those star pointed irises seemed to close in on themselves.

"You've nothing to fear of us, Swordarm. We expected someone to come, sometime or other. Fighting men like they make worse enemies than mere carvers and weavers. They left a curse in Drakewell. Most likely for you, I'd say. It doesn't discriminate much, though, and we figured the ones following them would be the best suited to do away with it. But if there's just the one of you... well, hope was always slim. Better if you stay with my folk and steer around it in the morning."

Dread snorted, bobbing her great head scornfully at such a thought while Sana took a moment to look east. She could see the warnings now that the greyness was dimming more to night. The sky glowed a pale orange with the powers of that not-so-distant place. She glanced down again at the young woman before her, then drew Dread back a step or two to let her pass. But as she followed her silence was one of cold, muted rage.

Fox transgressed with more than family honors, it seemed.

>>> <<<

Sana had expected Da to be the Wood Cutter's father or perhaps even her grandfather, nearly anybody but the short bearded, young dwarf who turned from the hearth cooking at their entry. He moved forward stiffly, his muscles clearly more accustomed to hunching his stocky frame over a workbench than walking about greeting swordarms. A pair of very small, star eyed children ran to hide behind his bulk. He stood with lips pursing, eying her closely. Yet despite her towering height, he didn't seem intimidated.

"My husband — Da." The Wood Cutter hung her axe on its wall peg as she spoke. Her basket had been dropped outside the door. "Those two are the Twins. They're our oldest. One in the crib is Rach, our newborn." She nodded at the slender figure who was fearfully half hidden in the shadows beyond the crib. "Prew there's my sister and that babe on the floor at her feet is her Sibby. Prew tends the youngsters and the vegetable patch for us, while Da does the carving and educating."

There was almost defiance in that last statement. Sana noted the jutting chin and sparkle of protective pride in the

Wood Cutter's manner, and she remembered that in some regions woodcraft was not considered a suitable skill for a dwarf. But as she glanced about the room quickly, she didn't miss the quality of the furniture nor the honored shelf of books. There was a loft over the back half of the cottage with ticks and straw bedding peeking out over the edge. Below that, beyond Prew's corner, was a carver's shop with tools neatly hung and shavings ankle deep. The smell of stew rich with meat was coming from the cooking pot and added testimony to their comfortable level of affluence.

Sana gave the young man a measured, respectful look. Skills with woodcraft she could only appreciate in the abstract, but education and warm kinship was something different. She tipped her head faintly, "Anyone of learning who boasts a loyal family as well is indeed a someone with treasures. I am honored to meet you, Carver Da."

Displaying a poise older than his twenty years, Da accepted her compliment with a smile and the hint of a bow. The expression was mostly hidden by his bristly beard, but the corners of his round eyes crinkled unmistakably. "And you, Swordarm? Have you a name?"

"Most call me Sana."

His gaze shifted to his mate with silent inquiry.

"She hunts the ones who destroyed Drakewell. I suggested, it be better to avoid the village altogether."

He nodded, growing somber. "If you will suffer a straw mat by the fire, you're welcomed to cup and sleep with us."

"Thank you. I'd like that."

"We've a barn of sorts," the Wood Cutter turned about brusquely. "I'll show you where your horse and gear can go."

The barn was actually bigger than the cottage. It boasted a mule-and-crank turnsaw, a pair of mules separately stalled from a milk cow, and a larger workbench for carpentry.

"It'll take me a minute to hobble the mules and turn them out to the corral."

"Not on our account, please." Sana forestalled any protest by ducking under Dread's chin and back out of the barn. Her mare followed obediently, and Sana had her unsaddled before the Wood Cutter could join them.

"This ain't proper!"

"It's common sense." Sana decided the fence would probably break under the weight of the saddle alone, so she wedged her gear into a corner between a covered water barrel and the barn. Dread voiced a low rumbling whicker of approval. "Your beasts can't handle a wolf pack, if they come in hungry. Dread can."

"Wolves just howl this time of year. It's winter when they get bold." There was a note of uncertainty in that young voice, however.

"If you could spare any grain, she'd be appreciative." In full agreement, Dread tossed her head. Sana chuckled as she gave the mare's ear a playful tug. "Greedy."

The Wood Cutter frowned, still considering the risk of wolves, but she brought the oats and hay, then filled the trough with fresh water as Sana groomed Dread in silence. There was nothing but moonlight to see by at that point, yet it had grown into a peaceful eve with only a coolish mist in the air and the frogs came out piping.

"May I know your name?" Sana asked quietly, stepping back as she finished with Dread. She didn't turn to look at the woman who leant against the fence rails. Instead she squatted down to stash away her combs and brushes.

"You'll laugh some." There was already a hint of humor in the other's tone. "My father named me Flute."

Sana did look at her then.

"He fancied himself something of a bard. As elves go though, he was not the best of singers. He made better pipes than he could play. He wanted to call Prew something just as poetic, but Ma decided his being fanciful once was more than enough. He accused her of being too practical like any other human, but he let her decide." With a wry twist, Flute admitted, "I can't even whistle, let alone sing. At least Prew can carry the melody for a lullaby."

Sana smiled as she shook out Dread's blanket. "Does your axe much care?"

Flute laughed softly. "Never asked it."

Dread's great head bent down and around to nuzzle against an arm. Sana clucked to her gently as she smoothed the cloth over the grey flanks. The creature arched her neck, chin high, and stood very still to allow Sana to buckle the chest straps.

"Amazing," Flute breathed. "You're a head taller than I am, and still you only clear her shoulders by a few inches."

"She's big enough," Sana stroked that thick muscled neck above her. Dread wuffled softly, nibbling in her hair. "I wouldn't have her any other way, though."

"And the grey colors?" Flute thrust a chin at the mare and blanket. "You wear grey. You ride grey. Your saddle leather's even bleached grey. Are you part of somebody's militia? Or with some clergy's guard?"

Sana remembered those comrades in the Order of the Blade. Her voice echoed her heart's sadness as she shook her head in answer. "No, neither. Once I aspired to wear a black uniform. But it wasn't meant to be."

Dread butted against her, rebuking her for wasting time in regrets. She grinned and hugged that huge head quickly, before turning to sort out her overnight stuffs.

"Have you see a lot of fighting...?" Flute faltered at Sana's sharp glance. "I only meant... well, you don't seem so very scarred, but those swords on your back and hip hang more than comfortably. And there is only one of you after a great number of them."

Sana considered that, then rose with a faintly sad smile. "Scars can heal, both on the inside and out."

Flute stepped away from the fence and placed herself squarely in front of Sana. She studied her guest in a long moment beneath the moonlight, until quietly she came to ask, "Is there a chance you could defeat this demon-creature they left in Drakewell?"

When Sana didn't respond, Flute shrugged a shoulder in a gesture of helplessness. "We don't know anything about fighting soldiers let alone demons. We know Drakewell isn't important enough to risk King's patrols in saving — doubt he'd even know where we are on his map. We do some woodwork, some weaving... a little fur trading. We host the caravans with good meat and hearty ale. But we don't kid ourselves, Swordarm. No one's going to miss us. They'll turn the southern side route or maybe the northern river crossing into a wider track, and they'll take their merchants around the trouble. That leaves us with nobody to sell our goods to... and that means we go from always knowing we'll have enough to eat, to only hoping we will. In that case, most of us will need to pack up and try somewhere else." Almost embarrassed, Flute pushed a pebble aside her with toe. "My family's been in these parts for more generations than we can remember. I don't want to move. None of us in the area do. We're an odd mix of human, elf and dwarf even for this region. And this place — I started to build it with Da and Prew when I was barely twelve. I don't want to leave it now. I don't ever want to leave it."

The words hung in the night air. Neither woman spoke, until gradually the sounds of crickets and tree frogs crept in again. Sana drew a deep, slow breath. Her lips pressed tight, heart raging as she looked above to the orange tinted clouds that drifted across the moon. Her voice was soft and low as she finally admitted, "I'd rather die helping gentle folk like you, Flute, than harassing my enemies' sort. But I need to know more about this demon-thing, before I know if I can defeat it."

"Da calls it a Chimera."

Sana winced at the hope in Flute's voice.

"He's been studying the thing. He can tell you more after supper."

>>> <<<

"I recognized it from my wizard's book," Da explained quietly, after Prew had taken the children off to the loft and bed. He brought the leather strapped parchments down from the high shelf as Flute cautiously moved the lantern to the far end of the table. The crinkled pages turned in reluctance on their four metal hinges, but the sketches of fanciful creatures with scribbled inscriptions and smudged arrows were all too familiar to Sana.

"Where did you come by the book?"

"My grandfather wasn't from these parts. He'd been an apprentice with the woods warlocks, then done some traveling. This is one of his older pieces."

"A charlatan," Flute muttered, obviously remembering the man with fondness.

Da chuckled. At Sana's expectant look, he grinned outright. "Grandfather was something of a self-proclaimed fortune teller."

"Ahh... and since futures are always in flux, he kept changing them by hinting at what they might be."

"Yes, he used to boast of the disasters he'd averted. But it's difficult to gain any credibility when you only predict things in order to make sure they don't happen. Around here, he was an amusement that gave travelers another excuse to spend money among us. Not many in Drakewell took him seriously."

"He taught you to read?" Sana ventured to guess, and Da nodded. "Did he teach you his science as well?"

The young man glanced at his wife uneasily. Flute suddenly smiled, a bright affectionate gentleness that reached out and hugged her husband. Sana glanced away, feeling for the moment very much like an intruder. "I know of those early trials, Da. I was holding my breath every day, just hoping you'd come back out of those woods in one piece and unchanged. When you quit trying, there wasn't anybody as glad as I."

He swallowed and awkwardly nodded. His sensitive dark eyes returned to Sana, however, full of both relief and regret. "I had no innate gifts to train, you see. And I don't have the memory for chants and hand signs, they were too much like fine dancing."

"So you mastered your gifts of wood and family instead," Sana amended quietly. He nodded looking to Flute again, and inside of Sana something cried a little for those gentle things he shared with Flute, knowing they were never to be part of her own life. She cleared her throat and pointed back at the book. "And now you believe from this that the demon-thing is some sort of chimera?"

"Aye!" He straightened quickly, blunt fingers sifting through the pages again. "From time to time I've used these as references for my carvings. Drakewell had an inn that went by the name Chimera, and I'd redone the placard for the owner. So I know its — yes, here!"

Sana sat back in her chair, straightened arm braced against the table as she recognized the beast of that picture. It was an older, more faded sketch than the ones she had been tutored with, but the details were accurate enough as were the apprentice notes written in the upper corners. "Was this Chimera Inn a popular place in Drakewell?"

Flute shrugged. "Most of the caravan chiefs and traveling nobility stayed there. They had reasonable fees and more often than not, music for cheer."

So that explained why this particular creature, Sana thought. Foxsun had never been very creative, but he'd have thought it a grand joke to loosen that thing upon its own town. Drunk and bored, he might have even done it from sheer malice without ever knowing of her approach.

She sighed and leaned forward. "Did it look exactly like this?"

"No," Da pointed to its two slender horns. "These are wrong. It has a smaller horn lower on its forehead, then a longer one above."

"Spiral or smooth?"

"Spiral."

Meaning, magic warded and nastier than its simple-minded, hunger driven cousins. This thing was a demon in the truer sense of the word; it fed on fear and blood lust, not on mere meat.

Again the creature stared at her from the book, mocking any resolve she might have to defeat it. But the image wavered as her thoughts turned inward, and a more deadly vision rose in her mind's inner eye. Its lion-like muzzle snarled, triangular ears flattening again a massive head. Dull brownish hair matted in curls against its skull and cheekbones. A scruffy goat-like beard straggled beneath its chin. The strong, thick neck was covered in the same grubby coat, extending into a coiling body that twisted about a barren tree trunk or ruin wall as a snake might attach itself to a single tree limb or vine. Its small wings batted. The thing shuddered, lifting the top half of itself by both body strength and flight. But it angled its head menacingly, quickly, despite its initial feign of clumsiness. Eyes glinted, a gem green glaze where pupils should have been, and its snarl turned into a roar of hot fire.

Sana shut her eyes, nostrils draw tight against the metallic stench of that evil flame. She blinked, dispelling her inner sight as Da's voice registered again.

"I don't know if it's true," he was saying, "but there is some magic to its fire, because it burns stone as easily as wood. The entire village is nothing but sandy rubble now."

"And the people?" Sana's flat tone echoed her bleak expectations.

Da's head bent, his tongue suddenly tied. Flute touched the back of his hand lightly, then stood to come round the table to stand beside him. Her hands kneaded his shoulders as tears misted her own vision. She shook the stray hair from her stinging eyes. Her chin lifted bravely as she managed an answer. "Most are dead. Or at least gone. There was no sign of them left, not even bones. The folks on the town's edges, they got away — some. When they tried to grab belongings, they didn't make it. Prew was doing the marketing; she was almost one of the ones we lost. Both Prew and I lost cousins. Da lost his parents and sibs."

Her husband covered his face a brief moment, then shoved himself up and away from the table. His expression was a torn mask of agony. He pushed out of the door and left them for the night beyond. Flute drew another shaking breath, and her fingers curled, knuckle white around the chair's back. "He's been back there more than anybody. Says someone's got to know what it's doing or we'll all end up like the townfolk. He's afraid it'll leave Drakewell soon and start hunting other places...?"

Mutely Sana nodded.

"Then he's right?"

"He is."

The young Wood Cutter looked to the open doorway. Her murmur was almost to low for Sana to hear as she amended, "I knew he had to be. I just didn't want to believe it."

Jerkily, that frightened gaze centered back on Sana. "And you, Swordarm?"

"Can I defeat it?" Sana's heart went cold. Very deliberately her grey eyes returned to that book, and her finger began a slow, intricate sketching of that winged picture... in a mage's preparatory spell. "Most likely, yes. In any event, I will try."

Sana did not look up, did not invite the question that hung between them then, but Flute could not bring herself to ask the price this risk would cost the Swordarm. In the end, the woman fled to find Da.

As those footsteps faded beneath the sound of the fire's

crackle, Sana closed the ancient book and sighed. That she could defeat this toy of Fox's, she held no doubt. Probably, she would even survive it. But the bond this Wood Cutter and Carver shared reminded her of a different sort of quest, one which she would most likely not live to pursue.

If it had been simply revenge, she would have held no regrets at abandoning the chase. But the choice was no longer hers, she knew. There was a much grander scale to her half-brothers' ambitions than mere wealth. There would be too many like Flute and her kin left to be hurt, if the Triplets went unchallenged. Just as there had been no choice left her comrades and tutors in the matter of the Holy Order, she still found no choice in wearing Her Gray.

The knowledge did nothing to lessen the emptiness inside. The Star Strider had never been a gentle taskmaker.

END FRAGMENT

* * *

Winds & Light

Was Chris Anne trying to escape Aggar? Maybe she was afraid she would come to be known only as a writer of Amazons and Shadows. Yes, she loved Aggar and talked about returning to that mythology in many different forms – a role-playing game (which fascinated her), an anthology of stories by other writers (which delighted her), and even a comic or graphic novel. But went it came to writing another Aggar novel, she always set out to create something else... and Aggar crept up on her.

Once again, Chris Anne was exploring a theme "untethered" by her own Aggarian mythology, allowing herself to run with ideas and plots without having to bend them to any rules. But, just like with "Under a Crimson Sun," Aggar kept tugging her back. Eventually, after writing almost 40,000 words (about a hundred sixty manuscript pages) of nonlinear chapters of "Winds & Light," she stopped and wrote a corresponding outline for "Oceans of Aggar."

It was years before I connected her outline (sent to me hand-written, once again) with the inspiration it grew from. The outline was rich with metaphors about the power of wind, light and a world ruled by song. But the outline was on Aggar and it took many, many reads of "Winds & Light" before I finally saw the similarities.

As I mentioned before, Chris Anne had a gift of keeping the heart the same while changing the surface.

Some readers of "Shadows of Aggar" and "Fires of Aggar" were disappointed when hundreds of years passed between the two books. But this, too, was part of Chris Anne's process. She never wanted to become bored or complacent. She believed that a thriving culture is a culture that changes. Amazons would integrate into Aggar. Shadow guides would become more and more rare. The benevolent Council that assigned Elana to Diana would become the malevolent Choir to be found in "Oceans of Aggar."

When readers wrote Chris Anne and said they wanted to live in the time of Elana and Diana for ten or twenty books, she always answered: "Please write them! Write them and send them to my publisher." Because of that singular, unwavering response, Blue Forge Press is dedicated to publishing all Aggar-based fan-written works. Just contact us.

Summary

In a time long from now, when we are barely remembered by even the oldest of mystics, a new world was shaped by the great Barrier Winds, and a new people were born. A folk of faith and strength, they became known as the Chatu, and with their holy shaman they listened to the whisper of the Winds and learned from Wind-Blessed Dreams. They lived in the lands of both the Ginia and Nana Hills and rode the vastness of the Barren Ranges, guarding the balance and order of all Today's world. But east of their Ranges and north of their Hills, another folk came. These were the people of Nyor, a group of selfish and greedier interests who followed the cruel teachings of the Choir. In the course of things, conflict grew between the Chatu and the Choir. Until finally one Spring, a woman fled the Choir's wrath and sought asylum among the Chatu. In this, a legend was begun... a legend of Winds, of Light, and of two women's love.

Preface

The three flames of the hanging lamp suddenly flared, and the old woman paused, a stick of incense still in her hand. There was a stillness about the room, the thick crimson tapestries and gilded edges of cushions seeming to hold everything in a hush. Then from nowhere, a breeze swept in and the candlepots sputtered and died. Overhead brilliance of the bronze lamp grew. The topaz gold of the Shaman's eyes began to turn, darkening to a shining flint as she listened to what only she could hear. The aged hunch to her shoulders lifted. The pewter grey of her braided hair became a lustrous silver-blue. The power of the Barrier Winds filled her, and she heard their whisper of the dangers rising upon the Plain of Today.

The ancient lines in her face hardened grimly. She drew

a slow measured breath, a gesture of determination, not weakness. The Winds lent her their strength, and her eyes closed as she sent out her mystic's summons.

In the Nana Hills at a scout's Hill Post, on the southern edges of the village territories, a protector spun about. The two she'd been speaking with went silent. Then everything around the small long house went utterly still. The ponies quit grazing, a ground squirrel perched on its burrow's edge... beyond, in the forest, the birds quieted.

A stiff wind blew down from the spring skies. It swept around the hilltop clearing, but not a blade of grass was moved. Then it stopped as it touched the young woman who had turned. Her golden eyes narrowed within the mask of her amber headscarf. Sun glinted from the gilt of her satin jacket and trousers as she waited, senses straining for some sense of meaning.

:Tamtcha!:

Her head jerked up at that faint touch of the Shaman's mindvoice. The Winds exploded in a whirlwind dance that caught her alone. She hurried for her mare.

>>> <<<

Along the edge of the Nana Hills and Barren Ranges, northeast from the village a bit, another looked up sharply and reined in his pony. The elder was alone, mid-way between two scout posts on his ride. His bleached leathers and pale headscarf blended well with the straw hues of the range grasses. As the windclatter of those hollow reeds faded, he and his spotted pony almost faded away in the stillness of the scene.

A few feet to the side, the harshness of the Ranges abruptly stopped and the forested Hills began; his tawny gold gaze fastened to those trees. Then the leaves there stopped their rustling, too. Experience told, and Kahl did not wait for the Shaman's mindtouch.

His pike's point flashed as his pony wheeled and set off at a gallop.

>>> <<<

"Lightsinger?!!"

The great roar reached Tamtcha even before she'd pushed through the heavy tapestries into the Shaman's room of sanctuary. She tore the her headscarf off as she joined Kahl, and her gold eyes darted from the one elder to the other with concern. Like her, Kahl removed his scarf, and the three tigereye gems braided into the narrow kownband glinted upon his brow, fiercely reflecting the magic and light of that sacred lamp above. Her own kownband's gems blazed as brightly, shimmering against the blue-black of her hair even as the bronze lamp glittered against the shadowy blackness of the arched ceiling. The very air around them tingled with apprehension, and she tossed her short braid from her shoulder in a conscious effort to relax those tightened muscles in her neck. Her gaze finally settled on the Shaman. Her voice came low and calm, "What has the Choir done, Nahessa?"

Stiffly the Shaman turned away from the Eldest as Kownbearer. Kahl dropped his eyes and made an obvious effort to release some of his antagonism, and the old woman drew a steadying breath of her own before saying, "They've done nothing yet."

Tamtcha studied Kahl for a moment more as Nahessa moved to the far side of the table and seated herself on the low cushions. Her once-foster father glanced at Tamtcha briefly and, gave a quick nod of reassurance. He was not a man normally given to rash outbursts. Together they joined the Shaman at the table.

"Tell us more of this lightsinger, Nahessa," Tamtcha prodded.

Nahessa suddenly looked weary. In a habitual gesture, she reached back and freed her long braid from some snag on her tunic's rough gilt. She seemed to leave them, staring into the mother-of-pearl inlays upon that rosewood table. But neither Tamtcha nor Kahl hurried her, and eventually she lifted her mortal, gold -shaded eyes to them. "The Winds speak of one who runs from the Choir, Tamtcha. She is a lightsinger."

Now it was Tamtcha's turn to frown. "One of their pawns

escaped? How — I didn't know a singer could perceive the outer world well enough to realize there was something beyond the Choir's will? Aren't they bound and bred within the Crypt's innermost walls? Without even the sky freed above them?"

Nodding slowly, Nahessa affirmed her words. "This one is different in some way. She has been sent by our Windbrothers."

"From the Wind's Temple in Nyor then," Kahl amended.

Again Nahessa nodded. "Her name is Anzund. She has grown up amongst the Windbrothers, not within the Crypt. But she was discovered recently by the Choir and was forced to flee the Pachin Mountains. She was — is attempting to cross the Barren Ranges."

"Alone?!" Tamtcha sputtered in shock.

"Yie, and on foot."

Kahl grunted, his bushy grey brows lifting high. Tamtcha was equally impressed.

"So she is gifted with the mindvoice and the power of the light songs, but she heeds the Winds' ways of peace and balance." Kahl opened his hands in query. "Why hasn't she spoken to you sooner? Why has she waited until she is forced into such drastic actions before seeking your wisdom, Nahessa?"

"She is not gifted with the mindvoice of the Choir's lightsingers, my friend. Somehow, she is different. I can not clearly grasp why or how, but it seems she hears as you do, yet speaks with the light chants. She could not have spoken to me from Nyor, and the Windbrothers' High Priest chose to keep her presence among them secret."

"Understandable, if she considered the Temple to be her home," Tamtcha pointed out. "The fewer that knew of her existence, the safer she would be."

"Until now. Now she has dire need of the Chatu. She seeks us to beg sacred asylum. Yet she has become lost among the range grasses, and so the Winds call. She is held dear enough to Them that the Winds Themselves are the voices calling for her help. It has not been her pleas that I heard, but Their own."

"You have been Dreaming?" Kahl pressed. "Do you know where in the Ranges she is lost?"

"I have been Dreaming briefly, but no, I did not find her among the grasses."

Tamtcha felt a chill slid down her spine, and her chin leveled. "Then you have glimpsed her windsoul on dreamquest."

"Yie."

Kahl stiffened. Tamtcha felt her fingers curl into fists even as she saw Kahl's do the same. For this Anzund to have slipped into that nebulous limbo as a windsoul meant that the Winds Themselves had summoned her; she was either very close to death and They were preparing to take her from the Plain of Today across to the Plain of Yesterday, or she was a holy woman of immense importance to Their balance of Today.

"The Choir, too, has begun to seek her amongst the Dreamings. They will soon find her—"

"And she is unprotected," Kahl growled. "Alone on footwander. Alone on dreamquest... this Anzund is either desperate beyond imagining or foolish."

"I would say desperate," Tamtcha breathed, feeling her heart pounding... already anticipating what the Shaman would be asking.

"Very desperate," Nahessa agreed. She looked at the Eldest as Kownbearer, and he shifted uncomfortably beneath that knowing gaze.

"Yie, I am too old. I admit it." He gave a grunt of impatience. "Even if I can still plan a caravan's ambush, I'm not the best choice for wrestling rabid yotes or marching forever through who-knows-what."

"So the task falls to you, Youngest as Kownbearer. Would you accept?"

A mask of stoney grimness closed all fear and doubt from her expression, hiding her heart from her oldest friends. But this lightsinger Anzund was seeking the Chatu for their sacred asylum, and it was not something Tamtcha would have denied any living soul. Especially not to one fleeing the horrors of the Choir. "Yie, I will go. She has need of a protector."

"She is still a stranger," Kahl murmured, concern turning him back to Nahessa. "Is it right to ask a Kownbearer of the Chatu to risk so much, knowing so little about her?"

"The Winds whisper of her need," Tamtcha reminded

him quietly.

And Nahessa's voice grew suddenly stronger as her eyes went flint black, "Call her Shaman's Daughter, kin of my lodge and once-child of the Temple. Know that the young Kownbearer seeks to behold the beauty and the power of all this one will be. Know that the Eye must seek the Essence yet again."

Kahl's golden gaze narrowed, doubts leaving him despite experience and responsibilities that might have demanded more caution. Tamtcha felt a steadiness take her, too. The Winds... always the Winds... the Shaman was to be trusted in all things.

"Is the quest accepted, Kownbearer?"

Tamtcha looked into those black-irised eyes and quelled the tremor that touched her heart. She reminded herself that she had founded the Lodge of Weazlbear Claw only two years ago through the single-handed defeat of that evil creature. She had earned the kownband in facing droughts and fighting Nyor's greedy caravans. She had earned the tigereyes she wore, and she had accepted the responsibilities of the Tryad that came with them. This was simply one more thing her people needed from her... one more thing the Winds demanded.

"There is no choice," she answered finally. "She has need of a protector."

"There is always a choice," the old woman murmured. "You are Chatu. There is always a choice."

"I am Chatu," Tamtcha repeated. "I choose to follow the Winds."

The Shaman nodded very, very faintly. "Then today — this means you must learn if you trust your heart or your cautions. Your loyalty has never been lightly given."

The magic of the Shaman began to creep around them both, distancing them from the elder Kownbearer. The scents of apricots and dried barks subtly began to fill the room. The light of the lamp overhead began to dim even as the slender tallows of the beeswax candles mutely flamed to life. The Shaman's hands reached forward to capture Tamtcha's upon the smoothness of that table, and the scent of the smoky vapors grew stronger.

"Know that there are many paths one may take through

the Winds' forces. Know that there are many quests declined and more that are never noticed. Know, Tamtcha, Kownbearer of Chatu, that the dreams of quests are charged with decisions and that choices are weighed against each heart's need—"

The azure blue of a summer's twilight skies enfolded them. The protector and Shaman sat across from one another. Between them lay an empty fire ring. Their hands clasped above the ash and charred embers. Swirls of damp mists like foggy fingers of wet spring mornings moved about them. There was no ground beneath them, only blueness. There was nothing near them, save for the grey, cold stones of the fire ring.

"Know, Tamtcha, protector of Chatu, that there is never a single path from beginning to end. There is one path which is true for each soul. Stray from it, then return when you must. Or find it and follow it only. Only you will recognize the order of Today's Plain and the feats that your windsoul must seek."

"And if I decide wrongly?" The words were spoken steadily, but quietly.

"Any measure of worth must come from within yourself — choose what you may live with, the loyalties you must live by." Nahessa's voice gentled as did the gaze she bent upon the other. "Your quest, my youngest of kowndaughters, is for balance. Heed the Winds. It is in your heart to decide what need They have of you."

Her hands were released. Tamtcha watched, unblinking, as the Shaman's figure faded, and the Kownbearer was left alone. Her gold gaze dipped down to the ash of the fire ring. It would be lit and brightly blazing the next time she sat here, if she survived to the end of her quest. If she did not, then she would simply return to the Shaman's Lodge. Or at least her body would... only the Shaman ever knew what happened to those windsouls that went missing for months after the failed dreamquests. Only the Shaman knew what it took to heal the anguish that springs from that kind of failing.

Silently Tamtcha rose, pushing up to her full height with ankles still crossed until she was standing. And then she did nothing for the longest of times, except stand and wait. Until finally, she felt it.

Turning to her right, she lifted her face into the breeze. The brush of the air strengthened, blowing back the loosened strands of her black hair; only the kownband bound it at her forehead. Unconsciously she reached for her headscarf on her shoulders, but it was gone. She glanced down at herself then and found the streaked, bleached leathers that she now wore were the plainskins she usually hunted in when on the Ranges. There were no arrows in the quilted slots at her tunic's back, however. There was no pike in her hand. She glanced down at the dull amber boots and sash, feeling vaguely better about the knives there. Her palm smoothed across the curved handle of that twelve inch blade at her waist, and the coolness of the stone made her skin tingle; incredibly, it was made from a single piece of tigereye. She half-lifted her boot to glimpse the hilt of the knife sheathed there; it shimmered a pale, pale pink and was made of a rose quartz.

The strangeness of the weapons was accepted. They were pieces to the quest's puzzle; the understanding would come later. Tamtcha felt the cool touch of that breeze again. She looked into the growing denseness of the mists. The Winds beckoned her there. She set off to find this lightsinger.

Chapter One

Taking a deep breath, she savored the sweet tang of apricots, and a soft smile formed as Anzund's pale eyes flickered open. The rich, liquid brown of a tigereye gem swam about her. The Winds seemed to approve of both her and her venture; the Dreamquest was beginning in the midst of a sacred soul stone. Yet the fact that she had not been born and raised among the Chatu was also accounted for. Across her lap lay a long staff, the defensive weapon of an Acolyte.

The colors thinned mistily around her as she stood, until only glittering tendrils of the starry bronze dust lingered. She took a long time in studying the patterns swirling in the air before her. Then with a graceful dip of her hand, Anzund chose one. The others vanished immediately. Her fingertips tingled lightly, directing her along the sparkling wisp.

The glitter widened its span and dropped down to form a trail beneath her feet as she walked. But she didn't have far to go. The last of the mistiness cleared away before a translucent sheen of rock. Too dark a stone for amber, too flawlessly clear to be topaz, a hillside of brown obsidian held a single cave. The footpath glowed brightly as it disappeared within that cavern.

Anzund's stride never faltered.

>>> <<<

Tamtcha walked for nearly an eternity. The hardness of the places beneath her feet changed as she went. At times it was cushioned, like the springy texture of a high pasture where the ponies kept the grasses cropped short. At times, it was so firm as to be harsh, like the rocky stones placed along the Nyor caravan routes. The sounds brought by the Winds altered with the footing of the unseen path. The arid grass scents and ringing calls of the northern vagabonds danced about her and then passed. The bleating cries of smasheep and the laughter of Chatu children playing in watery streams slipped by. But the Winds' touch never turned her aside. She walked, as if she were a ghost through the sounds and smells and textures of those hidden scenes. Yet always, she kept her face turned fully into the breeze. Her feet kept following, and once again the mists and scents of spiced fruits would surround her. The scents of apricots gave way to green apples, and then to tangy citrus. The spices grew richer, with the scents of the cinnamons and cloves became thick enough to seem like dust. Then the Winds' touch would sweep it all aside again, and a new piece of the Today's Plains would echo in the blue and mists... echo with its temptations to pause and turn. Tamtcha merely walked on.

She grew thirsty. The sounds of water and spring rains grew more prominent. She grew hungry. The sounds of feasting and celebrations came more often. She became annoyed at the foolish simplicity of the ploys, and then the sounds of battles and dying Chatu rose instead. Her hand closed about the tigereye knife in her sashed belt, but she did not stray from the Winds' touch. Those sounds too, finally faded.

Then from the mists' swirl rose a stone. Once a column of some sort, it had fallen. It lay cracked and shattered as if it had once been a mighty tree which had been struck down by lightening. The Winds' touch led her across the rubble to the weather- worn stump that was still standing. The masonry was coated with a chalky dust, and Tamtcha vaguely remembered these sorts of ruins in the lower forests of the Pachin Mountains. They had marked a Temple of the Winds which had been abandoned early in Nyor's history, and the place had offered shelter to the small band of Chatu she'd traveled with; it had been the journey just after her Naming and they had been trading with the Windbrothers, semi-precious gems and mother-of-pearl for the Chatu holy liquors. Tamtcha saw a woven saddlebag was laid upon that column's stump, and a flask of the Shaman's liquor as well as a loaf of the Windbrothers' bread was set on the pouch. A handful of dried fruit was also there.... Rueful to find the sacred meal of Dreamings so courteously provided for her, Tamtcha straddled the fallen width of the column and settled down to eat.

The Winds' touch swept around her in a gentle, circling motion. It had become the faintest breath of a breeze, almost without her being aware of it. But even as she finally noticed this fact, the mists and blue around her were retreating. The coolness of a dampened forest kissed her skin. The thick, dappled shade of the towering pines and oaks melted into being, and the chattering cry of careless birds echoed around her.

Tamtcha looked about curiously as she chewed, barely surprised to find the stone column beneath her had indeed turned into a decaying tree trunk. The rich smells of moss and green greeted her, almost drawing a smile from her. The rushing sounds of water falling from some nearby height explained the dampness to the area. But the thing that took her interest was the slender staff leaning against the tree stump. She took a long draught from the leather flask's spirits and eyed the dark wooden pole again. It was obviously a pike shaft with a rod of steel at its core, but it lacked both the hand grip and the steal point which she was accustomed to. In fact, it lacked any kind of grip or three-edged point. She finished her mouthful of bread, gathered the rest of the food back into the saddlebag with the flask and shouldered the things before rising. She was not the type to take journey food for granted.

Curiously she squatted beside the stick and simply looked. There was a place cut into the staff where the grip would eventually be bound. There were also the grooves on the very top to screw on the pike point. The wood, however, was not really brown at all. It was an amazingly deep shade of maroon, and there were very fine, honey- hued lines marking the grain of the stained wood. Cautiously, Tamtcha extended a finger and traced one of those lines. The satin smooth finish boded ill for a sweaty palm; without a grip, the hand would certainly slip in combat. But there was nothing else about the touch that seemed odd. She picked it up and stood. Hefting it with one hand, she noted it's balance with approval. Once the point was fastened, its weight would center perfectly at the grip grooves. It's slender length was well crafted too; there wasn't the faintest hint of warp in it.

The roar of the water seemed to grow as a dampish breeze lifted Tamtcha's hair and chilled the nape of her neck. She glanced over her shoulder into the woods, then with a satisfied nod and staff in hand, she stepped onto the trail.

The path wound back and forth as it climbed, crossing small trickles of waterfalls that were canopied by feathery ferns and black wet, rocky slopes. She found signs of animals and Chatu, and it was not hard to see why this lush place might find room for the windsouls of both to live amiably. At a high junction, perhaps half way up the hillside, she saw the trail divide completely. From the scuffs of booted prints and smasheep hooves, it was plain that the local travelers usually went west from here... deeper into the forests and away from the droning sound of that waterfall. But the Winds' touch, or rather the only breeze left to follow, was strong and came along from the eastern path. Tamtcha turned for the sounds of the churning waters and that damp breeze.

The path grew rockier. The footing grew a little less certain as the dirt was mostly washed away here, and the trail was left with almost nothing but the dampened bedrock. The ferns and mosses still clung to the shelved stone beside her. And from the steepening edge below the trees and vines grew to offer a cheerful greeting. Even though one was standing half way up each trunk's height at that point, it was comforting to have their crowding company... they weren't about to let anyone fall without a solid holding to catch at.

The noise of the waters became louder as leaves and ferns began to drip, and Tamtcha felt the fine spray on her face and eyelids. She took in the sweet smell of the earth, and then paused, finding herself in the last dark inches of shadow before the stone landing opened into the sun. Beyond she could see only the tumbling wall of white waters that rushed by. Slowly she emerged into the rainbows of mists and the thunderous cloud of the falls.

The perch jutted outward from the hill, a small plateau suspended mid-way between the tumultuous whirlpools below and the falling tons of water above. The wind whipped about her, tossing the wetness against her and soaking her leathers, but Tamtcha was beyond caring as she simply stood in wonder, gazing at those rising mists and falling whitewash. The sunlight streaked and danced, scattering prisms and arches of color. The falls and their light were dramatic against the green, almost black backdrop of the wooded depths, and yet it seemed so pure in its clean, cutting descent that cleared the tangled depths to the pools and rocks below.

A glint of clear gold beckoned and Tamtcha turned to see a flight of stone steps carved into the hillside next to the falls. Above that something flashed again, and she saw another broken column standing on the rocky tier up there. Lightly she bounded up the wetted steps, finding their grooved surfaces were safe but well worn. Then she paused and wiped the water from her face, pushing the dripping strands of her hair away as she looked at the strange podium's gift. Again there was the broken stump of the column that resembled the Windbrothers' temples, but this time there was only the stump. This time, there was no food, only a bow shaft and a single, long arrow. A faint frown pulled at Tamtcha's lips as she noted once more that the presented weapon was unfinished. There was no string to the bow nor was there a head to the arrow. And like the pike staff, there was no grip bound to it.

She slipped the headless arrow into one of the slots in her tunic's quilted backing. The short bow she tied into place on the outside of her shouldered saddlebag. Then with the wind and waters rushing down from above, she continued up the step-like trail.

Her calves ached. Her heart was pounding. She grew hot, although the waters' spray was icy cold. She kept climbing and ignored her body's shivering. She reminded herself that she had been colder during the winter hunt, when the blizzards had separated her small party from the high mountain lodges for three days. Her body memory rekindled and attested the truth of that fact, and her trembling ceased. Her mind focused again on the falls beside her, and she saw a strange dance of lights above.

Then suddenly a great bellow rang out, and Tamtcha spun on her rocky stair step, crouching quickly as she strained to see into the forest's depths below. A squeal... a cry of humanness or of panic so high-pitched that it seemed human... ripped through the trees. And then everything fell quiet. Too quiet... even against the roar of the falls, the forest's silence was haunted by that death. It was an eerie quiet that made Tamtcha sweat. She'd never thought to hear that awful sound again... not alone again.

The sounds of the woods began to emerge finally, tentatively. A half-hearted peep, then a fluster of wings and leaves ventured forth first. The tension seemed to lift. The noises offered some reassurance, and Tamtcha warily let herself believe in that respite.

The last time she had consciously heard that grisly bellow had been nearly two years ago... on the day the weazlbear had lifted its claw to strike. It had lifted its head to bellow out that savage delight of victory even as it had slashed downward with its razored nails. That boastful anticipation had cost it its life, as with its eyes half-slitted in ecstasy of its kill it had missed Tamtcha's desperate last ploy. She had thought of herself as already dead... or she never would have made that roll into the swiping paw. She never would have pushed upward, arching herself and the pain away from the ground and into the mammoth body that hunted her... her knife never would have slipped down its very throat and aside, cracking through the great jaw hinge and down into the death cut across the jugular. She never would have lived, if she had expected it to die in her place.

But she had lived. And the panic receded as she reminded herself of that. She had lived. The evil had died... the weazlbear had lost because she was not afraid to do what must be done, even if she knew there was only the riding of the Winds left for her soul afterwards. That was what Chatu was to her, Tamtcha realized finally. She was Protector not only by name... but by soul.

She straightened from her crouch slowly. If the quest was to face that evil again, then so be it. The Winds' touch was suddenly very warm and gentle upon her face, sparing her the icy ping of the waterfall for the moment. Tamtcha felt a smile grow as she glanced above, and then she resumed her climbing.

The route eventually led to a landing beside a darkened chamber entrance. There were no more steps above nor any trail to the side. The water dripped from the outer edges of the crevice and the black-grey rock glistened in its dampness. But Tamtcha moved warily as she approached the place. The weazlbear's cry had not been forgotten.

Inside a sputtering rasp suddenly lit a dozen torches set in the circling wall. The chamber wavered in the bright light, making Tamtcha blink as the smoke billowed a bit, seeking that ceiling crack somewhere. Then the shadows settled and she found herself standing before a ring of straw. Dried range grass had been carefully laid, long lengths alternating with shorter lengths to form a sunburst around a center stone. There was no trace of the Windbrothers' column work, but then this was an ancient Shaman's Stone, and its sacredness preceded the Windbrothers' ways. The altar itself was of red amber, the very orange-crimson richness of berry juice. Translucent even in the shadowy shimmers of this cavern, the power of the altar illuminated the gifts in its depths. The slender, snaking line of a bow string laid tied to a glinting, steel-edged arrow tip. Beside those lay the three-edged blade of a deadly pike point.

Tamtcha came only as near as the edge of the straw sunburst. Atop the altar sat a leather grip. Its casing was opened, thongs ready to tie it into place upon a weapon. The small beads that dangled from the ties were made of both tigereye and rose quartz. Tamtcha glanced down at the knives she wore, feeling the war of uncertainty rising within her. She had never known this sort of quartz to be particularly important for anything, but the tigereyes were only too familiar as the Chatu soulstones. Cautiously, she decided to take some comfort in the fact that the grip held both stones and didn't seem to imply one was less holy than the other.

The Winds' touch became cold, pressing from the back of the chamber and passing directly across the altar to reach

Tamtcha. It chided her for her slowness. It taunted her with the need to move on with her quest. Resolutely, Tamtcha stepped forward and placed herself squarely before the altar to wait; she was not ready to leave. The bite of the Winds died. Instead the amber stone took on a fierce glow, and the warmth gushed up. An orange flame erupted high, lifting the grip. Then abruptly the flame vanished. The leather piece almost dropped as Tamtcha fumbled to grab it from the air.

But she did catch it, amazed to find it wasn't in the least scorched by the fire. She frowned as the Winds swept in from the back of the room again. Stubbornly she refused to move, and the drafts left off with their urgings. The amber altar offered nothing more, though. Her frown deepened to a scowl, and she laid the pike's shaft horizontally across the altar. Nothing happened. As she lifted it away, the grip brushed the pike and its beads rattled. She froze, staring hard at the pieces she held. The beads continued to shake, rhythmically like a prayer chime. They stretched the length of their leather ties as if alive and reaching for the pike's shaft. Below in the altar, Tamtcha saw the faintest of glows begin around the pike's point. She moved the grip apart from the staff quickly, and then drew out the bow. Again the small beads began a staccato rhythm, but this one with a different tempo. Within the altar the bowstring and arrowhead began to glow.

Understanding finally, Tamtcha slipped the grip into the saddlebag, and the altar cooled to its reddish translucence. The weapon she tied the grip to would be the one the altar completed for her. The bow and arrow could be used or the pike; she could not have both. She sighed faintly, and sympathetically, the Winds seemed less impatient as they called her into the back passages.

The cavern narrowed into stone steps, and again she was taken higher. The sky was a blue patch far above, and the roar of the falls rumbled about her in the stairway. And then she was standing in the open, on the very top of that cliff amidst a dozen rushing little streams and raised sun-warmed rocks. The Winds whipped around her, and within a pike's throw the cliff sheaered away and the waters fell. She looked behind to where the forests and hills rolled outward, and she saw the telltale trail of smoke from village lodges. Then she turned to gaze across the river and saw the huge trees banking the eastern shore, dark green against the almost blue-white sky.

It was not until she brought her eyes down from that horizon that she noticed the still figure on the center rock of the falls. Nearly at the edge of the drop, a small, slender woman sat with legs crossed and eyes closed as her face tipped back towards the overhead sun. A braid of blonde hair sparkled with mists, and the bleached leathers were a match for Tamtcha's own.

"Anzund?" It must be, Tamtcha thought. But her cry could scarcely have carried across the river's roar. And the woman was obviously intent on her prayers. Tamtcha began to make her way across the waterflows, jumping between the exposed plains of flattened rock. As she went she saw the light song rise. Glassy veils of sleek colors shimmered and then vanished. Sparkling bits of rainbows in the mists gathered and wove a spiral of light, twining about the woman's figure.

"Anzund?!"

An answering shriek from behind spun Tamtcha about. But the creature that had challenged her was no human... the weazlbear she had heard below appeared at the plateau's side. With scarcely a pause, the huge beast lunged forward. Tamtcha found herself dropping gear and drawing knives. A claw reached out from its loping run and her blades sliced as she went down to avoid the blow.

It backed off with the touch of steel, and Tamtcha rolled to her feet, a knife in each hand as she faced the thing across the waters and flat rocks. It was not quite as large as the one she had met two years ago, but it seemed somewhat quicker. And it was ugly... uglier in the bright daylight of the plateau than it could ever have seemed in the forest's shadows.

On its face, jagged white lines slashed through china-blue eyes, leaving a grotesque impression of blindness. The pointed ears that lifted forward were tufted with black hair. The pugged muzzle held folds upon folds of blackened skin that pulled back into a slobbering snarl to show brown-boned teeth and tar-black gums. Tamtcha shifted her footing slightly, securing her stance as those lips curled back again in that low, assessing rumble. Her skin crawled as she remembered the stink of that hot breath.

The weazlbear rose, swaying from side to side to better see and smell its opponent. Like a giant sloth, the beast had a massive shoulder frame and a powerful, long- armed reach. It usually swaggered about on all fours, walking on the curled backs of its fore claws. But when it battled, the creature was more agile on its two hind feet. For all the world of monsters and ghosts, it looked like a man clad in shaggy fur and armed with clawed gloves as it stood before an opponent, head held high and arms spread wide.

Tamtcha swallowed the fear, clamping it down into a tight ball in her gut that would center her balance and stop slowing her mind. The creature folded its arms inward, one claw almost folding into the other in one of those remotely human-like gestures that could so unnerve a protector. In the distance behind the weazlbear, Tamtcha glimpsed the spiraling trails of lodge smoke. The weazlbear half-turned, following her gaze and grunted as it too saw the village. Its white-bright eyes came back to her and then moved beyond her to the center of the falls. Tamtcha did not need to look to know it was eyeing Anzund.

It ventured a step forward, watching her shift her feet but not retreat. Subtly, then with growing fervor, the animal began to rock its torso. A low grunt pushed out with each quickening breath, and Tamtcha tightened her grip on her knives as the creature's mouth ran with the drool of its mounting excitement. She wished fleetingly that she was closer to the edge of the falls, because she had no illusions about the deadliness of mere knives against this beast — and then it sprang.

They went down rolling. She curled tightly into its stomach and the slashing claws swept through sheer nothingness even as her own blades raked in, bloodying its underbelly. But it caught her before she could scramble back, and the swipe flung her through the air. There was a resounding crack within her skull that silenced the searing pain from the gashes, and then she slipped into an icy place of darkness.

The rush of cold, cold water pressed against her, nearly choking Tamtcha as it covered half her face. It pulled her back through the blackness. It brought her back to the shallow run-off of the falls plateau. It froze the skin to numbness in her collarbone and left cheek where the three bloodied rakes of the claw were. She shook her head, desperately striving to pull herself to consciousness. She had not killed it. She could not afford to lie here, sprawling weaponless.

Tamtcha rose to her knees, breath heaving through her numbed carcass. She blinked, the sunlight seeming harsh. Her ears roared and she couldn't tell if it was simply due to the falls or if the noise was from inside her head somewhere. She lifted a hand to her forehead, finding some solace in the feel of the familiar kownband and in the shading of her eyes. She pushed herself up to her feet, and blinked, concentrating... and the brightness of the sunshine resolved into the dancing pattern of a light chant.

The Nyor woman stood now rather than sat, but that was not all which had changed in the scene. The weazlbear was held frozen, shimmering with an unnatural brightness. Yet even as Tamtcha watched, the outlines of the creature faded into that brightness. As if a Shaman were fading into the Winds, Tamtcha realized, but here the beast was fading into light.

With a gust of whirling wind, the transformation was completed, and a swirling light creature surrounded Anzund. It snarled with the angry hiss of wetted coals. It swam with silver-laced crimsons and turquoises, white claws of light leaving trailing, menacing lines in the air as it traveled. It held no hindquarters now, only a wisp of something... of powers that propelled it around and around the standing woman.

Tamtcha felt her throat tighten until she could barely breathe. She stood, transfixed in her place upon the plateau with her mind dulled by fears and dreads and unnamable suspicions.

:I can not hold it long, protector.:

Tamtcha started at the glittering curtain of light that gently invaded her head. The young woman within the circling beast had finally reached out with her mindvoice.

:You must kill it.:

Tamtcha shook her head uncertainly. "It is but light...?" Then louder, so as to be heard above the falls and wind. "There is nothing my hand could kill!"

:No, this is a windsoul.: The woman nodded slowly to where the saddlebag and weapons were strewn. :Your sacred arms will kill it... will sever its connection to this Plain. Then the windsouls of the village beyond will be safe.:

The beast snarled and clawed out towards the protector as Tamtcha moved for her weapons. But the whirling currents of light and wind kept the weazlbear's soul bound to the smaller woman as if chained or caged.

Frantically Tamtcha dug out the altar's grip and pulled at the wet leather knot that bound the bow shaft to the saddlebag. Her fingers felt clumsy. Her senses seemed numbed, and she struggled with a muttered oath even as she kept glancing back to that strange light song of woman and beast. The weazlbear ghost mounted upright, stretching its stringy haired arms high with its snarling challenge... and within its very center, motionless Anzund waited.

On one knee, Tamtcha hesitated as the bow finally freed. Shards of light danced and vanished about Anzund. The shape of the thing did not leave. The form of the woman never wavered. The Winds' roar seemed to grow louder... the falls noise became even more deafening, but Tamtcha could not close her conscience to the questions rising.

"Lightsinger! If I pierce this windsoul with my arrow, what prevents the weapon from passing on into you?!"

The woman did not answer.

"Anzund?!"

A hand pointed, reminding Tamtcha of the village in the forest behind her. And this time there was but the softest whisper of a mindvoice; it was as if the words were suspended within the sparkling light of a glass prayer chime. :You are Chatu Protector and Kownbearer. You must not let it reach the village.:

"I am Protector," Tamtcha repeated hollowly, feeling the life drain from the soles of her damp booted feet. Without conscious thought her hand set the bow aside and chose the pike shaft. Her movements came as if indeed she was dreaming then. The grip was laced to the staff and the amber fire of the distant altar blazed, capping the pike with its Winds Blessed steel. She stood, slipping her hand through the thong before grasping the grip. The weazlbear bellowed. Claws clacking in furious impotence, it raised itself towards the sky again. She felt the shiver of deathpain slide down her own back. "I am Chatu Protector."

:Don't do this. You've been hurt.: The mindvoice was gentle, unaccusing in its urgings. :The risks are too great. If you should fail, it will turn on the village. I can not hold it—:

"And you, Anzund?" She did not even know that she had asked that aloud.

:I am only a stranger among you, Kownbearer.:

"A stranger named Shaman's Daughter!"

Tamtcha left no further argument. She feigned a forward jump and lunged aside, swiping the pike across the mid-section of the screeching creature. Anzund fell as if cut herself, huddling about her knees with a gasp. The weazlbear hollered with evil delight despite the silver lava-like drippings of its own windsoul's blood.

:Quick and clean!: Anzund gasped.

"Release it!" Tamtcha cried, circling and dodging the slash of a claw. "Release it to me!"

:Only as you kill it!:

"Then death is — NOW!" and she hurdled herself and pike in an arch through the heart of the light form, sailing above the crouched woman. The creature exploded into a fiery orb and substance! Woolly coarse and muscle hard, it clutched Tamtcha as they went spinning out. The pike drove through. The shaft buried to the grip and her hand. The Winds sang. Light turned to chaos... and then they were falling, and only the mist and roar of the waterfalls was left to surround them.

>>> <<<

Tamtcha heard the sound of running water. A soft, damp pad touched her cheek where the claws had struck. Her chest felt heavy and ached, but the air managed to fill her lungs. The scent of the Chatu holy liquors was suddenly very strong, and then the fiery brew was coursing down her throat. She sputtered and almost gagged. When it was done, she found her eyes had finally opened.

She was still in the forest. The waterfalls could not have

been too far away, but the denseness of the foliage suggested that she was below the plateau. The last memory of the leap that took her and the weazlbear over the edge was very real then, and she shut her eyes briefly to adjust to the fatality of that lunge.

:You are not dead yet.: The words danced through Tamtcha's mind amidst the crystal shimmer of a prism's rainbow, like the sound of a prayer chime turned to light.

The protector looked up then and found herself cradled in the lap of the young lightsinger. Amusement crinkled the corners of pale grey eyes. Something much more tender curved those lips into a smile.

:I am not as incompetent as all that, you know.:

Tamtcha felt lost. "Incompetent?"

:To let you die in a mere fall.:

"You wouldn't have?"

:No.: A soft humor was reflected in the indigoes of that mindvoice. :I admit I don't have the ability to deter a weazlbear very long, but it's not nearly so difficult to catch a Chatu windsoul... especially when she wants to be caught.:

"And... I did want to be caught."

:By me?:

"By you." For a hushed breath, eyes met and held... and Tamtcha felt as if the very Winds Themselves caressed them.

Then, :I have something for you, Tamtcha. Can you sit yet?:

"You know my name."

Again that tenderness touched the woman's smile. :I caught your windsoul. In that moment, I could not help but know you. Now can you sit?:

Tamtcha found she could. She settled herself gingerly, noticing the small fire that Anzund had built. It was only then that the protector realized how late it had grown and that the shadows had not come simply from the forest's trees but from the descent of twilight.

:These Wind- Blessed Gifts are to be returned to you.:

Tamtcha looked at the pike and the single knife. For a long while, she merely stared at the pieces. The knife was the rose quartz handled one that had been in her boot sheath. The pike was the same she'd taken up against the weazlbear, except now the leather grip dangled with quartz beads... the tigereye stones were no longer there. Warily she raised a hand to her headband.

:Your kownband is unchanged. The three stones are still Chatu soulstones.:

"But this quartz...? Do you know what it is for?"

Gravely, Anzund held Tamtcha's gaze. :It is my crystal of light power.:

Tamtcha took the Winds Blessed weapons, remembering the strength in the woman as Anzund had stood amidst the weazlbear's windsoul and urged Tamtcha to choose the arrow. Her heart stirred, and suddenly quiet clearly she saw the value the Winds placed in this woman... and she understood her own wish to be saved by this woman so that they might share more than a single moment of a dreamquest.

:You will not remember much of this,: Anzund murmured softly.

Tamtcha thought it was said with a strange sort of reluctance. She tried to lightened the frown with a crooked grin, "I'll remember enough. More than you, I dare say, since it was both the Winds and the Shaman that sent me after you."

:No, I'll forget nothing.: Anzund's grey eyes lifted again to meet Tamtcha's. :Remember, I was once a holy Acolyte of the Windbrothers. And I am a lightsinger.:

"Who Nahessa names Shaman's Daughter," Tamtcha nodded slowly. "I think I understand."

:Does it... anger you?:

"No, I'm sure it's best that one of us remembers this clearly. But I still have a question."

Anzund encouraged her with a faint nod.

"When you are settled among us, do you... will you remain within the Shaman's Lodge as you once thought to remain in the Winds' Temple?"

:I don't know what will happen. The Village Circle must dictate the terms of my acceptance, mustn't they?:

How could she have forgotten that? Tamtcha felt her heart might just break at the thought. But she gathered her courage and accepted the fact that how she felt would not sway the Honored Providers of the Chatu Lodges into anything. Even the Shaman would accept their judgment in the matter of this newcomer.

:Tamtcha?::

She glanced up as the woman knelt beside her and suddenly found a soft kiss being pressed to her lips. Her golden eyes reflected puzzlement when Anzund drew away.

:I wished to catch you... as much as you wished to be caught. Remember that, if nothing else. Whatever else our roles are to be, if you will have me — I want to be beside you.:

Tamtcha smiled wanly. "May the weazlbears beware."

Anzund did not answer her smile. :Unfortunately, they will be.:

Tamtcha frowned at such somberness. But fingers pressed against her lips to prevent another question. :You are done here. It's time to go home.: With that the woods around them began to blur, only the small camp fire blazed clear. :I will remember your words, my Beloved Kownbearer.:

"I will remember my loyalties," Tamtcha murmured, lifting the weapons trimmed in that rose quartz, "...and my love."

Their fire grew into a bonfire. Surrounding it appeared the stone ring that had once stood so empty with ash and blackened embers. Azure nothingness chased away the forest. But the wisps of mists were pale, pale ghosts of clouds now, and Tamtcha found herself back where she had begun. Nahessa nodded a silent greeting from the far side of the roaring flames.

Tamtcha glanced about them in concern. "Anzund?! She should have—"

The Shaman smiled in reassurance. "I have taken her already. She is exhausted from the magics and from before, from the trek her body was forced into across the Ranges. With rest and care, she will be well. Now it is your turn to return. "

Then they were sitting at the table in the Shaman's room. The bronze lamp burned overhead, its three wicks blazing as brightly as the bonfire had seemed to.

"Kahl has already gone to speak with the Circle."

Tamtcha drew a long, slow breath and felt her muscles stir from that strange limbo of Dreamings. She let her consciousness wake at its will. She allowed the safety of the Shaman's magics to cradle her. Her left cheek felt stiff. She raised a tentative hand to her face, but there was nothing different about it. The tails of her kownband were still woven into her dark braid. The glittering brocade of her red satins seemed a bit heavy, almost awkward, but she knew where she was. She knew who she was. She looked at Nahessa curiously, and the old mystic smiled.

"You did well. What do you remember?"

"Anzund... there was sungold in the color of her hair, storm grey in her eyes and — such strength. I saw windlights in the touch of her mindvoice. And still..." Tamtcha's brow folded in confusion, "...there was something more. My path... somehow I am to walk with her, Nahessa."

"Are you content in that?"

"Yie." Almost unexpectedly, Tamtcha felt a faint smile turn her lips. She nodded more confidently, "I am warmed by it."

"Yet the rest slips away even as you reach back for it."

"One can not travel back, only forward."

"You remember my teachings well. Now I charge you, remember your feelings equally as well. She will have need of a protector in the days to come."

"As she faces the Village Circle?"

"Beyond. Now, my kowndaughter, take your gifts of the Dreamings and seek your lodge to rest."

For the first time, Tamtcha noticed the weapons atop the mother-of-pearl inlay on the table. They were laid between the two points of the open-based triangles; at the point of Today within the Barrier Winds' glyph. The pike was beautifully crafted with small quartz beads dangling from the center grip. The knife was a hunting blade, also with a rose quartz handle. The carvings on the knife drew Tamtcha's attention, and reverently she lifted the piece to examine the images. The carving was of a swirling, mythical weazlbear; it sprang from a watery pool as a lone protector attacked it with a pike. The ribbons of pink and white in the quartz moved through the scene, softening the dire circumstances of the battle with their colors. Tamtcha smiled, feeling her heart touched with a fondness even though she could not say why.

She stood and bowed deeply to Nahessa, a hand cupped beneath her heart. "Fair day to you, my friend... and thank you."

The Shaman nodded gracefully. But as Tamtcha left, Nahessa only wondered at the vagueness of the Tomorrow she glimpsed, and she frowned at the darkness they might all come to face.

>>> <<<

Anzund paused at the edge of the forest, looking down into that small valley of the Northern Gate guardians. The sun had begun to set, creating shadowed silhouettes of pines and birch, while the Chatu below set about lighting their village. It was as always, Anzund found... after three years of watching, she still did not tire of the beauty night brought here.

Strings of candlepots slowly lit, tracing the narrow paths and footbridges. The intertwining lattice of shallow streams glistened as they began to reflect the lights of both candles and stars. Above a sky of indigo deepening in warm blackness and yet more stars emerged. Then one by one the lodge house lamps appeared. Their three wicks glowed safely within bright brass fittings as chains drew them up to nestle in the arches of center beams. Each lodge hoisted their lamp, each path from stable to Shaman was outlined, each stream glistened and together they spun a wondrous web of white gold light.

Her breath caught and Anzund listened for the chaning of the very wing. Breezes were about to turn and come from the thin pass beyond, up from the Barren Ranges instead of down from the forested Hills. Then it happened—for an instant, as the air currents still just before shifting, the lodge chimes tiled. A hush took the valley and Anzund on its edge. The rustle of leaves stopped. Tree frogs and crickets went quiet. Only the babbling streams below seemed unhindered. Then with the gentlest of sighs, the reversal came, and the sun-dried scent of the range grasses swept in. And with it the chimes of reed and crystal stones began to sing again.

A village of light and wind, Anzund thought, her own heart singing. This place she had only imagined as a an Acolyte among those of the Temple, yet not it was the place she called home. More than that... it was the place of those who'd adopted her as one of their very own. They had accepted her without grudge for her Choir-like power of lightchants, without fear of her mute strangeness that allowed her to speak with only one at a time and only through her mindvoice – a mindvoice colored by light songs no less! They hadn't even seemed repulsed by her small, fine-boned and very blond appearance; she looked every bit like the Nyor city-bred servants of the Choir, and it was accentuated here among these folk of tall frames and ebony hair. Even the pale gray of her eyes was odd compared to the brilliant tigereye hues of these Chatu. By all Holy, they should have greeted her with only suspicions. But their hearts had proved as fearlessly bright as their soulstone gazes, and these Chatu had trusted their Shaman and the Winds in Anzund's coming. She had hoped for safety, prayed for some way tolerance and restrictions... at least until the Honored Providers of the Village Circle had gotten to know her and she could somehow prove her worth. Even Tamtcha had clearly expected only a begrudging acceptance for her. But each of the Circle had asked only one question of Anzund, and amazingly, her answers had satisfied all.

"The sound of a prayer chime turned to light," Kahl had later said, "can reflect only truth. Your mindvoice sings with such light. To turn you aside in any way would betray the very Winds we follow... and our own souls. Our providers know this as do I... at least, I do now."

That was the only time the Eldest as Kownbearer had ever referred to his initial misgivings of her arrival. Since then, Kahl had been supportive of the Shaman's naming of Anzund as provider and daughter, and he had even endorsed her rather unorthodox, monogamous marriage to Tamtcha.

Anzund started down the path again, feeling the wistful touch of a guilty conscience at that last memory. Tamtcha was a strong woman, a quiet woman, who led by example and patience; Anzund had been half-expecting the Tryad and Circle to forbid their marriage when she'd asked for Tamtcha's fidelity. After all, she had been suddenly acting as an outsider and exerting outside customs. That was not necessarily indicative of a perspective any of a kownbearer's spouses should have... if anything, Anzund was sure a kownbearer's First Provider should be even more circumspect in Chatu manners and customs than most. But then she had still been quite new to the Chatu. She had come to learn that they tolerated differences with a matter-of-fact acceptance she'd never imagined existed. Because she was not raised among them, they were even more lenient of her preferences. Because Tamtcha was an extraordinary protector, evidenced by her election to the Tryad at an age younger than any before, they also expected Tamtcha to be extraordinary n her tastes. To Anzund's surprise, everyone in the village had actually believed their marriage made perfect sense.

But it had also meant that Tamtcha's newly founded lodge was till largely empty, even three years after their welcoming. Anzund had come to realize that multiple marriage served very practical function outside of the bedrooms in the keeping of the lodgehouses. It took a number of providers to tend hearth, raise children, weave and mend, and still coordinate with the Circle to bring in crops and care for the mountain herds. It took an additional assortment of skills in the lodge protectors to hunt both wilderkal on the Ranges and forest game in the Hills, guard the fields from venomous rake snakes and rabid bandi, traffic messages and goods to other villages in the Hills, and–most importantly in this northernmost border–guard the Chatu against the thieving caravans of Nyor. A single couple simply could not adequately cloth and geed themselves let along meet the village responsibilities expected of a lodge, especially not when the protector tended the work of the Tryad and the provider was Shaman's Apprentice.

So at Tamtcha's suggestion, Anzund had arranged for Weazlbear claw to adopt a Wanderer, a woman protector by the name of Zhrin who was skilled in both weapons and hunt. After that Weazlbear Claw had begun to grow a bit more in the usual, polygamous manner. There now five of them, three protectors and two providers totaled, and gradually they were becoming more autonomous from Tamtcha's foster-parents' lodge. But there were still no children, still none designated as Childbearer. At it was Chaiz was the only male in Weazlbear Claw and neither of his two protectors had the slightest interest in mothering children... no matter how much they loved him nor how much he would have loved raising small ones. And Anzund knew that despite Tamtcha's loving assurance, the

First Protector of Weazlbear Claw sorely mourned the absence of youngsters.

>>> <<<

"You're awake?"

Anzund tossed a nod back over her shoulder as Tamtcha slipped through the tapestries to join her at the bathing pool.

"I thought you'd be asleep by now. Or at least resting."

:I am overly rested, thank you. And Sappen was kind enough to light the wood chips this afternoon, so the water's deliciously warm.:

Tamtcha leant over the tiles to dip a hand into the pool and sighed, eyes sliding closed with pleasure. "Remind me to commend his foresight. This is precisely what these old bones need ."

:Hmmm...: Anzund accepted her lover's slow kiss in belated greeting and then gently stroked aside the damp, dark hair that had freed itself from braid and kownband. :You look tired, Beloved.:

"Very tired, very sweaty, and believe it or not, chilled through and through!" With that she took herself off to the wash trough on the pool's far side, shedding clothes as she went.

:Why wouldn't I believe you? It's cool tonight and you've been dancing since sunset. I'd imagine you'd be quite cold once you stopped moving.:

"Yie, what was a blessing at first is less so at the end."

Anzund watched quietly, admiring the grace of her protector's body as Tamtcha soaped down. Their eyes met, and she blushed at being caught. Tamtcha gave her a crooked grin before dousing herself with a pitcher of lukewarm water.

:So, how are you all doing?:

"Fair enough," Tamtcha shook her hair free from its band and bent to wash it. "We're sore, but ready for Harvest Markt. We practice now to keep our stamina up."

:You and Baij managed to agree on all of the steps for everybody then?:

Tamtcha grunted, head half-buried in the side trough as she lathered her hair well. "K'ntro, the youngest protector of

Sparrowhawk Eye, gave us the last set the other night. Both Baij and I agreed we should use it."

:Oh?:

"Unlike most of our younger, over-enthusiastic protectors, she grasped the need to conserve a little strength for the wee hours of the dawn." Tamtcha sighed and emerged from the water to bury her face in a small towel. Another sigh underlined her weariness. Then with comb in hand, she finally climbed into the pool with Anzund. "She presented a very nice piece depicting a hunt-and-track that can precede my old weazlbear kill... the one Baij made me resurrect?"

:Uh-hmm,: Anzund hid a smile at Tamtcha's disgruntled tone.

"There isn't a leap or tumble in her entire piece. Instead she's relying on stretches, turns and timing. It's perfect for our needs. A nice sensible change of pace to let us catch our breaths and loosen up again. Has good use of pike and bow too."

:Sounds as if she has a talent for the planning of the dance.:

"Yie. It's a shame we've only noticed it this year...."

When she may not be around for next year, Anzund finished silently, and then amended... when so few of us may be.

"By the Winds! Such waste this war brings."

Mutely Anzund drew near, setting Tamtcha's comb aside. A tender hand guided the Kownbearer down onto a lower step. With a grateful moan Tamtcha consented to her kneading touch, and slowly Anzund began to rub the tension from those strong shoulders.

"This dance... first I worry we've asked too much and then I worry it's too little."

:It's important to you... to all of us. That's why you demand it be as near perfect a balance of stamina and skills as possible.:

"Yie, for this Challenge Dance above all others must be — this year's when it will not be merely symbolic. Idiotic, isn't it? To choose which protectors will become warriors and which will not based upon their performances in a dance!"

:No,: Anzund corrected, words spun into a soothing mixture of green and gold light. :It's tradition, and as Kahl says, there will be more volunteering because of pride and need than are fit to ride the Barren Ranges. You need to find those physically capable of riding long hours and fighting longer ones. This is not some trapping party you'll be leading. They can not pace themselves to suit their personal convenience.:

"Yet too few have ever fought so much as a wounded bandi, let along an armed rider or a caravan's footsword."

:But that is because the Gate of G'nia and the Southern Gate have done well, just as your own protectors here have. Outsiders do not march into the Hills of the Chatu. Besides, who of you would begrudge those inner villages their generations of peace?:

"No, I would not. But I could wish for more who understood what we will ask of them. For their sakes... for all our sakes, I don't want us to fail because of sheer inexperience. Yet I know many of them will fall, because of it."

:You will do what you can, starting with the dance.:

"Followed by the winter's training."

:Yie, then the rest will be left to the Winds.:

"Winter...," Tamtcha scowled darkly into the waters.

:You're thinking that there's too little time?:

She pursued her lips consideringly, then shook her head. "Nahessa says the protectors travel from the G'nia Hills and from the southern coast already."

:Those battle-tried protectors of the other Gates?:

Tamtcha nodded. "It will be mid-winter before some even arrive. But with their help, we may have enough time."

Anzund nodded, her hands turning their attention to Tamtcha's stiffened neck. :Maglind was wise in suggesting the protectors' meeting lodge be enlarged and that new ones be built for group-living and winter weapons' practice.:

Tamtcha chuckled at the irony. "A traveler's lodge in the Northern Gate? Who would ever have suspected we'd need to house so many that we'd build one, let alone a half-dozen."

:But you expect to fill them all.:

"I hope to." The weariness returned. "I hope for more than that... for enough to fill every empty pallet in the village before spring comes. Baij agrees... he has even arranged with the Honored One of Ringcoon Hand tend the Kownbearers and hunting chiefs in his Yote's Fang. That will be good for morale.

At times, we leaders have doubts best left unshared with even our most devoted followers."

Anzund understood that. :How many do you think will come in all?:

"A thousand perhaps. Not nearly enough."

:Nyor may be a large city, Beloved, but the Choir doesn't control much of the province outside the city walls. They do have limits on the number willing to die for them. And their relations with the countryside... that too will make it difficult for them to keep a large force supplied should the fight become a long one.:

Her brow furrowed, and Tamtcha shook her head, trying to ward off some muddled apprehension. "I feel as if we're overlooking something. Something... intangible, yet somehow it's so obvious that we should be preparing for it."

Clear eyes of grey studied Tamtcha without derision. Then frowning faintly, Anzund sought to remember all she knew of that distant enemy. But in the end, she found of nothing specific. :I'm sorry, I don't see what it could be.:

Tamtcha heaved a despairing sigh and muttered, "If I look but do not see, can I say I am aware?"

Anzund stilled, seemingly startled. :Where do you know those words from?:

Her protector shrugged, "Only an old saying of ours."

:No,: Anzund gnawed on her lip, disconcerted at the misty memories that rose from her childhood in the Temple. :I had a nurse, an Acolyte that had come south from the Storm folk... you speak the first words of a verse of hers. It is the dialogue between the Eye and the Essence... the verse that begins a creation tale.:

"We too know of an Eye and Essence. They came out of the Chaoses to give birth to the Winds. How does the Storm's verse go?"

> :If I look
> but do not see,
> can I say
> I am aware?

If I come
and leave unseen,
am I not
less than a ghost?

Then return and
I shall search to
see your Essence.

Recognized,
then will I thrive
beneath your Eye.:

Slowly Tamtcha nodded. "The Storm remembers the same beginnings then... it shouldn't surprise me. Once both our folk were closely bound in kinship and belief. But it seems to have little to do with the Choir's rising powers now. Or not?"

Try as she would, Anzund could bring nothing from that odd piece. :I can only think of the obvious — that many of the Storm serve the Choir. But that sense of not-quite-rightness you have? I do feel it. I'll speak with Nahessa. Maybe she'll better understand what is missing.:

There was nothing else to be done, Tamtcha realized, and for the time being, her conscience agreed she could relax. Drawing a deep breath, she did just that. Anzund smiled as Tamtcha sank back into her arms, and tenderly she tipped her lover's head back for a kiss.

"Very nice," Tamtcha murmured, eyes still closed. Then she grinned, "And what about you?"

:What about me?:

"How has your 'overly rested' day been?"

:I went riding some, on that new pony you got for me. And I admit it — you needn't look so smug with yourself — White Tail and I do suit each other quiet well.:

"Just as I said?"

:Just as you said.: Anzund dropped a kiss on her nose and then playfully bit it.

"Ou! Hold off here! What have I done?"

:Verged on the edge of arrogance.:

"Is that all?!"

:No,: Anzund laughed with a teasing riot of lightburst, : but you'd have to see Sappen for the full accounting. He's the only one keeping records on you, at the moment.:

"At the moment?"

Her eyebrows wiggled threateningly, :I may start my own!:

Tamtcha laughed and gave up. But as Anzund's arms drew her back again, she was surprised to admit that the tension of the day had actually worn away.

:Ahh, speaking of Sappen. He brought your outfit for the Challenge Dance, when he came by with supper. He asked that you try it on tomorrow to make certain it fits loosely enough for your so-called acrobatics.:

"Sounds like my irreverent once-sib."

:Whom you still adore despite his wit.:

"I admit I do. What is he up to these days?"

:Mostly tending your lodge, Dearest.:

Tamtcha chided herself for that oversight. "I should be more grateful than forgetful. When I think about it, it seems he must nearly live here."

:It would probably be easier for him, if he did. At least he'd have fewer to cook for.:

"Maglind still has him charged with evening meals for the children?"

:Children — and trail fare for protectors.:

"Hmmm...," she toyed with Anzund's fingers for a bit, tracing the watercrinkles on their tips. Then somewhat cautiously, she ventured, "It would be possible, you know, for Sappen to become part of Weazlbear Claw."

:Not by marriage, it wouldn't be,: Anzund quipped, but she was also undeniably serious.

"Well no, not to me certainly."

:Then short of having Maglind disown him and disgrace the poor man in the eyes of the entire village... or having Red Eagle Talon blown to the ground in some tragic accident, how do you suggest we adopt him?:

"Not him, but his sweetheart, Zharin. She's a wanderer and quite eligible for adoption."

:A wanderer?: Anzund frown suspiciously. :Aren't those the protectors exiled from lodge and village for unforgivable transgressions?:

"Occasionally," Tamtcha chuckled, amused at her lover's lack of faith. "Do you really think I'd consider that sort of ruffian fit for your lodge, Love?"

:Well, no... but then I think you're a little crazy to have welcomed me in the first place, so what do I know?:

"Fair enough. All right, it is true that a few wanderers are exiles. They've had their band and tigereye taken from them, and they're less than welcome at most any hearth. But usually they travel off beyond the Chatu boundaries or else seek out another village's shaman and ask to become a learner."

Warily Anzund nodded. That fit with what she'd been told by Halin and the learners themselves. Although honored for their teaching and history-keeping, the learners always seemed to be more observers than participants in the Chatu lives... and they were the only ones who never wore a tigereye's band. :Then what about these others you call wanderers?:

"They are just that... wanderers. They are protectors who disown the Honored One's lodge and travel. They sell their skills, usually of pike and bow, and move from village to village learning about people and places as they go. Often they travel beyond our boundaries with trading goods to the southwest continent. A few come north to see the grass ranges or the Storm folk. But they always return to settle again within our Hills.

"Zharin is one who came north. She hunted caravans and wilderkal with us the year after Sappen was named provider. She left here to earn a Welcoming Store.

"At the time, Kahl was unimpressed with Sappen's declaration of love. Both he and Maglind refused to consider adopting Zharin into Red Eagle Talon. As you can imagine, Sappen has a way of flirting that would make anyone suspicious when it comes to believing in real affection. But he surprised us all. He continued to dance the circle fires and ride with numerous suitors, but he's turned aside anyone growing serious as he waits for Zharin to claim him as First. And every year Zharin faithfully comes to Harvest Markt with a lengthening list of trader's favors owed for her services."

:Ahh, that's right. Only providers own property. So without a lodge behind her, she'd have to wait to be married before collecting anything other than basic food, clothing or weapons.:

"Just so, but her Welcoming Store has grown considerably in the last four years. And Kahl has admitted to being a bit more impressed."

:So why hasn't Sappen simply married someone and take Zharin to be his Second?:

"Not exactly very flattering to his First... I mean, we do tend to approve of love and emotional attachments and all of that, you know?! Just because we marry more than one person, doesn't mean we don't feel expect to feel something very special for each of them!"

Anzund blushed. :Sorry, my prejudices are showing again, aren't they?:

"Yie...," Tamtcha kissed her gently, "but don't think I regret having you to myself. I'd court you again, if I had to." Then withdrawing a bit to Sappen's matters, Tamtcha settled back into her lover's grasp saying, "There are practical reasons Sappen sees in waiting for her, too. He's not sure any Honored Provider other than Maglind would agree to the arrangement, and he doesn't want to risk loosing her for good. After all, a wanderer has disowned the authority of a lodge once... that doesn't always bode well for future family relations with the Honored One nor First Protector."

:And you'd expect this wanderer to do well with us? An Honored Provider who looks like a Nyor enemy and who's a lightsinger too? And you with the authority of the Kownbearer?!:

"I do," Tamtcha countered quiet calmly. "I know Zharin. I think she'd be just as enamored with you as Nahessa and Sappen are. And I think you'd find her very supportive of both of us and... and she'd empathize with the separations we feel from so many of the others. After all, she grew up feeling alienated because of her desires to travel. And since leaving her provider's lodge, she's been kept somewhat on the outside of village life wherever she goes."

:Yet you respect her,: Anzund realized abruptly. :Despite her differences, she has somehow impressed you with her skill and honor.:

"Yie, and she respects me... for my abilities and not for

my infamy."

Anzund knew what a rare find such a friend was for Tamtcha. She studied her love for a moment, before, :Are you really serious about this... adopting her and bringing Sappen into the lodge?:

Hesitant silence hung between them, telling Anzund far more than Tamtcha's words ever could have about how hopeful her protector was. Then Tamtcha shrugged. "It's not my decision. It's yours as Honored Provider of Weazlbear Claw. But it does seem viable."

:It does... very. Will she be at the northern Harvest Markt this year?:

"Undoubtedly, and she will be one of those who returns with us to prepare for spring. Unless ill fortune has befallen her in the past year."

Anzund nodded slowly, still uncertain herself. It took some consideration to change how she had been thinking about Weazlbear Claw... as hers and Tamtcha's alone. But she was finding it more and more difficult to balance Nahessa's demands with the more traditional roles of providers. And she wasn't agreeing to share Tamtcha. She smiled abruptly. The thought of someday having children and other adults to fill the long length of this lodge was not at all uninviting. :So, you will introduce me to this heart throb of Sappen's, and we shall see.:

Tamtcha grinned outright. "Was I wrong about White Tail?"

:A pony is quite different from hearthkin, my Love. Don't grow too arrogant on me!:

Chapter Fifteen

The night was moonless, and the stars were hooded with thin wisps of clouds. Fires blazed brightly, flames leaping twice the height of any apprentice. The shadows swirled in a charcoal grey mist around the fire's clearing. Yet within that mistiness, faint traces of magenta and deepening purples wound about, blurring gazes with half-imagined shapes. In the distance, above on the hills and beyond wooded slopes, the fires of another gathering flickered... the protectors' Challenge Dance had begun in the Harvest camp and their music boards of long, hollow half-tubes sent out rhythmic plink-plinkette sounds into the night. But here beneath the stars and between the three great fires, the wise women and apprentices of the Shaman's Lodge met for their own challenge.

The breezes murmured, and the thin, metal chimes which hung in the trees sang. The mindvoices of the shamyn chanted in eerie silence, their bodies swaying to an unheard rhythm. With their eyes closed, hands upon knees, and faces turned upwards to the winds of the night, the women's prayers went on. They sat between the bonfires, forming a triangle with roaring flames at each corner. Their young apprentices sat within that boundary, forming yet another triangle. But the apprentices faced the shamyn, waiting and watching as the elders bound them all together in magic.

Anzund felt her heart pounding, and her breath seemed shallow. She moistened dry lips and swallowed hard, eyes never leaving Nahessa's rocking figure. The Oldest Shaman was dressed as the others in a Healing Jackets of lavender. The grey hair was unbraided, but knotted with tiny bits of bone and bark. It made Anzund shiver to remember that this was how she had met Nahessa, just after her first waking in the Northern Gate village. It made her shiver to remember that the Choir had been responsible then, even as it was now, for the need of such garb. For the shamyn and their chosen were gathered tonight to heal the wounds of jealousies and bickering that any village might hold against another. They were here to heal the Winds' Today of any grudge the slowness of its Chatu tenders might have inadvertently caused. They were here tonight to heal and to unite, so that the Choir might never divide... so that the Chatu could ride with the Winds' blessings and strength come spring.

And they were here to choose the Keeper of the Rites, be it shaman or apprentice... they were here to find the one who would ride into war with the protectors to be the voice and hand of all shamyn. They were here to find one strong enough to be entrusted to wield the power of Winds and Chatu, to stand against the Choir Pawns, and to stand against the temptations to abuse that very power which would be the hope of their people.

The tree chimes rang out again, rippling with the

gathering magics of the mystics. The fires reached higher, and trails of glittering sparks began to swirl off from the tips of the flames. The shamyn's prayer gathered them closer, the bodies of each woman straining as shoulders stiffened and worn lines deepened within faces. Then suddenly high above, the Winds and lights joined and found life of their own, spinning as one — no longer dependent upon fire nor tree chime. Sparks descended in a flowing stream, circling over shamyn and apprentices. Colors bolted like lightening striking, and the river of windlight tumbled around its path even faster. Together the shamyn's stilled and their eyes opened. The cascading power dipped and slid down, almost to the ground, and flowed in that narrow chasm between the triangles of elders and apprentices.

The energy prickled the skin on the back of Anzund's neck. Her silken tunic fluttered as the rushing sparkle and splay went by. The air seemed cool, like the forest's green depths on a summer's hot day, and her head felt giddy as if she'd been galloping headlong into the Wind. She blinked, trying to break the mesmerized feeling that held her staring so blindly into that brightness... and as she did so, the swimming windstars halted.

Not a breath was heard. Not a single woman, apprentice nor shaman, moved. In the space of an instant, their world hovering precariously balance... their souls being weighed and their deeds being judged in utter silence.

Then suddenly the sparks eclipsed the brightness of a sun. A mighty stream of golden light shot up for the stars. It began to twirl about itself, like a spinning wheel's thread, and strands of pale rose and blue hues appeared on its outside. They bound the gold so tightly that the pastels began to mesh into a single sheath of lavender. As the gold within grew more restricted the core glowed even brighter, causing more strings of rose and blue to rise and bind it. Until suddenly the colors darkened in density and the gold was contained wholly within a glove of indigo. The goldness glittered and flashed as a crack or thin hole was found here and there, but the velvety reed of deep, dark purple held. The dazzling column thinned, stretching into the infinity of the night, vibrating with the power of Winds and light. Then thunder cracked in the starry skies above, and the band of power whipped back from the heavens in a powerful arc.

Anzund screamed with a mind's cry of silent terror as her soul was ripped from her body's shell. Within a heartbeat all that she knew of herself, of shame and pride... of good and bad..., was flung into her consciousness, and all that she could be was shown to her as possible.

She blinked and the breath rushed into her lungs as if she'd been drowning. She found herself standing in the middle of the apprentices' triangle, hands trembling as she held them out in front of her. She felt alive with the night's breeze brushing her cheek and yet she felt alien to this body of hers. Her hands turned over slowly, and sparkles of light danced across the backs of her wrists and fingers. She gazed down at where her feet stood, braced and planted firmly against the uneven grass footing; there was a glow about the edges of her boots' trim.

There was motion around her, and she looked up as the shamyn and apprentices stood. They formed a single triangle about her, and she saw not only the shamyn that had been seated with her earlier, but the windsouls of every shamyn of Today's Plain. Behind and beside the elders, the windsouls came to complete the triangle, and she knew what she did not want to know... that she had become the Keeper of the Rites.

The low chant of welcome and thanksgiving began. Feet began to move in the steps of the Shamyn's Dance. Anzund felt the panic rise to grip her again, but suddenly Nahessa was dancing across from her. That calm, dark gaze caught and held her within the fearful chaos. The old woman's grimness softened into a smile that was both encouraging and unsurprised.

:Yie, the Chosen One. You answer to each of us and yet to none of us now, Anzund. You draw upon all of our powers. You have become our Shamyn's Apprentice.:

Anzund remembered the day when Nahessa had given her the lightwand and she had accepted the responsibility of learning to use her special gifts. Now she realized this Oldest of Shamyn had known then what her task would be.

The powers within her stirred. Anzund felt the fear recede. A quiet determination grew in its stead. She had been chosen by the Winds' Light and by the Chatu's Heart. She would do what was needed.

And in that a moment, Anzund knew too that this sense of duty was what Tamtcha had felt when the Kownband had been passed to her.

Tamtcha woke abruptly. Sleep vanished with the suddenness born of scouting instincts that scented danger. Her breathing went shallow and quiet as she listened in the darkness. The sounds from the woods and wind crept in through the lodge house windows. Smells of lamp smoke and oiled woods tainted the air familiarly. At her feet, the two otter-like rat'ta'tats lay frozen, slender noses lifted in search of an intruder's scent.

The bed beneath her creaked as she rolled from it, but she swallowed the curse as she shrugged into a short robe. She'd never thought to master a stealthy leaving from Anzund's framed bed; Chatu sleeping pallets rarely made a rustle. The rat'ta'tats' dark forms flowed to the floor and entwined themselves about her ankles as she paused beside the felt curtain of the doorway. There was the dim shape of a knife in her hand.

A muffled clack brought her out into the living area, crouching low on the thick layers of carpets. To her left she saw the faint outline of Zharin's strong frame and across the lodge, beyond the reflections of the bathing pool, Devon's lithe figure was barely visible. Both protectors huddled low waiting for her commands; like her, both women were armed with their hunting knives. She hesitated, listening to the stillness, the rat'ta'tats beside her with whiskers twitching. The quiet held that unsettling quality of wrongness.

She touched a furry head lightly and the sleek little creatures slipped off into the flickering shadows. As usual, the bronze lamps were at half-glow and lowered from the ceiling arch, coaxing a warm coziness into the midnight hours. Tonight, however, it only created a dimness that Tamtcha mistrusted.

Shrewdly her gaze scanned the blacker corners, looking for that something which was out of place. Her breath caught, then she was moving towards the slumped figure that lay near the back ovens and kitchen pumps and in an instant the rat'ta'tats were chattering with their alarmed compassion.

"Anzund?!"

At her frantic hand signal Zharin retreated to the side room to fetch Chaiz as Devon hastened to the herbs room for his medicine rolls. She forced the tumbling pups aside to kneel and gently turned her lover, cradling her close as fingers shakily brushed the golden hair back from the damp forehead. "Anzund!"

Eyes fluttered open, glazed and unable to focus. A hand lifted and grasped for Tamtcha's arm as the slender body shivered violently, teeth snapping. Her long robe was soaked with water from the spilled pitcher, but Tamtcha could find no sign that Anzund had fallen against anything else. She pressed a hand against the flushed cheek and felt the fever, but it puzzled Tamtcha even as if frightened her. There had been no sign of illness at their late supper.

Lights of yellow and orange chaos struggled to enter her mind, and Tamtcha tightened her arms about Anzund's trembling figure. "I'm here, Love. Tell me again."

:Shaman — bring Nahessa.:

"Yie, I'll fetch her." Tamtcha swung Anzund up into her arms and carried her back to bed. Stripping the water-chilled robe from her, Tamtcha tucked her in beneath a thick quilt and paused to light both of the braziers. A worried glance cast towards her lover sent her hurrying for her finger flute hanging near the lodge entrance.

Outside Weazlbear Claw, she raised the small flute and trilled a rippling half-measure. Night sounds stilled, and again her piercing notes flew. Then she turned, lowering the lamp in the arch and feeding the wick until it brightened. She pulled its chain, lifting it high again and an answering flute called to her. Below in the village figures stirred, stepping out to see which lodge lamp marked the call for the Shaman's aid. Tamtcha ignored their attention and, assured by a repeating flute song that help was coming, she ducked back inside.

It seemed to take Nahessa forever to arrive. Tamtcha had never felt such helplessness as she knelt beside her provider, holding tightly while Anzund clung to her with both hands.

:Don't. Let. Go.:

Tamtcha squeezed her eyes shut to block the menagerie of light bursts that assaulted her. "I have you," Tamtcha slipped onto the bed, gathering Anzund and the quilt up into her lap. "I'm not letting go, Sweetheart. I'm not letting go."

:Hurts—:

"What hurts? Love, tell me what hurts?" But Tamtcha could raise no further response from her. The shivering only grew worse as sweat ran from her brow.

"How did you find her?"

Tamtcha looked up in relief as the Shaman entered with two Learners close behind. "In the back. She'd fallen fetching water. But...?"

"No," Nahessa squinted, peering into Anzund's eyes as she gently forced them open, "this did not come from the falling."

"She showed no distress earlier. She said nothing of feeling ill today."

"What has she said since?"

"Just that she hurts."

"Yet you sent for me," Nahessa rocked back on her heels and faced the other squarely. "Why not call your neighbor, Sappen? Or a Learner alone? Many others are competent healers."

"She — she asked for you."

The grey haired elder nodded, lips pursed. "Did she leave you before sleeping?"

"Yie, to meditate. She does her lessons for you nearly each evening before retiring."

Grimly the Shaman glanced behind herself and signed something to her Learners. One left, herb bag in hand. The other began to unpack one of the rolled bundles, setting others aside as unneeded.

"What is wrong?" Tamtcha whispered, fearful of the answer and of the solemnness written upon the elder's lined face.

"She is being courted by the Choir's lightsingers," Nahessa said gently, placing a reassuring hand upon Tamtcha's own. "The ones she fled from Nyor sing to her. Somehow, her songs tonight rode the eastbound winds, and they snatch at her, even now as we speak."

"They know she is alive?!"

"They have known for some time. But they do not know where."

"And now?"

"They are still ignorant. They cannot come to her. They must wait for mistakes and then lure her into their Sanctuary. Their seduction is sweet, when they will it. I doubt she even knew what she wandered into, until it grew too late to retreat."

"Can you return her to us?"

Nahessa looked mildly surprised. "Of course. She is Chatu, apprentice of my own lodge, provider of yours. They have no claim upon her soul unless she gives it willingly." A hand waved impatiently at the shivering woman before them. "Does this look as if she's willing?"

The Learner returned with a bowl of crushed herbs and water, and chastised, Tamtcha held her silence. The second Learner began to light the incense straws she'd set about the room, pausing to add something to the braziers that sent rosy smoke into the air.

"Leave us now, Kownbearer." Nahessa unwounded Anzund's hands from Tamtcha's, grasping them securely in her own. "Your part is done for the present."

Heart in her throat, Tamtcha glanced about at the three of them, then one last time at Anzund. She managed a nod and complied.

>>> <<<

:Should I have hesitated, Nahessa? Was I being arrogant to assume the task alone?:

The Shaman took Anzund's hands, meeting the woman's distress with nothing but reassurance. "The only question of importance, Daughter, is will you dare to try again?"

Anzund nodded, pale and apprehensive. :Unless you forbid it.:

"Alone?"

Panic flared at the concept, exhaustion and fright mingling to hold her thoughts frozen for an instant. Then she found her courage and the words. :If I must, I will.:

"But if not?"

:I would rather... not go alone.:

Approval sparked within those golden eyes, and the old woman settled down on the bedside, folding Anzund into the thick quilts. "So, I would say there is wisdom in your judgment rather than arrogance. Wouldn't you?"

Relief made her breath catch, but Anzund shut her eyes against the pain that knowing her own fear's depths had caused. She was ashamed at how much she dreaded facing that Dreamquest alone again.

A damp cloth pressed to her forehead, cooling her fevored flush and her self-chastisement. She looked back to Nahessa to find the old woman nodding. The Shaman reached to her with a gentle yet colorless mindvoice, :I see you understand a little more of yourself... and your task.:

:Some. The fault was not in my powers. The circumstances were merely more complicated than I'd anticipated, and I... I did allow my fear to distract me.:

"A dangerous stumble," but Nahessa's tone held no rebuke. "You did not, however, allow it to defeat you."

A weak smile sprouted. Anzund only half-believed that.

:Still, there is another thing that does alarm me.: Nahessa placed the damp cloth back into the herbal water, and with a silent gesture bade the hovering Learners to remove the basin and medicines. Anzund lay still as tender fingers probed the faint bruise above one eye. With a satisfied "tsk" the Shaman left off with her study.

:You mean, how did the Choir invade the Dreamings without your knowledge. Don't you?:

"Yie." Now that the Learners had gone, Nahessa fell back into speaking. "Given my lifetimes of experience and your prior flight from Nyor, I should have anticipated their actions. I know they are patient. I know of their vigilance against attack... their vengeance. You are not a prize they'll willingly forget, even after all of this time."

:But since they don't believe in the Dreamings, Nahessa, why would you have cause to expect I'd meet them on Dreamquest?:

"They do, however, believe in 'a place of otherness' and

on occasion, that leads them into the Dreamings — just was it so, when they hunted you from Nyor."

:Yet they can not touch the Dreamings without disturbing the Winds, Nahessa. Surely that means the Choir hadn't been in the caverns long?:

"Or is that the concern?" Nahessa lips curled at the sour taste of those words. "Is it that they've grown so powerful that they can hide from me even with the Winds' crying to me?"

Anzund frowned, cold creeping into her at such a thought. That the Shaman was human enough to doubt her abilities at times was not the devastating concept to Anzund that it would have seemed to others, but the implications—? No, the Winds would not have let Nahessa's powers wane before there was another strong enough to take her place. It was not their way, and no matter what enchantment the Choir wielded, they'd never silence the Winds without so much as a breeze of warning. Her ashen gaze fixed upon Nahessa with a compelling strength, and her hand sought the elder's boney grasp. Their fingers folded together, and Anzund understood that Nahessa sometimes needed others to accomplish the Winds' bidding too, which meant Nahessa had not neglected anything; she had not been meant to forewarn Anzund, because Anzund was already following the Winds' path.

Then suddenly their gazes both dropped to their clasps. Right hand to right hand they held, wrists bound by the providers' bracelets of leather and single tigereyes — magic to magic. Slowly a warmth rose, creating hazy waves of heat. A burnished sparkle, akin to the Dreaming's trail that Anzund had followed spun out from those tigereye stones and entwined about their hands. Then a sweet, cool breeze kissed their skin; glitter and heat vanished in an instant.

Shakily, Anzund pulled free. Still staring at what had been, frightened by the powers the Winds had given her in their confirmation of her suspicions.

"Speak, Daughter."

Her startled gaze flew to Nahessa's, and her mindvoice was hushed in silvery frosts, :Perhaps you were not meant to see the Choir? What if instead, I was meant to fail tonight?:

Nahessa's golden eyes narrowed. She nodded almost imperceptibly for her apprentice to continue.

:What if the Winds are using the Choir's duplicity to our benefit?:

:Yie!: Nahessa rejoined with her own mind speech. :A balance of the longer needs against the briefer moment!:

:By not allowing me to succeed, we learned of the Choir's persistent interest in me and—:

"Their fear of you."

:And we both experienced something of their powers. We understand that they have grown stronger... are growing stronger yet.:

"Yie, barely could they ever catch any Chatu before in the Dreamings. Yet now, they not only lured you into their snare but snatched you back for the barest of moments after you had returned here."

:So now we are forewarned. They grow in strength and audacity. And...: her words stumbled into a splay of hesitant scarlet and rose. Nahessa squeezed her hand encouragingly, and Anzund gathered her fears together. :I was prepared tonight, Nahessa. But I did fail. The path will be guarded more closely now, since they know I must attempt the route again. It means I need to go with another.:

"You have need of a protector," Nahessa conceded. "Indeed, you have need of Tamtcha."

:Again.:

"You remember something from your initial meeting, I gather."

Awkwardly Anzund nodded. :You never asked about it. Do you — but you must know, I could not defeat the Choir's weazlbear alone."

"So now you worry that you're somehow dependent on her to amend the strength of your own lightsongs?"

Anzund's sheer silence was telling.

"You equate dependence with weakness, Daughter. There are many kinds of dependent relationships... some are to be avoided. Others court the Winds' own balance. No one of us will ever truly stand alone and prosper. Against the Choir, this is doubly certain."

:And if I should hesitate again and if she were hurt because of me? Nahessa, I could not bear that.:

:Nor could she, if you were injured because she was not

there. Anzund, it is time to remember your vows to both her and yourself. She is your First Protector. And she is our Kownbearer. She is not some fanciful child. Let her use her skills, Daughter, so that you may use yours to provide her — all of us — with the Winds' own blessings.:

Her heart felt only dread at that need. The risks were so great.

Nahessa rose from the bed, brooking no further arguments. "I'll send her to you."

:Nahessa? Please—?: The old woman paused at the plea. :Does it have to be her? Couldn't it be someone else? The Weaponsmaster perhaps? Or Zharin? Have I no choice?:

"And what would it do to your Tamtcha—?" Stoney faced, the Shaman left her.

:It would destroy her....: She closed her eyes to the world. The pain of exhaustion and unshed tears multiplied the despair, and her heart squeezed tight beneath her breast. It seemed too much for one night. Then memories of those slashing slivers of white light invaded, overwhelming the last of her sanity. Her body recoiled and shaking her head, she rolled into the pillows to bury her voiceless gasp of her sob.

"Shh-shh, everything's all right now. I've got you."

A careful touch gently pried her fists open, sure fingers curling over the backs of her hands and between her own fingers too interlock their clasps. Then her arms were tenderly spread to ease their cramping, and the warm, whole length of her lover laid down atop her to cover her protectively. The overstuffed shape of mattress and quilts took more of Tamtcha's weight than Anzund did, and suddenly, for the first time in this eternity of a night, Anzund felt safe — hidden and safe.

"That's it," Tamtcha soothed, lips brushing a kiss across Anzund's temple and through her hair. "That's it, my Love. You're home... with me."

Tension began to lift slowly. Their fingers uncurled, and gradually Tamtcha drew away to sit as her hands moved to stroke this blonde hair from Anzund's damp cheek. Then those pike calloused hands moved again with a greater gentleness, kneading the tight muscles of shoulder and neck.

"My hands — only my hands," Tamtcha murmured, not

deceived into thinking such anguish vanished totally with touch. "the Dreaming done for now... you're with me. Be here with me."

A long shivering sigh took her, but afterwards Anzund found she had indeed returned to their home. Tentatively she flexed her fingers, drew a deeper breath, and then relaxed as she discovered she could trust herself not to slip away into that ice-white cavern again. Tamtcha's hands stilled, spanning the bare skin of Anzund's waist and it was a steadying kind of hold on her... as if her beloved was prepared to catch her if she fell.

She gave a last sniffle, wiping her face dry in the pillow's linen, and turned onto her back to face Tamtcha. Those steady hands let her move but never left her waist. She managed a watery smile, feeling somewhat awkward. Yet glancing down she realized how little of her there was beneath Tamtcha's wide-handed span. She covered Tamtcha's hands with her own quickly, desperate in needing to be held onto.

:I feel very, very small.: Her lightsong barely sparkled at all in that fearful admission, the words were so soft.

Tamtcha smiled in a tender reassurance. "Frightened."

:Panicked,: Anzund corrected, but her mindvoice was a bit stronger. :I was careless first. Didn't... didn't see until it was too late. And then I... just... panicked.:

"That can seem worse than the danger threatening — to feel so lost, without control."

Grateful... amazed!... at Tamtcha's calm perceptiveness, Anzund finally found courage enough to meet her lover's gaze. She saw no rebuke there. :Thank you.:

"For?"

:Understanding.: Anzund tugged on Tamtcha's wrists. Her protector let of of her long enough to shed the robe and slide in beneath the covers.

:Nahessa said...." Anzund struggled for more words; only light bursts would come.

Tamtcha smoothed the blonde hair back from Anzund's forehead, waiting with patience, but it was still all too much. Pain skirted across Anzund's expression, and in a needless yet somehow comforting gesture, Tamtcha placed two fingers against those trembling lips to urge the lightsongs silent. "There's been enough tonight. Tomorrow or after... whenever you're ready, not before... you can tell me."

She found her words then in a desperate ribbon of silvery pink. :Hold me!:

Her protector wrapped her near in warm softness and steady strength. Anzund burrowed in close against her neck as the tremors began again. :I feel so fragile.:

"You're not," Tamtcha murmured, tightening her hold. Cautiously, almost timidly, Anzund cupped a small breast in her palm. Tamtcha edged back enough to give her room. "Go on—"

The nipple was soft and cool to Anzund's lips. Hesitantly she took it, gentle with her tongue. It puckered sweetly in her mouth as it responded to her need. Her hand closed over Tamtcha's ribs where those slender, weazlbear-clawed scars were; Tamtcha's strong arms surrounded her again, and with the tangible reminders of her protector's power, Anzund clung tighter, suckling harder.

"Beloved—"

Then harder still... half expecting protests for too much, yet needing more, she grew almost frantic. But the hand stroking her hair never restrained her. The reassurance was unfaltering. The knots inside her began to unwind. Exhaustion slowed her eventually, almost sending her drifting towards sleep, until the tiny core of panic rekindled at the vague thought of the nightmares that might come.

Anzund strained closer with a sudden fierceness, and this time it was different. Tamtcha stifled a low groan and fought against the desire to arch into that fiery taking. Startled, Anzund realized the self-control her lover had been exerting all along. Her need changed then, from one of taking to giving. She needed proof that she was not so very insignificant after all.

She shifted her weight into Tamtcha, who willingly laid back to let her mouth move to that other breast. And this time it was different — as Anzund teased with teeth and tongue and lip, Tamtcha's hands curled into fists full of pillow.

Anzund smiled a thrilled, little triumphant smile as that last remnant of panic vanished to be replaced with confidence... insecurity banished beneath the evidence of Tamtcha's joy. She slipped her hand down into that treasured nest of dark curls, finding them damp and lush with her lover's wanting.

Tamtcha arched, then pressed Anzund's hand against her urgently — unable to wait or go slowly. Fingers slipped into folds and satin wetness. With the skill born of all their past loving, she answered her lover's demand. Surrounding — entrapping that swollen bud within her fingers, she recaptured another dusty rosebud by mouth. Rhythm of hand and tongue matched.

Tamtcha's breath strangled in her throat as she half-lifted in an arch and then froze. For an endless moment she hung, suspended by the pleasure and desire and unexpectedness of it all. Then she was shattering into a million glittering pieces like Anzund's lightsong... no, she was Anzund's lightsong!

She gasped out, "Please!" and Anzund went still, covering that wetted nest with her palm and laying a flushed cheek against Tamtcha's breast. Tamtcha collapsed back and arms reached desperately around Anzund.

:I'm still here, Love.: She heeded that movement of vulnerability by hugging her protector close.

"Now... now I am the one so fragile."

Anzund looked down at her with solemn, pale eyes, lips tender in their growing smile. :Fragile, wonderful — cherished, my dearest Heart. Always, always cherished.:

The kiss they shared was exquisite, ever so very sweet.

>>> <<<

Anzund glanced behind at where her protector sat, and amused, she had to smile. :You look as entranced as a ra'ta'tat on in a fluttering field of poppyrose, my Love.:

Blankness blinked back from those golden eyes, and Anzund laughed fondly. She caught Tamtcha's face in a gentle grasp and made her look down towards her. :What amazes you so?!:

Tamtcha took Anzund's hand and lips turned inwards. A whisper of a kiss brushed against that pale wrist, then she nibbled lower over the knots of her provider's band, featherlight touches reaching past the leather to tantalize skin into desire. Anzund gasped with a bolt of sapphire, snatching away. Eyes seductive and bright lifted to hers. Commandingly and yet wholly silent, her lover entrapped her... daring her to deny those bonds that bound, and hearts pounded as breaths caught.

Until suddenly Anzund found the humor. She laughed, a broken sparkle or two at first, then a splay of soft hues laced with shimmering silvers.

Her lover's mouth twitched with a forbidden smile.

:You witch!: Anzund muttered and turned back to her work. The warm richness of Tamtcha's chuckle followed her. There were not many who would call this Kownbearer a witch. Then, there were not many Tamtcha would have trusted to tease.

"I do love you."

The hushed words wrapped about her like a soft, worn robe. She nodded and continued unpacking the incense and crushed leaves. It was still special to be told.

Her Kownbearer stretched out beside her with something of a flop, a deep sigh telling of deeper contentment. Tamtcha rolled to her stomach and propped herself up on her elbows to watch the arranging of things.

:Don't touch.:

Tamtcha nodded. Her fingers curled, interlocking obediently on the pillow before her. "What does all this do?"

:Nothing very mystical,: Anzund returned. She grinned crookedly at Tamtcha's surprise and gave a shrug. :Mostly the incense and tea is to make the passage easier for Halin. And the candle flames will help me focus.:

"And the others? You asked K'ntro to bring both Sappen and Zharin."

:We are a family,: Anzund returned quietly. The reminders of Spring rose again. :And for this child of all we may have, there is the least certainty of who will be present to raise her. I thought each of us should be part of her beginnings... the bonding with the others may be helpful, if you and I are not here later.:

For once, Tamtcha did not rise to the somber threat of Tomorrow. Her thoughts had drifted along their own course, and her voice was musing as she asked, "Will she be a lightsinger, you think? With your fine bones and gold hair...?"

Anzund smiled and shook her head, bemused. She had

never seen Tamtcha quite so charmingly distracted. :We shall have to have children every year, if this is the effect they're to have on you.:

"No, what?" Tamtcha quickly came back to her. "But do you know? Can you... I mean, if she will be a singer?"

:She will not be.:

"You can be so certain?"

:You forget, Love... lightsingers are Choir Pawns — slaves. They have been isolated and inbred for dozens of generations in order to produce their talents... and passivity. Their traits are recessive. They will not mix with others and dominate.:

"But your talents have."

:Only some... I have limitations to my mindvoice, remember? And I hear well enough. Nor as slender as I am, am I quite as fine boned as my mother must have been. No, our daughter will not sing. This child will be even less affected than I am, because she will be another generation away from the Choir's folk.:

"Yet you know she will be a daughter?"

Anzund looked at her sideways. :For a breeder of ponies, you are being amazingly dim-witted, Beloved. Or have you neglected to mention some strange force in your genes that can produce a male child without a male parent?:

Completely unperturbed by the fact that her common sense seemed to be deteriorating, Tamtcha shrugged and then pointed. "Your tea water's boiling."

:Oh dear!: Anzund pulled it quickly from the brazier.

"So... what do I do?" Tamtcha watched attentively as Anzund strained the water through the crushed leaves into an odd assortment of cups.

:Can you trust me?:

"Without limits."

:Then that's all you need do.:

"Trust you?"

:Yie, and let me sing to you.:

The answer brought a faint nod of satisfaction, and from the corner of her eye, Anzund noticed that she did indeed have her protector's trust. There was no awkward tension nor furrowing frown to suggest loyalties within that proud heart.

She remembered the Dreamings that had demanded so much from this woman, before that quiet confidence could be extended. Her hand went over, covering Tamtcha's two where they lay.

Surprise reflected in the questioning gaze that rose to hers.

:I hope I never do anything to earn your doubt.:

Tamtcha smiled with a softness that suddenly made her look young and innocent.

"Impossible."

The Winds stroked her cheek with a lover's touch and yet not a strand of Tamtcha's loosely -braided hair stirred. Beneath the amber and roasted golds of her quilted tunic, her breasts ripened and grew sensitive. The magics whirled around her, brushing the nerves of her skin into a tingle. Her body hummed... sated and full in such mystical tenderness.

A glimmering, heatless fire of colors danced around her. Suspended somewhere within the Dreamings, she stood amidst a head- high circle of lights. Further out that ring mixed and blended with other hues, but here around her place they were made of sheer lavenders, inky violets and indigoes that gleamed with the translucence of mother-of-pearl. Then within this wondrous haven, Anzund joined her... a rosy cloak of power enclosing her.

Tamtcha smiled and found an answering one upon Anzund's lips. Eyes of grey, staring at her through that pink mist, claimed her and bound her to utter stillness. Anzund stepped closer. Doubt never murmured; Tamtcha felt only the richness of their love grow tangible.

The indigos shimmered and flamed, eclipsing their bodies and sight as Anzund came near enough for touch. It felt then as if a breeze swept through Tamtcha, from front to back, leaving her fresh and alive inside as it ended. The ring of light retreated a few paces.

She turned about to find her beloved standing motionless, cradling a golden glow of life within each hand. Sparkles of stardust swam within the two auras. Fragments of lightening crackled and reached out, trying to span that little space between Anzund's hands — trying to join the two into one.

Anzund walked away from her, slipping through the sheer curtains of flickering indigoes as if a ghost were walking through lodge walls. Beyond her place, Tamtcha looked to see Halin seated among the faint outlines of half-present windsouls. Her family of Weazlbear, Tamtcha remembered then; everyone had assembled for this blessing.

She watched as a liquid gold of auras began to appear. It came first as spindly thread, then thickened to flow like glittering lava. And the Winds wrapped their new curtain around Halin and Anzund.

Suddenly, Tamtcha found herself blinking at the dimness, and they were all back again in the small room of Weazlbear Claw. Sappen, K'ntro and Zharin appeared faintly bemused. They were sitting behind Halin who was shading her eyes as if she'd been nearly blinded. Anzund knelt before her, watching in gentle concern. Halin smiled shakily and murmured something that made Anzund nod, tenderly touching the side of Halin's cheek with reassurance.

Then Anzund looked back to Tamtcha, and the protector's breath stilled at her beauty. Those grey eyes were glittering like gems, bits of rose and gold and indigo alive in them.

Anzund smiled at her. :It is done.:

A glow of vibrant joy leapt through Tamtcha, and tears brought sparkles to her own golden eyes. She found her voice gone, and Anzund nodded slowly, sharing that same wonderful feeling.

And in that moment, despite the Choir and the Chaoses, Tamtcha thought she finally understood: No matter what Tomorrow might bring, they had won... somehow, in the hope of this child, they had all won.

>>> <<<

:Why is it that no matter how frightened I am, when I curl up in your arms—after a while I'm really not afraid anymore?: The stillness in that strong body told Anzund to continue; Tamtcha was listening closely. And in some way, she realized this was part of her answer. :Is it because you listen to me so well?

Wrapped close in your grasp, I can be safe for a time and yet know you don't dismiss my misgivings out-of-hand?:

"Do you mean it's an opportunity to step back and reconsider things?"

:Maybe," but the word came with reluctance. :That isn't all of it,"

"No, not all of it, although you give me at least that much yourself."

Startled Anzund turned over to face her lover.

"Did you think I hadn't noticed?" Those burnished gold eye crinkled at their corners with the smile. "All those evenings that you'd chase me from the Village ledgers and trade maps? All those times you've cornered me in dim lodge corners and begged to be off to bed and loving? Could I help but notice how your demands so deftly maneuver me away from my fretting frustrations?"

A rueful grin answered her. :So much for subtlety."

"Once or twice maybe, but three years of it?"

Mischief sparked in Anzund's pale lightsongs. :I haven't heard any complaints from you... until not."

"You've still heard none," she growled, hugging Anzund close and setting her chin into the warmth of the blond-gold hair.

A very contented sigh replaced all hint of teasing. Anzund nestled nearer, enjoying the smooth-soft strength of her woman's arms about her. :I never forget what has been troubling me, but even so... you're right. The frustration seems to lessen.:

"Uhm-hm. It's always easier to deal with difficulties knowing someone believes in you."

Anzund pushed away a little and looked up. In concern she touched Tamtcha's cheek, and her mindvoice reached out with ribbons of rich blue, worried protests, :All of us believe in you, Beloved. All of us—not just those of Weazlbear Claw, but everyone... the village and Shaman too."

An off-handed sort of shrug replied.

:We do!"

"Differently, most see me as the kownbearer foremost – as a courageous, indomitable protector of Winds and Life."

:At times ..." Anzund observed somberly,:... you are."

"But not always."

:No one is one-thing always."

"As says the shamana's wisdoms?"

:As says your Honored Provider!:

Tamtcha smiled again, a knowing calm aura about her, and Anzund found her own ire dissipating. She chuckled at that suddenly and allowed Tamtcha to wrap her close again. :I see what you mean after all. It is easier knowing someone knows you—:

"And believes in you for best or worst."

:So tomorrow?:

"So tomorrow we will go Dreaming, and together we will meet the Choir."

Chapter Eighteen

Anzund paused in her undressing to listen. A shoulder bare, the heavy quilted shirt hung nearly forgotten as her hands clenched the maroon fabric in her tenseness. There were muffled voices above the clack and clatter of dishes. Halin and Sappen were putting out the breakfast settings for morning. A burst of laughter choked off abruptly; that was K'ntro's triumph over the southerners at some board game, most likely. The faintest skritch of pen and parchment came through the bedroom wall adjacent her, and she knew Tamtcha was still at work. But beyond the sounds of her lodge, Anzund heard... no, felt!... something more coming.

A cold tremor rippled in her stomach. Suddenly she was shrugging back into her shirt and her feet were moving. Sappen and Halin looked about startled as she swept out of her rooms. Her hand pushed both chimes and curtains aside, but Tamtcha was already rising.

:You feel it too?:

"Something, I don't know what," Tamtcha mumbled, barefooted and sleeveless as she hurriedly followed Anzund to the lodge's entrance.

Outside spring had barely arrived. Mud splattered snow and half-frozen puddles vied with patches of new grass. Twilight had descended to caste cast a dreary grey veil across everything, and the dampness had kept the potted candles along the paths from being lit.

Tamtcha shivered from the chill, listening to the utter silence that had fallen. Anzund took a step or two further away from the lodge as the rest of their family joined them. Yet the eerie quiet hovered, swallowing even the rustle of garments.

Anzund turned slowly, watching... waiting. The village below was empty, not another soul was to be seen. Her breath was white from the cold. Her eyes blurred from the icy sting of the air, but there was no wind... no sound from forest nor folk. In the corner of her eye, Anzund saw the Shaman and her learners appear before their lodge. Then she was looking above at that dismally grey sky.

A crack broke, hurting the ears and shaking the ground. Overhead a jagged black bolt of lightening streaked across whitened skies. Then suddenly a screech and then a grinding, soul shrieking whine split the air, and the sky shattered again in the black streaks as the earth continued to rock beneath their feet. Like ink spilled and bleeding across a table, the liquid blackness leaked out from the ragged, ebony lightening, until everything across the sky became mirrored, polished onyx.

The heavens flickered, twilight grey then black then grey again as Today rebelled at the invasion.

Abruptly, the jet black sheet was gone. The wailing ceased. The ground steadied — and Anzund heard the Winds return with a mournful howl of their own.

She rounded, a slender figure cloaked with grim strength, and Tamtcha came forward, ready for her commands. :Fetch your weapons, the holy ones from your Dreamings.:

The Kownbearer ducked inside.

:Halin — bring my lightwand. And the Lodge Coat.:

The protectors straightened as her pale gaze fell to them. :Zharin, take K'ntro. Find both Kahl and Baij. Tell them, the Choir has sung. Tell them not to wait for Tamtcha before making decisions.:

Zharin nodded and pulled K'ntro along, explaining as she hurried them towards the village. Below people had begun to pour from their lodges, and the evening clamored with rising panic.

:Sappen...,: Halin returned with both lightwand and

coat. :You and Halin represent Weazlbear Claw now. Take the Coat, with Maglind call the Village Circle together and tell them this is the Choir's doing. Urge them to send the protectors to the burrows. How much the Choir controls... where they are singing — we have no answers, but we can not wait within the village's hills any longer.:

"They will ask for war votes then."

:Turn to Nahessa. Let Weazlbear Claw support the Shaman.:

"Yie!"

:And Sappen — remind them of the child Halin carries... of the hope we've all seen.:

His hand closed over hers briefly, silently. Halin came forward, handing her the lightwand and hugged her quickly, and then they were gone. Anzund felt her throat close painfully as she shut her eyes. For a moment, she wondered if she would ever get to see that child.

She blinked the unshed tears aside and found Tamtcha standing there mutely, that golden gaze missing nothing. Anzund tilted her chin upwards, challenging the Choir's powers as she remembered that weazlbears had fallen before them.

"I sent the southerners to ready the practice lodge for meeting and to gather the protectors. I told them the kownbearers would come as soon as they had finished with the Village Circle."

:Yie, they will not have long to wait.:

"And you? Do you seek the Shaman or take another path?"

:I go Dreaming, Kownbearer. And it may be that the Shamyn's Apprentice will have need of a protector.:

"Then you have need of me." The rose quartz beads of her pike grip rattled as Tamtcha tossed the weapon lightly, her hand slipping through the wrist thong and closing about the grip again. She had finished dressing, and the dark violet of her tunic rippled with its silky sheen as muscles moved, despite the thin quilted padding; the motion made the black embroidered leaves dance as if tossed by the Winds. In its bootsheath, the rose quartz of her knife handle glittered almost indigo, reflecting the violet of her trousers.

She looked as deadly as the warrior-protector she was,

Anzund thought. Her own gaze fell to the short wand in her hands. Its maroon and honey lacquer matched her own silks' colors. She wondered if they had truly known so little this morning when they'd dressed. She murmured a word or two of rose then blue, and the lightwand she held shifted, stretching. The spell finished and soberly, Anzund hefted the long, slender pole with its embedded crystal head. The balance felt even, readied... like the power within her.

The staff planted firmly in the ground. A gaze cold with purpose lifted to Tamtcha. The protector nodded once. Together they turned and set off towards the Shaman's Lodge.

The tip of Anzund's lightstaff dipped, parting the air before them. Within a dozen steps, Tamtcha found the blueness of the Dreamings had swallowed them. It was disconcerting. There was not even an ashen fire pit to mark the quest's beginning, only the vastness of an empty sky to march through.

"Where are we going?" If there was a guiding breeze, it was too faint for Tamtcha to feel.

:First to the Barrier, to see what await us.: Even as she said this, Anzund pointed ahead and the fiery auras of the Barrier Winds became visible. Behind her Tamtcha visibly stiffened, but her protector's step did not falter.

"Is this the division of Tomorrow or of Yesterday?"

Anzund glanced at her, slightly surprised. :Either and both. Has Nahessa never brought you here, Love?:

Somehow the endearment softened Tamtcha stoic reserve. Awkwardly she shook her head.

:The Barrier Winds separate us from the Plains of Yesterday and Tomorrow,: Anzund reminded her, pausing in their journey to point to their right. :There in the distance, you can see the other side of Today.:

Tamtcha squinted, making out a fine line that shimmered. She turned back to the Barrier on her left and saw the small wall of fire had grown into a rising cliff. The heat was scorching against her face. "This is the edge of the Today?"

:Yie.: Anzund led them forward again. She seemed impervious to the heat as she walked within an arm's length of the roaring inferno. :That surprises you. Why?:

"I'd thought — aren't the Dreamings the crossing to the other Plains?"

:In part, images... windspirits... dreams pass from one Plain to another and are caught on the edges here. But they usually can not travel much further unless called by some power... and it takes a great deal of power. Here, it is easier to show you.: Anzund took her hand and led them into the flaming golds and oranges. A coolness enveloped them, and Tamtcha saw the arch they walked through was commanded by the staff Anzund wielded. But though the heat was held at bay, the mighty gusts of winds swirled and tugged at them in caution. Still further on Anzund led them, and the golds grew to emerald and then into a rich blue until finally a gale force of indigo swept by. The lightwand lifted high and a stillness abruptly descended. They walked into a pale blueness of infinity, a writhing line of rose below their feet. Gentler winds blew now, tugging at them from every angle.... pulling at hair and clothing alike. But the whip-like force was completely lacking in this place of peace.

:There beneath you... that pale line is the intersection of the Barriers you saw in Today.:

"How can that be? The Plains are infinitely wide."

:No, the Plain of Today is finitely defined between Yesterday and Tomorrow. It shifts constantly as we move from one moment to the next, but it is the eye of the storm, the calmness of the present... the simple being of what is. It's the only time when all paths intersect and a concrete existence emerges.:

"But our past...isn't the Plain of Yesterday the reckoning of all that has ever been?"

:All that has ever been, all that was ever intended... windsouls freed from the physical to reshape the understanding of what was and of what could yet be again. Yesterday churns and rushes into Tomorrow with all the woes and guilts and unmet challenges of Today's misdeeds and triumphs.:

"I do not understand, Beloved."

:Think of Yesterday and Tomorrow as a whirlwind of being and desires. Ideas... dreams dance and court one another in a careless a manner. Yet in the center is their creation, our Today. The tighter the circle, the more force — the greater the power generated. Only the most powerful of desires can be spun into light... and finally be flung into the center to materialize in Today, for that split second of concrete reality. From the infinity of possibilities into that... : Anzund waved her lightwand at that thin rose line and suddenly it roared up before them into another wall of fire, this one dancing with flames of red and oranges. :Into the finite to create "us.":

"Created because we — as windsouls — once dared to dream and dream with such passion that we found the power to cross the Barriers into existence."

Anzund nodded, proud of her love's reverent comprehension. She raised her staff and passed it between them. Suddenly they were below again, standing beside the furnace of gold and orange flames.

"Why does it create the fire?" Tamtcha asked as they continued their march.

:It's not fire, not as you know fire.: Anzund trailed her lightwand along the Barrier as a child would a stick along a sapling wall. Rich blues and magentas rippled and vanished at the skimming touch, but the staff did not burst into flames. : The sensation is hot. But the heat comes from the friction of the rushing winds. Interrupt that rush and for the briefest of instants, you tap the power... like a paddle wheel's shelf catching the diverted water then has the power to turn a millstone.:"

"So it's not flame, but the Winds themselves."

:Yie,: and Anzund's mindtouch was shushed with turquoise and dusky grey-blue lights of her own. :In all their power and splendor.:

She paused abruptly, and in concern Tamtcha drew closer, turning to follow Anzund's gaze across the Plain to the far Barrier. It was closer than she remembered, and she realized that Anzund had not brought them back through those flaming Winds to the same place they had left. Then she saw what had caught the attention of the Shamyn's Apprentice; a blackness was carved into the flaming tongues of wind. A hollow, inky hole that even now was shrinking as they watched... the winds stretching to cover the emptiness and repair the Barrier.

"That is the Choir's doing," Tamtcha muttered, feeling a coldness settle within her at the desecration of the splendor —

at the monstrosity of carelessness that would free whatever half-formed dreams or desires might be beyond that edge. She did not need Anzund to tell her of the perils of such half-conscious figures being loosened upon Today; the White Chaoses had been both the destruction and beginning of the Shamyn's memories and had been made of just such madness.

Anzund turned, facing something unseen. :They marred the Barrier of Yesterday as we know it... the Winds send us there.:

Tamtcha watched Anzund start off, but she could not feel what called them. Her face settled with the cold grimness of a warrior, and she went to follow.

Tamtcha shivered at the dampness that penetrated the quilted batting of her tunic, and one-handedly she fumbled with the buttons on her shoulder. It had grown much chillier since the mists had closed about them again. Her hunting instincts didn't like the utter silence that hung about them either. She was accustomed to a walk through odd noises and baiting distractions, but silence was all she heard this time... her eyes fell to the slender, determined figure that marched before her. Irony twisted the protector's lips into a half-smile; Anzund... for all of her petite build... now barely resembled the child-like, battered figure Tamtcha had found amidst the range grasses. Tamtcha felt her heart soften with pride and a bit of wonder as she again realized this Shamyn's Apprentice had chosen her as a beloved protector. The thought eased the cynicism from her lips, and even the deepening chill of the dreamquest fear couldn't quite reach through to her soul.

Anzund glanced up slightly as Tamtcha's long legs brought her forward and they walked two abreast. She reached out and caught Tamtcha's hand, lifting it for a brief kiss before releasing her. Gold eyes reflected her smile, and Anzund shrugged slightly self-consciously. :I'm glad you're here with me. Thank you.:

Tamtcha grinned crookedly, then gestured ahead. "Can you feel the Winds we follow?"

:Yie.: Anzund's hand on her arm brought Tamtcha to a

halt. She had them wait a moment, then a breeze gathered itself and blew a bit stronger, beckoning them on. Tamtcha nodded, satisfied and they continued.

:I see the trail more than I feel it,: Anzund confessed.

"How so?"

She sighed, frowning faintly while searching for words. : A pale haze within the blueness of this fog? It's like a pony's kicked up of dust trudging through the glare of a hot afternoon.:

Still uneasy, Tamtcha shifted her shoulders beneath the satin indigo; her palm felt moist around the pike's grip. "The quietness is uncanny. I'd feel more assured even if I heard a battle fading in-and-out."

:We're moving too fast.: At Tamtcha's startled look, Anzund elaborated, :My doing.: She tipped the crystal head of her staff towards Tamtcha. The rose quartz glowed. A soft warmth as translucent as a sun's ray in the forest's depths washed down Anzund's hand to slip beneath their moving feet. The pooling hue of pink spread forward, anticipating their trail only by a step or two. Behind them it vanished as completely as if a cloud had swallowed a sunbeam.

"Have we so far to go then?"

:A ribbon of the Barrier Winds was torn out by the Choir's chant and bent into unnamable shapes. The trail we follow... the light-dust I see was thrown up by the passage of those we chase. The Winds' breeze that you feel when we slow is the — the desperateness of the Plains' Winds to right the madness before a greater damage is done.

:As to how far we go? I don't know. It depends on the mischief these Choir Pawns intend to reap, and on the others the Winds may summon to help. At the moment, I expect the poor monsters are to be pitied more than feared. They're probably as disoriented and confused as you would be if thrown into a dreamquest without knowing Dreaming even existed.:

Mutely Tamtcha digested that... but her assessment as a protector varied from Anzund's conclusion that these Choir Pawns should be pitied. In her experience, cornered and confused animals were generally the ones to be most feared; pity could become very expensive in those circumstances.

They marched for what could have been a full day or a scant handful of hours. Time ceased to have any true meaning. Fatigue was equally as useless a term. The liquid mist from Anzund's lightstaff rose from their ankles to swirl in slender tendrils about them both, and the tightening clench of overworked muscles eased even as the weary, hungry rumble within their stomachs receded.

:A gift from the Winds,: Anzund explained, after the first rose-spiraled dance. She had shrugged, unable to accept credit for the magical restoration. But Tamtcha noticed that after the first unexpected demonstration of power, it was Anzund who summoned the nourishing mist whenever either of them seemed to be slowing.

And then quite suddenly, the azure fog parted and they stopped. Before them, through a kind of whirling portal a barren, mud-bricked village lay. Dusty, rutted roads ran between dilapidated buildings, and black-crisped timbers hinted at the fires that had burned out the porches and slant-planked roofs. Window shutters hung half off their hinges, ashen remains of the catastrophe that had driven life and hope from this place.

Tamtcha sensed the rage that lingered here as she noted the white-washed outer walls which were streaked with ebony, clawed marks of soot. Unadorned mud bricks were gouged with similar shapes, brown singed rather than black in those deep grooves.

The wind blew. Grey ash and dust mingled, tossed into their faces as they hesitated at the edge of that damp fog. The air still smelt of wood smoke.

Anzund coughed, her concentration distracted for the barest of instants, and the village-world swept in and around them.

Tamtcha crouched, spinning to survey the road and forest behind them. But there was nothing. The pitted trader's road merely disappeared over a small rise into a leafless, winter woods. Nothing moved. Nothing made any sound above the hollow call of the Winds.

Slowly she straightened. The pike end went into the ground. Her lips pursed thoughtfully as she leaned on her weapon; these Choir's Pawns were not to be underestimated.

She looked at Anzund, approving of the narrowed eyed assessment the other was making. "What now?"

Anzund's mouth thinned, anger turning her knuckles white in her grasp of her staff. :They have been and left. But they are still relatively near... somewhere — there.:

Tamtcha looked along the line of pink sparkle that drifted forward as Anzund pointed. It followed the road that forked east of the village. A last, long glance into the sordid rubble of cinder and brick assured the protector that she was relieved not to have to trudge through that graveyard.

"Did it take lives?" she asked abruptly, setting off just as quickly.

:Not as you know them.: Anzund hurried to catch up with her.

"Windsouls then?"

:Yie.:

Tamtcha had grimly expected that truth. "Do you know yet what kind of creature we hunt?"

:I do.: Anzund offered nothing more for a good many strides, but Tamtcha did not press. Finally, a very weary sigh of lightbursts danced through Tamtcha's head. :Do you remember the legends of trollincraigs?:

The protector frowned, then shook her head. "Vaguely. They're ghosts of the Barrier Winds, aren't they? Some sort of lost souls or something."

For a brief moment, Anzund allowed amusement to color her mindvoice with a ripple of silver in blue. :Is there really a predator you know so little about?:

Tamtcha gave her a crooked grin. "Next you'll tell me they're in our Chatu lore, but unheard of in Nyor."

:You're right. Only the shamyn have accounts of them.: Those shamyn's tales rose in Anzund's mind and her teasing faltered. Somberly she amended, :They are older than the Learners' Scrolls. They live only in the Shamyn's Memories.:

Tamtcha sobered. "They come from the Old Worlds then — these trollincraigs? From before the Shaping of the Plains in the White Chaoses?"

:Yie... in the Times before Time. They were shaggy, non-human creatures of peace and solitude... towering, two-footed beasts of fiery orange hair. They favored the mountains and wooded heights away from men and women. But the Chaoses changed them — sought and found them even in their mountain refuge and engulfed them along with everything else. Shamyn say they grew enraged... fury-blind at the betrayal. After living so peaceably and always, always leaving to allow the savages of human-kind more space... even when it meant time and time again that they just left everything and moved on... to still be destroyed by the human-kind follies embittered them. They rose in anger and flung their very souls in outraged protest against the human-kind.

:Memories tell of that pain tainting the Winds as the Barriers rose. That embroiled passion swept into the Winds' divisions between the Plains and was caught... held. And those great ogres of the mountains were caught themselves — their souls banished to death in the Chaoses and yet their outcry of protest was left demanding vengeance. Their desires imprisoned them in the end, and they became half-souls neither living within Today nor seeking peace within Yesterday. Their impressions sank into the fiber in the Barrier Winds. Their ghosts, as it were, slipped into the dancing hollows and crags of the fiery cliffs of the Barrier itself. And there they roam now, sliding from one rippling chasm to another, raking and striking endlessly at the human-kind souls that pass across into life or into death... waiting for their own deaths which may come only when a human-kind passes in agony, taking their own half-soul on to the next Plain with them:

"On to Yesterday," Tamtcha amended.

:Always.:

They fell silent and walked on through the icy winds that swept across the rutted road. The scraggly, naked trees flanking the route seemed to shiver about them, and icicles occasionally broke from grey limbs as windy hands shook them. But there was no sign of snow. As frozen as the ground and forest were, the ice-sheathed tree limbs and glassy ground puddles were the sole sign of winter.

It was a cold that leeched the life heat from their bones as they went. The pale white of the sun overhead was in a faded, near colorless sky. That heatless disk was only a dismal reminder of warmth and hope.

With a disgusted, impatient frown, Anzund shook her

staff briefly and glared a reprimanding word or two at her quartz. A deep lavender-rose spark kindled within the crystal's depths, and then suddenly the spiraling fingers of a warming mist began its dance of renewal about them. But this time the color was darker... velvety rich... and its touch was almost tangible as it enfolded them both protectively.

The tension eased noticeably from Tamtcha's tall frame. Her questions returned. "Are these creatures windsouls or material beings? Or are they made of light and fire like the Barrier Winds seem to be?"

:Neither... a little of all three. They're half-souls, still part of Today and yet they have the power of the Barriers to wield. They are two-legged, two-handed — still orange-haired and shaggy, much like a weazlbear when they take physical shape... much like a dense shadow within a fire's flickering when they're within the Barriers. They are rare, very rare. I'm surprised the Choir's chant caught them. But they travel in pairs or small packs, so I suspect there's more than one ahead of us.:

If that information unnerved her, Tamtcha gave no sign of it. Anzund couldn't help but admire that bravery. Her own heart thudded painfully, and she prayed for the strength to match that calm herself. :If you think of weazlbears as evil incarnate...?: Tamtcha nodded, still listening closely, :Then think of the trollincraigs as rage embodied. They do not stalk. They're frenzied and — and frustrated and—:

"A desperate, dying savage whose been tormented beyond reason." Tamtcha shivered, imagining herself living in such an enraged limbo along the Barriers. "A kind of madness."

:Yie, but a strong, brutish madness. And a magical one. They tap the sheer power of the Winds', Tamtcha. They ice a tree with a glazing cold stare. They burn a building with the hot swipe of a long-nailed hand. They may not have the intellect of the weazlbear, but they haven't the sense to retreat either.:

"Do they have the sense to work in cohort? You said, they travel in small packs, how well do they communicate with each other?"

:Poorly... not at all. That will be our advantage.: Anzund smiled weakly. :We deserved a few, don't you think?:

A single brow lifted skeptically, "Name another."

:Your weapons. They are Wind Blessed. Plunge the spearhead of your pike into the heart of a trollincraig, and the Winds will sweep its half-soul into Yesterday's peace. And we do have my magics.: Her eyes turned mockingly back to the road. :The Shamyn's Apprentice is not the least of sorcerers, especially one who is a Lightsinger as well.:

Tamtcha's crooked smile rose, but her feet suddenly came to a stop and she turned.

:What is it?: Anzund halted.

"These trees," Tamtcha waved to the roadside. "Notice a difference?"

Anzund glanced around them quickly. The icy sheaths to the trunks and limbs had receded. Frost sparkled here and there, but the solid encased shells had gone. The road too was hard and frozen, but the patches of ice had disappeared. Anzund studied the rutted ground again, noting the scuff of crumbled edges at the gutted wheel holes.

Tamtcha moved forward cautiously, examining the frost and tracks with a scout's eye. "There are three of them."

:They're following their hunting tendencies, I think,: Anzund murmured as her protector's gaze shifted up from the ground and back to the trees. :For whatever reason, their unholy terrorizing has subsided to a duller fury.:

"So the trees aren't being blasted with raw ice whenever their gruesome gazes are falling to the wayside?"

:Or so I'd guess.:

"Hunting... seems to be a calmer sort of thing for them to do."

:The mere sight of us will undo that.:

"What about our scent?"

:I don't know,: Anzund admitted honestly. :They're not suppose to be capable of tracking — or ambushing, even if forewarned.:

"And when was the last time any of these trollincraigs were loosened to the Dreamings?"

Anzund's silence was confirmation enough of Tamtcha's worst suspicion. She drew a slow, deep breath and nodded grimly. The shadows were lengthening. "Can your staff hurry us again? I'd rather meet these things in the daylight."

>>> <<<

The bellow of rage rose from beyond the hillside, announcing the trollincraigs before they were seen. The two women paused in the relative safety behind the small rise as Tamtcha checked the quartz- handled knife in her bootsheath and the knots on her pike's grip. Her hand strayed to her ebony braid ties as Anzund stared at her staff's rose crystal, those grey eyes mere slits. An almost audible "pop" ignited a star burst within the crystal. Tamtcha shaded her eyes and blinked as tears stung, but she couldn't turn away. Pure power shimmered in a brilliance that hurt. The translucent hue of the rose quartz was almost burning white in its intensity. The crackling sparkles were nearly as colorless — and yet, there was a pale pink and a powder blue hue that alternately seemed to tease the senses, just at the corner of the eyes where the dancing slivers of light seemed to disappear.

:It will blind you, if you stare too long.:

Obediently Tamtcha's squeezed her eyes shut and laid her hand over the lids. The darkness soothed the ache that had begun in her distraction. She wiped the teariness from her cheeks, turning away deliberately before venturing to look at anything. The twilight coolness eased the last of the stinging, and she nodded, casting a grin sideways at her companion. "I can see where it could melt the ice of these trollincraig gazes."

Abruptly the greying twilight was broken by groaning shriek. The Winds and the barren wintry forest seemed to pick up the agony of the cry, and an echo reverberated in the emptiness around them. It faded only slowly as the third or fourth repetition died. Together they looked towards that small hill.

:Of the three, you must kill only one... through the heart,: Anzund reminded her protector. :The others will follow without your pike.:

"Through the heart, you say — like the weazlbear we took at the Falls?"

Anzund glanced at her in quiet surprise.

"I remember more than you might think, Love. Especially here on Quest."

That fact pleased her, gave her courage, and Anzund

took her staff in two hands. The brightness of the crystal steadied and drew in on itself a bit; the power was not dampened, merely better contained in preparation for the focus Anzund would soon guide it towards.

"I'll slip around into the woods and—"

:No! We must stay together...and in the open. I can't protect you from their magics, if I can't see you.:

With a short sigh, Tamtcha reassessed their position. Lips thinned and she nodded. "Makes it simple then."

Dangerously simple, Anzund thought, but she kept the words to herself. Tamtcha hesitated again as silver-blue tendrils of crystal's mist began to creep around her. Anzund shook the staff gently, and her crystal spilled forth more of the eerie shadows until they were both enshrouded.

:To hide us... briefly,: she explained, then they went on to greet their task.

The rise in the road before them had seemed higher than it was, but at the top it fell away steeply into a small valley of withered brown grass and a clearing in the trees. The grass was sheeted with ice crystals that glittered in the last faintness of the day. Below the road switched back and forth, descending the hill then breaking out to fork northwest and northeast into the bleak forest's fog.

The great bellowing cried out again, echoing in each of the three mammoth trollincraigs before fading in the Wind's own reply. Tamtcha felt her heart bulk balk for an instant, then resignation steadied her and she watched, gleaning anything that might lend her an advantage. But their sheer size was enough to daunt any warrior. As tall as a weazlbear standing upright, the shaggy orange -coated ogres had the bulk of mighty wrestlers. Yet they had the restrictions too, Tamtcha noted. Their torsos turned when they looked around, their bodies too muscle bound to allow quick glances over shoulders or straight extensions of arms over heads.

She watched as one tore a tree from the ground, the trunk as wide as the beast's own shoulders. It spun and hurled its club clumsily towards the northwest road. Tamtcha squinted, glimpsing a figure that stepped back quickly into the fog.

:There is another just beyond the fog's edge to the

northeast.: Anzund pointed to the shadow-like outline that blocked the other road. Tamtcha frowned; there was something familiar in that shape... Anzund nodded their attention back to the raging trollincraigs as a handful of fire was suddenly raked down the length of another tree trunk. It burst into flames even as the orange creature rammed the tree down with its shoulder. Another wailed as it bent forward; a hand laid to each of the ancient trees flanking him and roots creaked, the ground shaking even where the women stood as the roots tore and the trees began to topple.

:We must hurry. That fog marks the edges of this Plain's Dreamings. The shadows beyond... they're windsouls sent to stay these beasts from crossing the Barriers whole. In this shape, with the power of the Winds to turn against the Barriers themselves, they may just succeed. And that will end the world as we know it... the Choir Leaders are fools!:

Tamtcha grabbed Anzund's arm as she would have plunged down the hill. "Don't repeat their foolishness."

Anzund stayed. "From here you can see me anywhere in the clearing. Can you match their magics from this distance as well?"

Anzund's grey eyes swept over the small valley. :Yie:

"Then I go below. You remain here." A faint smile leant lent encouragement, "I may need you to catch me again."

Anzund forced a shaky, not-quite-a-grin something and gave a quick nod.

"Now — lift this misty cloak from me and see if we can't entice these trollincraigs back a bit from the Barriers' edge."

Tamtcha moved further along the hilltop, so that Anzund need not unveil herself too. The tigereyes of the kownband glinted with the gold determined fierceness of the protector's own gaze as she glanced back to Anzund. She nodded. Anzund clenched her staff, and the misting veil about Tamtcha evaporated.

A trollincraig turned and, amber eyes went red with rage — details seen so distinctly, so magic-bright even across the distances. Tamtcha felt the chill blow past her as a light, frosty breeze might blow. Her teeth bared in fierce triumph — a taunting grin. With a wordless, trilling call she raised the pike two-fisted to the sky.

The three giants rounded, then standing rigid, tipped their heads back and with orange manes flying they answered the war cry. But the protector was already moving, sliding... scrambling straight down the steep slopes and across the narrow road flats that traversed the hill's width. As they looked for her again on the hilltop, her feet hit the hard valley floor and the steel of her pike flashed forward as she came.

The one nearest, from the northwest fork, shrieked and heaved a boulder twice her size towards her. She spun, dodged and lunged, slashing at its black-leathered palm. Pain shrieked and she danced away from the valley's center and the other two beasts. Her target came after her.

A smaller stone, the size of a man's head, hit the creature's shoulder. It bellowed and clawed the air, but never did it turn on the beast that had underthrown. Tamtcha feigned with her pike and it snatched for the silver glint. The point circled above and back like a snake and bit into the furred forearm, then she was backing away again. And again it followed, roaring as it glared... and the brown grass underfoot went icy. She slipped to a knee, then laughing was rolling up and away again as the creature lunged full-length out onto the ground where she'd been.

Above, Anzund swore at the magic's slowness that had allowed Tamtcha's footing to ice under even though it had traveled the distance quickly enough to protect the woman herself from the deathly chill.

Her staff tipped and she glared with slate-grey eyes of power. Her left hand threw out the voiceless command and the silver-blue veil snaked up from the valley floor, hiding Tamtcha's private battle from the other two creatures. Even so, another tree was ripped from the ground but a golden bow pinged, and the tree fell rather than be hurdled to the valley floor as the arrow found its mark in the beast's arm. A knife whirled from the depths of the northeastern fog, and the other creature howled and was downed, its Achilles' tendon severed. Smoke and fire leapt high, savagely crossing the once-frosted grass to set the trees blazing.

Anzund shouted in silent anger, and the blaze turned back on itself as the downed trollincraig roared. Its orange coat went up in flames and it rolled, shrieking in panic and pain —

not thinking to smother the fire.

A pike of white ice flew at her and shattered nearly in her face as Anzund's staff spun up broadside to counter it. Gruesome half-laughter rang out at her from the standing trollincraig. She went down on her knee, still partly blinded by the ice dust, yet if the thing below thought she did anything but create a smaller target, it was disabused of the notion as her crystal staff batted a bolt of sheer blue light into its eyes.

It screamed and staggered, clutching its head as it too went to its knees. And Anzund looked frantically back to Tamtcha as another golden arrow plunged into the broad back of the kneeling beast.

The ground beneath Anzund shuddered as a piece of the hillside was gouged out and thrown at the dark-clad warrior. Anzund threw a lightburst of ruby and sapphire, and Tamtcha flung herself to the side. The earthen clod exploded still in mid-air, and dirt harmlessly spattered down as the protector came to her feet, charging under the clumsy bear hug and slashing the calf — leaving bone and blood showing as she moved out of reach. The creature charged her, pain-blinded and raging, and she swiped for its side equally as viciously as she bolted past and behind it. A fiery hand near caught her shoulder. The indigo silk and padding tore, flaming in an instant in the thing's clasp before it dropped as discarded ashes. She back away, shrugging her bared shoulder and conscious of the air's icy touch, but her golden eyes never left the magic-red gaze of her foe. Brown teeth of ivory, curved and long as fingers, bared with a roar as bloody-gummed and drooling it repeated its war shriek. Eyes closed as its head tipped back and its shaggy arms widened.

Tamtcha lunged. Her pike drove into its heart as its hands clenched about her upper arms and lifted. Rose quartz flashed and blinded her. Fire scorched through her. Her mouth opened to scream or protest but words strangled in her throat as ice and fire battled within her very flesh. Her hands twisted, blistering and yet somehow she clung to the pike and wrenched it forward.

Then suddenly she was dropping, the frozen ground slamming her hard as the air wrent with a shrill cry of death. The Winds howled and circled, whirling with gathering force that held the trollincraig's great form upright... stretching it tall, and its cry became the Winds' own.

A crack of thunder and brilliant light blinded Tamtcha completely. Instinct took over and she rolled — head huddled within her arms, she rolled away from the whirlwind of power.

The ground shook. Stones clattered down the hillside, and she blinked, forcing her eyes open to witness the blurred shadows of the battle that still raged.

Gone was the veiling silver-blue fog that had divided the valley. Gone was the forest and fog of the Barriers. In their place stood that raging inferno of light she had witnessed in the limbo-of-time-and-space place. It rose, fiery with heat and dancing with light from the grounds to the brilliant blue sky's infinity. It surrounded the valley, enclosing the whirlwind of death... enclosing the frozen, howling figures of the two injured beasts. It fenced the valley in with only the hillside behind them to see.

And upon that hill, Anzund stood outlined by the Winds' furor — by lights soaring for the heavens. Staff and fist raised in power, her head tipped back as Winds and light buffeted.

Tamtcha blinked and looked again. Fist and staff lowered and then commandingly struck upwards again. The light and wind formed a new wall behind the woman. Silver and gold separated and flamed, then separated again into prisms and rainbows of rushing color — a reflection of the vast Barriers before them all.

Howling screams pulled Tamtcha back to the trollincraigs. The two burst into orange flames, more deadly than the earlier fires. The whirlwind swept to the side to engulf the new pillars of fire. And at the moment — in the instant — when the forces of all three touched, a sunburst of amethyst ignited. And the half-souls vanished completely... all three.

Tamtcha was thrown back into the scarred hillside. She tucked tight as she was showered with debris from the valley's center as well as from above. The roar deafened her. The shaking loosened her bones... then she felt the world go stone still.

She waited, counting her breaths... nearly expecting the hill to fall and still bury her. But nothing more happened. A faint breeze pulled at her, almost curiously. The smell of green, wet grass teased her. And as she hazarded a look, she saw the sky was the most beautiful blue with a sun warming and high as if it were noon. She swallowed hard and found herself bruised but in one piece.

Cautiously she rolled forward to stretch out. The world spun a little sickeningly, so she paused, laying prone and up on her elbows. But it proved to be more her nerves than the earth in motion. She grinned at herself. After weazlbears and trollincraigs, it was a bit odd to be awed by a simple earth tremor, she thought.

Footsteps hurried and her stomach clenched as her head jerked up. Everything went spinning again, and she squeezed her eyes shut.

:Tamtcha.:

She tipped her head forward to rest on the sun-warmed earth, laughing at herself once more. She realized it was Anzund nearing.

:Tamtcha?:

The first thing she noticed was how amazingly calm that mindvoice seemed, and a peace stole into her with the mindtouch even as she thought that. The next thing she was aware of was the retreat of the throbbing bruises and aching muscles as Anzund's gentle hand touched her head... and then she opened her eyes to see the snowy streaks of sparkling white-lavender amidst the most beautiful, velvety rich indigo she'd ever seen.

Her eyes fluttered and opened again, but the marvelous crystal of raw amethyst remained. It took her a full moment to realized it was the size of two fists and set into a staff's wooden claws. But instead of being maroon-wooded and gold-veined as Anzund's staff had been, this one was a reflection of the stone itself... inky indigo with glittering, lavender-white veins.

She forced her head to tilt, glancing sideways to find Anzund on one knee and waiting patiently. Tamtcha's stare returned without comprehension to that small hand which held the staff even as it laid before her.

She swallowed hard and abruptly sat up, dreading what she was to find if the Shamyn's Apprentice had changed half as much as that staff. But before she could raise the question, the hand on her head slid to cup her cheek and lips of cool satin came to press against her own. Tamtcha felt the sigh gather within herself, and as she released it, she took her lover into her arms and returned the kiss with relief and gratitude.

:When you didn't speak, I began to think you were hurt.:

Tamtcha smiled wryly and met the beautiful, pale grey gaze before her. "Even a Kownbearer needs a moment or two to usher the wits together after such a clash."

Anzund smiled with a tenderness that banished the last of her protector's fears. :I love you.:

Tamtcha kissed her again, then softly vowed, "I will love you even beyond the Barrier Winds."

Anzund looked at her with a bit of amusement at so grand a claim, but she felt no need to debate it. :Can you stand, do you think?:

In response, Tamtcha rather unsteadily climbed to her feet with Anzund's help. But when she reached out to grasp the staff for more support her palm tingled uncomfortably, and she jerked away with surprise. "What's happened to that thing?!"

The grimness that settled about Anzund made Tamtcha regret her words. "It's all right. It just startled me. I'm used to carrying it for you once in a while... I expect that has changed?"

:Yie,: a strained smile appeared. :I'll have to do my own fetching for now on.:

"What happened?"

:It was the power of the trollincraigs... whenever one dies, their energy and the magic from the Barriers is freed. It is why you needed to kill only one — I could snatch that power at its death and turn it onto the others. By myself, I was not strong enough... even focused by my crystal. But after the first's death, I could force the other two half-souls to join their kin in Yesterday.:

Tamtcha studied the small valley about them, the green carpet of grass and the full-leaved trees in the forest. The two figures that had dimly been hidden in the Barriers' fog had emerged to sit by an empty fire ring beneath the cool, dark shadows at the forest's edge. She looked again to Anzund.

Those pale grey eyes had taken on that somber expression again. A vague, lavender sparkle teased the edges of Tamtcha's perceptions, and she was not surprised to find Anzund's clear gaze was not quite so pure an ashen grey now.

"What does the release of three trollincraigs' magics give to one called Shamyn's Apprentice, Love?"

:Has it changed me so much?:

In the plea Tamtcha heard the reflection of the fear she herself had felt just moments before. She chuckled suddenly and pulled Anzund into a strong hug. She planted a kiss in the warm, blonde hair and muttered, "I hope we live to be old enough to know how silly our insecurities are."

A sparkle of lavender and blue-silver laughter came with Anzund's gentled mindvoice. :I expect we won't, if we don't stop gallivanting around with the Winds' whims.:

"Yie," Tamtcha sighed regretfully, "duty."

Anzund answered with a sigh of her own.

"We've not quite finished here yet, have we?"

:No, we've allies to meet.:

"Allies?"

:They helped to stay the other trollincraigs from attacking you... and they helped the Barriers slow the beasts until we came.:

"Yie, allies. But why do I think you refer to future needs and not past?"

:Because...,: Anzund turned wearily, :you cleverly recognize truth for what it is.:

Tamtcha detoured to retrieve her pike from where it stood, driven upright into the ground. A brow lifted as she saw the dangling grip beads had lost their pale rose hues in exchange for the same rich amethyst which Anzund's lightwand had acquired. The gleaming tip of her three-edged pike point was equally as curious; the silver sheen seemed laced with indigo and lavender just as Anzund's own grey eyes were.

"I had forgotten," Tamtcha murmured, guiding Anzund on towards the fire ring and strangers.

:Forgotten what?:

"That I'd once made a choice between bow and pike for you."

"It was a well-made choice!" The hurried assurance sprang almost unbidden from the slender figure who was pushing herself up to her feet so rapidly. Tamtcha's cool glance swept over her, noting the tall lean frame and gold-blonde braid, but her eyes widened in denial and fear as she suddenly recognized the solidly built companion still seated beyond the stone ring.

Kahl's gaze grew compassionate and silently he stood. The kownband about his forehead glittered with now near translucent tigereyes. His lack of greeting only underlined his presence. The Youngest as Kownbearer trembled, stepping forward to raise the palm of her hand even as the tears formed in the corners of her eyes. The Once-Eldest held his hand before hers and as they pressed together, the light cool breeze of the Barriers brushed against their skins... separating them in that last ribbon of distances between life and death.

"Wh-when, Kahl?"

His arm dropped. The crimson and gold of his heavy tunic shrugged with the slow lift of shoulders. "Before the sky cracked with black thunder. Just before."

"There was more here for him to do," the younger stranger said softly. She faltered under Tamtcha's sharp glance.

"Gently," Kahl bid his once-foster daughter and added, "the spring has come, my friend... and she speaks truly. There was need of my eyes and courage in Yesterday. The tale I bring you is as important now as the Winds' Calling which brought the four of us here to the trollincraigs."

It was on the tip of Tamtcha's tongue to challenge his surprising recognition of such orange ogres, but reason chided her to silence and with an abruptly bitten off breath, Tamtcha's shoulders sagged. The passage into Yesterday would supply Kahl with a fund of history she could never hope to comprehend in her mortal Plain... and time to celebrate victories of any kind had not yet come. Her back stiffened; he nodded approvingly and directed her on the woman-stranger.

This time the oddness of those strong Chatu features mixed with that fair Nyor coloring registered, but in the same breath Anzund's utter stillness caught Tamtcha's attention too. Then eyes narrowing, Tamtcha suddenly... finally... saw the truth in those clear, clear grey eyes of youth.

"Anzund?" Her lover's hand reached out blindly to grasp her own. "Is this... our daughter?"

The proud tilt to that angular chin dropped; the child in the adult before them could not help her yearn for approval in her first meeting with her parents.

"Our daughter — our first of Weazlbear Claw...?" Tamtcha stepped nearer, topaz gold eyes assessing the strength of limb, the watchful intelligence... the beauty of her lover transformed into the heart of her people. "By the Winds' Blessings, what name do you use?"

With voice as bare a murmur as her mother's, the woman replied, "Mare's Gold."

"May'r...," Tamtcha repeated, reverently translating that precious title into the cherished ancient name of the first Chatu woman to tame a mountain's pony.

"Yie," Kahl granted somberly, "the golden hope of the Tomorrow's kin. Only this time, the bearer embodies the hopes and magics rather than gifts of simple, mortal skill."

"Bearer?" Tamtcha's glance darted between her once-foster father and her daughter-to-be.

"Yie," the grey eyes lifted, opening wide as gazes met and responsibilities rose. "I lead Tomorrow's windsouls. I was called... conceived by you to guard the Barriers and protect this edge of Today's Plain."

:You were conceived in love! And in desperate hope for love and future!: Anzund interjected, and the daughter-to-be turned to her for the first time. Fine lines of worry drew across her brow. :You were conceived in love, May'r. All else was... is secondary. You must know that!:

A tear of thanks gathered at the edge of the daughter's eye, and shakily she nodded.

Anzund turned a worried gaze to her beloved, repeating her assertion, and solemnly, Tamtcha raised their hands to show May'r their clasp. Her voice was gentle then in its low timbre, but no less forceful in its honesty, "This is our bond, my Daughter-to-be. This heartsong Anzund tells you of — this mortal love and the dreams that it yields... are dreams that became you. Do not doubt it, you are wanted. You're not merely a gilded token of the Winds' decree. If neither of us live to welcome you in Weazlbear, still know this is true... you come from the very heart of loving."

"A heart that extends to the people," May'r whispered, but there was pride and not regret in that knowledge.

"You are the best we could give to them." Tamtcha murmured. "They... are the best we could offer to you."

She nodded again, a wavering smile surfacing, and then as she swiped the tears away roughly, she raised her amber and gold encrusted wheelbow. Beads of tigereye spun in the knots of the pulley axels, and a golden plate on the shaft held the relief of a battle — a protector and weazlbear struggling amidst a river. "Your love is still recorded here. As I said, your choice in the pike over bow was a good one. That pike," she gestured faintly at Tamtcha's own weapon, "would have rendered me poor service today... limited me to but one toss across the Barriers."

"Ho-la." A respectful grin answered her. "You did well with the golden arrows."

Gratitude raced fleetingly across the younger's face, but their collective struggle was far from done, and May'r had not been summoned by the Winds' follies. She waved towards Kahl's patient form, sparing a reassuring glance for Anzund. She asked Tamtcha, "Should we all not hear his tale?"

Most people that comment would have startled, and that abrupt return to duty would have engendered an aching fatigue. But then most people were not Chatu protectors... even fewer were kownbearers. Tamtcha looked at her daughter-to-be and knew with pride, that she wore the kownband upon Her Plain of Tomorrow for both skill and judgment... and that she wore it well.

Tamtcha gathered Anzund's wearying figure close and drew everyone back to the cold fire ring. Anzund took strength from the arm that stayed about her waist even as they sat and forced herself to sit up a bit taller. May'r arranged her bow comfortably across her lap and leaned forward. Kahl's golden gaze met Tamtcha's as his arm dangled over an up-raised knee, then at a rueful lift of her brow, the Once-Eldest as Kownbearer pointed to the fire ring and called his death-vision back for inspection.

"It began on the edges of the Great Sea Cliffs." Images grew amidst smoky tendrils of purple. "The winds thrashed waters of darkest grey and threw the foam so high that it sprayed my face, making me taste that strange brine even atop those heights.

"I turned at the shrilling sound of our scout's flute... I turned west. And beyond the rise and dip of the blonde grassranges I saw the windriders of our Yesterday's Chatu. They came, trotting their ponies in good time — to save their beasts for battles to come. They were most from the Northern Gate and many wore the Tryad's own kownband from their time among Today. All wore the protector's tigereyes about their head, at least. There were also those from the G'nia, versed in the and Pachin mountain skirmishes against Nyor's thieves. Others were from the southern sea shores of Nana and the pirate defenses. But most were from our own place... well-versed in our Plains' wars with Nyor caravans and the mercenary Storm folk."

His somber gaze lifted from the swirling pictures within the fire ring, and Tamtcha saw reflections of those massing troops in the pupils of his eyes. "They ride dressed as May'r, in plainskins and weapons ready. They ride to cry bloodfeud and blasphemy, for the Three Plains of the Barrier Winds have been violated.

"We ride against Nyor's Choir Leader... the Dirktur and his demons."

Tamtcha felt the ice of deathdread slither down her spine. The Dirktur had been an empty, unfulfilled appointment among the Choir Leaders thought all the Shamyn Memories. That there was now that Chosen Leader meant some awesome power of life and destruction had intervened. If the Dirktur had been appointed, then the end of Today was being summoned. He could still the Winds, blight the earth and bring an awful new purpose to the living — a purpose of servitude to the White Light's Power... to the Wielder of the Storm's Eye... to himself.

"The Chatu assembled and stretched across the rise of the Ranges. Together we faced east to see the blackness of foul lightening streak out and fracture the sky.

"I stood and watched, my pony's head bent to my shoulder. I could feel her fear trembling even as I felt my own quivering in my belly.

"Until I was no longer standing among the grasses, but it was as if I stood above where the lightening had flashed. I looked down into the great Sanctuary of the dreadful Choir.

"The inner vault stretched high in thin, towering arches which made a circle of thirteen. And in each of the Heights, a single, black-cowled figure — a Leader — stood with hands folded in pious concentration. Those unwavering gazes were focused below on the wheels and wheels of lightsingers."

Anzund stiffened abruptly. Tamtcha's arm tightened, but neither interrupted. In the fire ring, pictures of those three circles of lightsingers rose... the circle of those seated within those kneeling within those standing. Their arms reached above towards the shadow-cloaked Leaders.

Centered above, there were crystal shimmers... curtains of colorless light flaming, flickering wildly in a mist. The shimmering unfolded like petals of a rose only to disappear into mists of flashing, painfully white light. The ground shook and the arching pillars trembled. Dust fell from stony buttresses while all the time the frenzied dances of white light swelled again... swelled and then began to whirl, creating a whiteness without the misty edges this time. Then the center grew to the black of blackness, and the outer whirlwinds of white hid the voiceless lightsingers swaying below.

The Sanctuary shook and blocks of granite and marble began to loosen. Still the Leaders' glazed stares commanded. Still their utter concentration wove the singers' mindlights... and the blackness cracked forth in a wicked slash that opened the roof to a sky of white-whiteness.

A pole — long, thin and clean in shape like polished rock — hung in the tiers above the lightsingers. It was an ivory slenderness hanging in a black emptiness. A mere sheet of the white wind separated the thirteen Leaders from that awful, mystical lightwand. Like a whip's crack, another jagged rasp of black lightening swept down and this one hit the tip of the wand.

The black, obsidian glass of pure volcanic rage... destruction frozen by the coldness of powers and hates came to top the wand. An ebony, translucent crystal upon a white shaft, it turned slowly in its whirling cradle.

And one blonde-haired man stepped forward from the Leaders. His hand alone dared to extend into the spinning winds. His grey eyes glazed with the ambition... and for the third and last time the blackness struck as he claimed his prize

The Sanctuary fell, pedestals crumbling as the other Leaders shrieked with their abrupt return to awareness and death. Light spirals dissolved as walls tumbled and floors heaved. Fires spewed forth to claim the lightsingers. And the One stood, transformed as his hand grasped that wand of power. Pupils dilated and eyes became sheer reflections of that crystal... globes of glossy, glossy black. Skin whitened like the staff, cold from lifelessness and yet ivory sleek from inhuman strength. Blonde hair became black and slick, ash white at the temples.

His gaze lifted, reflecting starless voids of midnight, and malice rang as the hand shook the staff high. The Sanctuary fell — and the Dirktur prepared for a New Age of Reign to begin.

Kahl blinked, shaking himself abruptly as if to cast off the tainted brush of the madman's mindtouch. His nostrils thinned with a sharp breath. The fire ring emptied of those chaotic images, and he glanced about at his companions. "Somehow... this man has summoned the Eye of the Storm — wrested it from the Storm folk's own magicians and bound it to the Choir's Lightwand." Kahl nodded at Anzund, "Even as you have somehow come to yield the Crystal of Essence, Anzund... I'd truly come to believe none of the shamyn still knew where it was hidden."

:Amidst the Ghosts of the Three Barriers... it has always been hidden by the windsouls themselves.:

"Ahh... that explains why the Barriers released the trollincraigs with such relative ease."

"The Essence?" May'r looked at her slender, mother-to-be with a rather startled respect, "Can you wield such a lightwand yourself?!"

Tamtcha grinned with a poorly hidden chuckle. "Anzund, Daughter, is not the least among sorcerers. She is the Shamyn's Apprentice, no less."

"And a lightsinger?!"

Anzund nodded, glancing with a silent reproach at Tamtcha's mocking. She knew her protector too had once underestimated a wayward traveler's abilities due to meager appearances. But then Kahl suddenly reclaimed her attention with that somber stare of his.

"You are she, are you not? The one the Winds have whispered of?"

Anzund looked baffled, half-shaking her head. :I don't

understand what you're speaking of.:

"It's said beyond the Barriers, that the Hand of the Lightsinger shall deliver the Plains. It shall be by your hand... will it not? By your powers and light?" He threw off his frown and his nod was decisive. "Yie, we will follow you, Anzund, if you will have us. We shall add our skill as Yesterday's protectors with the exuberance of Tomorrow's... add us to the Chatu of Tamtcha's bands. And perhaps you may find a way to carve this Choir Foe into teary drops of crystal dust!"

Tamtcha sensed the cold clench in the tautening muscles of her beloved. She said nothing, merely strengthening her encircling arm. Anzund found the courage to nod.

Chapter Nineteen

"Our most major problem is also our best strength," Tamtcha declared quietly. But all eyes followed as Anzund rose from her seat at the end of the map table. It was Tamtcha's voice, but tonight it was Anzund's words that she spoke for the others.

The lantern lights glittered inside the tent and in the silence of the pause, the kownbearers could hear the winds of the range grasses outside. They were divided by the length of the table, their favored runners standing behind them. Tamtcha with Zharin and Baij with a protector of Rake Venom — Anzund could not place the name tonight — sat to her right. May'r and Kahl with featureless shadows of windsouls attending were to her left. Anzund leaned forward, sketching the outlines on the map of the eastern ranges. Attention shifted to the ridge she indicated as Tamtcha spoke.

"Two days out of the Pachins lies the Ring Bluff. The grasses are barely hoof high to the east. Above on the western ridge, they're perhaps waist high."

"Yie, spring has thawed enough for a good growth," Baij supplied. Kahl nodded in agreement.

"If we meet the Dirktur there, we have a direct confrontation. Force against force. No raiding, no ambushes — very little hiding."

May'r's blonde head shook faintly. "No cover for my archers. After the first volley, they'll know we line the grasses above."

Baij grunted. "It's not the sort of fighting we do best."

"But it is the sort of thing we've been preparing for all winter," Tamtcha reminded them. Her right hand was raised slightly to sign that these words came from herself.

"Yours of Today have... not those of Yesterday," Kahl amended.

Tamtcha touched her heart with a slight bow of apology. Everyone turned back to Anzund. Her expression was steady, unreadable. Tamtcha continued for her.

"As I said, location is our weakest point. But — from the height of the ridge I can see nearly all of you. It means I can counter whatever magics the Dirktur throws at us. It means May'r's people have the visibility to use those wheelbows of theirs, and some measure of surprise for that first round of arrows, at least. Also, the wall of the Ring Bluff itself means your riders, Kahl, can practice the raiding and retreating that their range experience has trained them for. I can make it seem as dense in anyone's vision of Tomorrow as it is in Today. Your protectors can literally disappear in-and-out of it as if it were a hedge of grasses. Neither the Dirktur nor his followers — even those he might summon from your Plain — will be able to see to follow you."

Kahl's narrowed gaze marked his thoughts; this idea had merit to it.

"As for your wintering forces, Baij — they will have to do what they've been training for."

"Hold and divide the main force."

"More than that," Tamtcha inserted for herself. "They must either slice a wedge in to reach the Dirktur..."

"Relying on my folk to keep you from being cut off completely," Kahl saw.

"...or if he is too far in the rear, cause so much havoc that he must show himself in trying to muster more strength for his demons?" Baij nodded

"Yie," Tamtcha acknowledged, again for Anzund, "I must eventually be able to see him. Otherwise all that the shamyn and the Winds have lent me is in vain."

May'r frowned, pointing to the map's ridge again. "But from that vantage site you'll be visible to him -- almost from the beginning."

Anzund shrugged. Tamtcha scowled. "It's a necessary risk. He'll not be fighting with common foot soldiers nor even with Storm folk. From what Kahl saw, too much of Nyor's city was sent to ruin when he claimed his staff. And seizing the Eye of the Storm from those northern folk, surely sent their land into equal turmoil. So he will be relying on his powers and on Chaos' evil kin. None of us can stand against that demonic troop without the Winds' magics. I must be able to see you. And eventually, the Dirktur must be able to see me too. Or how else can we be matched off?

"Which is also why we must meet them quickly — at the Ring Bluff. Right now I may have some small advantage with my staff and the Winds' Blessings. I understand the Shamyn Powers... have been studying since before Harvest Markt to wield our Crystal. But if we delay...? Well, the longer it takes to confront this Dirktur, the greater his abilities to use his new staff becomes. It's certain that he doesn't yet know how to do all that he might be capable of doing. Delay and he learns. Delay and he weakens the Winds' Barriers by the day... for he steals their strength with his ambitions. And so he steals our strength to stand united."

"He is destroying the very fiber of the Plains," Kahl muttered. "He is a madman."

"We are all mad this spring," Baij observed grimly. "To willing ride into the slaying and horrors, we must be."

"It is necessary." May'r said it without the innocence of youth. She knew only too well how this onslaught would steal that naïveté from every Chatu child born in the next year... if any were left to be born.

Anzund hung her head a moment, and the others fell silent. Then, shoulders straightening, she glanced at Tamtcha who nodded. Grey eyes slipped from one member of the Chatu's council to another, and Tamtcha merely watched, knowing that shimmering mindvoice touched each. Then that gaze came to her. An audible sigh passed her lips, echoing Anzund's own fatigue, and the Shamyn's Apprentice touched Tamtcha's shoulder lightly before leaving the tent. There was yet more Dreaming to be done.

For an endless moment, the rustle of the tent's flap hung in the stillness. Then Tamtcha folded her hands together on the table before her, accepting her own role of leadership again. Being the Youngest as Kownbearer of the Northern Gate, Baij had become the commander of their village protectors and of those who had joined them for this fight. But their Eldest as Kownbearer was now Tamtcha, and because this war would be waged upon her Plain, she had become coordinator for all — those from Today, Yesterday and Tomorrow. They followed Anzund with hope and desperation, but the execution of the impossible... that had become Tamtcha's responsibility.

"We shall meet again in three days," Tamtcha reminded them, her voice strong in its quietness. "At that point, we should all be amassed at the Ring Bluff, and we should have a good two days to complete preparations for the Dirktur's force. Anzund will have a better idea of who or what we fight. Kahl's scouts will be actively harassing them... and hopefully drawing them south of the trade road to our chosen ground."

"And if we are not succeeding, we'll know that by our next meeting as well," Kahl noted.

"Which will still leave us enough time to shift north, if we must."

Baij nodded, pointing just west of the Ring Bluff on their map. "Our burrows here will not be fully supplied until the fourth day. But we've enough there now that we can make a northern shift without immediate delays for rations. Although we would need to rely on your aid in the transporting, Kahl."

A wry grunt and a smile came from the old protector. "As long as we don't have to eat it, we'll have no trouble moving the bulk for you, my friend."

Amusement rippled among them all. Yet underneath lay the unspoken concern. Neither May'r's nor Kahl's people were bound by mortal food constraints, but they were reliant upon Anzund's powers and the Winds' strength for nourishment... and they comprised more than half of this Chatu fighting force.

Tamtcha stirred slightly and frowned, her gaze fixed on May'r. She gestured at the map, asking, "Should we need to move north, how will your archers fair?"

A faint shake of the head answered her. Then May'r reached out to angle the map a bit more towards herself for a closer scrutiny. "The ground seems more broken and the grasses shorter. We might be able to find cover down nearer to the battle, but our range would be severely limited by that. We can only shoot at what we can see, Kownmother."

"And it would of course be better if you could see over the heads of our own riders," Tamtcha concluded tiredly.

"It would help if there were more details here," May'r admitted. "Our experience is too limited. I have only a vague idea of what this terrain really offers us."

"Could you spare a scout or two to ride with Kahl's protectors?" Tamtcha prompted suddenly, glancing at her once-foster father for his agreement. "Your protectors know that Ridge from Sea Cliff to Nana, Kahl. Her people could combine that with their own observations — bring her back a better picture for positioning."

"Certainly, we'll carry them. We could also take a few ahead with us to our appointed place. They could return to you and give you a detailed overview before Anzund arrived, maybe?"

May'r scowled, and Tamtcha wearily recognized how familiar that look of concentration was... she'd seen it in her own wall mirror a thousand times. May'r shrugged cautiously, "It may be possible."

A dark brow lifted and Tamtcha pressed, "What worries you?"

"We — I mean Us of Tomorrow — need Anzund's focus to find these places of Today. We seem to... slide aside from routes and destinations when we set out to explore for ourselves. As a group, it's clear we must follow her to the appointed site. There is no certain way for us to come unless she is first there to call us."

"Unescorted your scouts would fail," Kahl acknowledged gently, "but the Winds will permit our joint efforts, Kowndaughter. You need have no fears here. Your forebearers will not lose you."

All of them accepted his knowledge as fact and May'r nodded quickly. "How many shall I send you then?"

"A dozen," Tamtcha intervened. "Have them travel in pairs. And two should go with Kahl's harassing band of scouts. Your protectors may recognize powers from your own Plain, May'r, that Kahl's folks would miss."

"Fair enough."

Kahl agreed as well.

Baij heaved a sigh, and they all turned to him. He waved his interruption aside. "I was merely regretting my folks' inability to use their bowstrings. I know there are a few that could have added to your party's strength in taunting these devils south, Kahl."

"It is a pity," Tamtcha allowed, briefly remembering Anzund's demonstration of how simply Today's archers could have their arrows turned in mid-air and sent reeling back upon themselves, in flames no less. "But I have faith in May'r's protectors." She smiled sympathetically at May'r's own ironic conditions, "And you are undoubtedly regretting the lack of ponies."

May'r admitted it with a tilt of her head and a shrug.

"Well, you can't blame the poor creatures," Kahl grunted. "Why should they cantor into this mess? To them there's no reasoning, only joy in running. My folk merely have the foolish ones that grew overly attached to us during our times on Today."

"Or were those favored ponies more intelligent?" Tamtcha muttered, remembering Dancer's own quickness compared to other beasts she'd had. "Perhaps they grasp a little of the importance in this fight — after spending so much time with your in past needs, hmm?"

"Huh — would be a nice thought. I don't enjoy dragging them back into the mayhem after they've earned the peace. Be comforting to think they were choosing the path themselves." Then he scoffed at himself with a grunt, "Philosophy... gets us nowhere. We stray from our tasks, my friends."

Tamtcha tapped a finger against her lips, thinking he looked wearier than she'd ever seen him. Baij and May'r looked no better. She straightened, shaking her head a bit. "No, we stray from nothing. We are simply done for the evening... unless any of you have further concerns?"

Heads shook and stools creaked with shifting bodies. Tamtcha nodded, "All right then, in three days at sundown, we shall assemble on the Ridge. In the meantime, Kahl's and May'r's scouts shall be busy. I'll leave it to each of you to tell our kownbearers of our plans."

"And Anzund?" Baij queried.

"She will ride with us. Her Dreamings will take neither her nor myself away from this mortal time again. Our shamyn to the south will tend to that sort of journeying, if it is still required. Nahessa will tell Anzund, if there is news."

Relief spread through the others like a wind swept through grasses. Surprise turned to chagrin as Tamtcha realized how much they each needed the reassurance that Anzund's powers wouldn't turn her into some ghostly waif in this venture. They believed in those powers, but magic was such a very intangible, mystical thing, and right now, everybody needed a bit of physical reality to hope in. It suddenly made sense to her why the shamyn had endowed one of their daughters with their cumulative powers... and why they had sent that Chosen One out into battle with the protectors rather than commanding from their distant fires; when people were afraid, they needed the Winds' physical presence... even if those people were ruling kownbearers.

>>> <<<

Tamtcha eventually followed Anzund from the command tent, leaving that sprawling structure for Baij to use in briefing his commanding kownbearers. She paused beneath the gloomy black overcast of the night clouds. Above, only a patch or two of real sky broke through with its starry velvet. A few of the southern kownbearers appeared in response to Baij's summons, and she nodded briefly to them before forcing herself to move away. If she stayed, she knew all too well how she would become enmeshed in details again, and right now she had neither need nor interest in reviewing; Baij was perfectly capable of it, and she would be more supportive of his authority — and her own — if she left him alone to do his work.

She pushed her way into the smaller tent she shared with Anzund, and with faint surprise saw her partner seated cross-legged amidst a triad of candles. Eyes closed, the blonde woman sat in the stillness of concentration and prayer. But the dividing curtain had not been hung for privacy and her body was quite solid, lacking any of the translucence of a Dreaming.

:It's all right,: Anzund's soft mindtouch reached out to her. :I'm nearly finished.:

Absently Tamtcha nodded, then took herself off to their bed chamber at the side. The beginnings of a storm rumbled outside, and she glanced at the heavy felt tenting as the first patter of raindrops came. Undoubtedly the entire camp was going to be soaked for the next two days of their march, but it did mean that water would be in good supply.

:Shall I turn the lamps down out here?:

Tamtcha looked to find Anzund standing with the curtain half-pulled back. "No, please. Turn them out."

A rueful and very tired kind of grin answered her.

"I'm hoping Baij will be plagued with midnight disasters tonight and not myself."

:If you say so.:

Tamtcha shut her eyes with an inner groan and climbed into bed, shivering slightly from the roughness and chill of the bedding. She sincerely hoped tonight would mean sleep. After the past few days of first the Dreamquest, then the organizing and the march, she desperately needed a final good sleep. Last night she had arranged with Baij that she handle the problems so as to allow him that needed relief and time with his Honored One, Shel — one of the healers among them. Tonight, however, was Baij's turn to answer for Tamtcha. Both knew that the coming days would not allow them opportunity for another such break, but then their field chiefs were good people and the difficulties were dwindling rapidly; their chain of command was functioning well, better than either of them had even hoped, and as should be happening, she was being freed for the more difficult challenges of guess-and-double-guess.

The quiet sounds of Anzund changing into her nightshirt and the rain outside mingled, bringing Tamtcha a needed bit of peace. Her lover climbed in beside her, rolling over to press her back into Tamtcha, and the Kownbearer moved, scooping her near and spooning her naked body protectively about Anzund's smaller form.

:You're still wearing your kownband, Beloved.:

"I'm not moving again."

:Shall I take it off for you?:

"That means I'd have to let you go, have you squirm around to face me and then snuggle in again when you're done. Leave it be."

:You'll have a headache in the morning.:

"I have a headache now. And it's not from my band. It's never from the band."

:Yie... but what would you be without those three tigereyes, I wonder.:

Tamtcha frowned, eyes still stubbornly closed. "Why are you so awake?"

:I don't have the ability to simply shut the world out and drop off to sleep so quickly, Love. That's your gift, not mine.:

With an aggrieved sigh, Tamtcha hugged her. "Sorry, I didn't mean to snap."

:You have every right to. Should I go into the other half of the tent?:

"I'd rather have you here, even awake." A comforting hand squeezed Tamtcha's. "I suppose... I should take advantage of the fact that you really are here and awake."

:I'm awake. It doesn't mean I'm not exhausted.:

"I didn't mean that... although it is a nice idea." But it a mumbled, half-unconscious observation.

:You have questions, then?:

"Huh... just two." Anzund yawned and Tamtcha gathered her a bit nearer. "How was the Dreaming?"

:Blessedly short and uneventful. Our shamyn are say nothing's changed. It seems we'll meet on or near the Ridge as you suggested.:

It hadn't been much of a suggestion, Tamtcha mused. After their encounter with the trollincraig and the obvious problems they were all going to have if Anzund couldn't stay to high ground, it had become a fairly self-evident solution.

:You said two questions, not one?:

"Yie," she buried her face sleepily in Anzund's warm hair, liking the faint smells of candle spice and dreaming scents. "It's been bothering me... this Dirktur's fighting force, these demonfolk."

Anzund absorbed the coziness and nested feeling of Tamtcha's hold. Her eyes shut and she let the tension drain from her. Despite the seriousness of the concerns, the safety of the here-and-now was blissfully — finally — setting in.

"Why does he attack so soon, if these are all the forces he can muster? Why doesn't he wait until his followers in Nyor and at least some of the Storm Folk regroup and join him?"

It was Anzund's turn to sigh, and discouraged, her grey eyes opened again. :You don't understand the strength of his power, Love. This is no small caravan he leads.:

"I understand the size and power of his group. What I don't understand is how he can sustain that large a force without succumbing to exhaustion himself? Especially since he creates each of them to begin with."

:Quite simply... he is that strong.:

Tamtcha gave a grunt, vaguely feeling frustration stir. "From his own strength? Or from the strength of the crystal staff he wields?"

:He and the staff are the same, Tamtcha. Destroy either and the powers... the demon forces will break, and he will be gone:

"Have you just told me that I need to look after that damned staff of yours as well as yourself?"

A slender smile curled her lips and Anzund sighed again, this time with a very contented sort of feeling. She pulled Tamtcha's hand up between her breasts. It felt nice to be reminded of her protector's love.

"I guess you have." Tamtcha smiled herself at the wordless mindlight that softly danced about behind her closed lids. It didn't really matter, considering how close Anzund kept the thing... it was a bony lump beneath their sleeping pallet even now. "One more question."

:Hmm.:

"Tell me you weren't exaggerating, when you said your skills still lend you an advantage over him."

:That's not a question.:

"Were you exaggerating?"

:That's a question... no, I wasn't. I am a lightsinger and the Shamyn's Apprentice. I do have the powers to match him.:

"Then you watch over your own staff."

:Will you still watch over me?:

"Shamyn's Apprentice, Honored Provider or fleeing Acolyte... when have I not watched over you, my Dearest? Now, it's time for sleep." Tamtcha's arms tightened reassuringly. She felt Anzund's conscious effort to relax. Then as Anzund's breathing grew deeper, Tamtcha's own eyes opened. She stared into the tent's dimness at those three little lamp flames, and unbidden her own doubts rose again.

Anzund stirred suddenly, rolling over to face Tamtcha with sleepy grey eyes. A quirk of a smile chided the protector. : Is it my turn to tell you to sleep?:

Tamtcha smiled herself. Anzund sighed, a wistful despair coloring her mindvoice, :Then let me at least take this thing off of you.:

Obediently, Tamtcha bent nearer as Anzund's fingers reached around to loosen the kownband and braid. She found herself nuzzling into the softness of Anzund's nightshirt, breathing deep the scents of worn lint and sweetened musk.

:Hold still—:

She made some incoherent sound of protest and gathered her lover up against her own long length, burying her face against Anzund's neck. The skin tasted faintly of salt, and she found she liked the contrast of cloth teasing her.

Anzund sighed, discarding the kownband finally. Her fingers sank into the thick, dark hair — lifting it to her face as she stretched and arched into Tamtcha's grasp.

Tamtcha nibbled at the edges of the nightshirt's collar, then at the folds where the fabric bunched. She felt Anzund's hands molding to her scalp, sliding through her hair possessively, as she wound her way down through the paths of folds and tucks until she felt the rising press of that fine breast. Her tongue dampened the cloth, caressing the roundness beneath. Then as the nipple hardened she took it into her mouth, suckling shirt and all in a languid, sated taking... less intent on arousing and so content with their closeness.

Anzund's arms closed around her shoulders in a cherishing hug. A hand stroked the hair back from Tamtcha's face, fingers light against her neck. A mindtouch sprinkled with the palest of peach and translucent sea greens slipped into her, asking, :Be inside me?:

"Hmmm...," a hand moved to comply. Fingers searched tenderly into that lovely place of heat and folds. The dampness was faint, like the humid touch of summer before a rain. Tamtcha paused. "You're not ready, my Love."

:Please... just to be near, to be with me.:

She took two fingers into her mouth, wetting them for

her, and then carefully she entered. Anzund arched, wrapping a leg around Tamtcha's hip. Then, as her lover bore down, Tamtcha felt the tightness open and reclasp, fitting to her fingers as warm, rising dough might. Anzund relaxed, melting into her. The moist fabric of the shirt brushed against her lips. With a sigh of her own, Tamtcha accepted the gift.

Her fingers curled forward, gently seeking that special place of a slightly roughened texture.

:No...,: Anzund's hand closed on her shoulder. :Simply be part of me...?:

"Yie — however you want me." They stayed that way, curled close and dozing together for a long time. Thunders clashed beyond their small haven. Someone slipped into the outer room quietly, rifling through the map chest before leaving. A pony was led by to somewhere, its hooves going plop and then thwuck in the thickening mud.

Tamtcha found herself in a dream on a plain of soft, cropped meadowgrass — beneath a sky of blue. The air was hot like summer; it smelled of a faint trace of dust. The sun made her feel golden from her skin down to inside her very soul. She looked at the earth she sat upon. The sparse pale grass was summer grass, with a trace of straw stiffness to it. She put her palms to the ground beside her. The soil seemed welcoming, and her fingers curled deep. The sun had sown its touch here too, and the earth was warm... warm down as far as her slender grasp could reach. She gripped hard, feeling herself held fast in return.

She lifted her chin high, letting the sun wash over her. Breezes rose and tugged at her hair. Without a kownband to bind, her hair blew free... branching wide. Until suddenly she saw she was no longer sitting upon the ground, but she had become a proud, strong- limbed tree who stood beneath that golden sun. Limbs spread wide, with thickly clustered leaves riffling in the wind. And below, deeply set roots planted her in the ground. The precious earth fit 'round her, holding her sound... its nurturing waters forever hers to reach.

A lighter breeze stirred through her leaves... she woke feeling Anzund's drowsy sigh brush her forehead. Her lover lent her a gentle kiss atop her head, and then stiffened suddenly instead of rolling away.

"Wait," Tamtcha murmured, fingers still burrowed deep. Together they moved then, and Anzund smiled faintly at her tender care. Tamtcha slipped low, tongue seeking the soft depths of her fingers. Anzund stretched to meet her moist stroking, and stiffness yielded. Still Tamtcha bathed her with her tongue. Fingers slid in and out caressingly... aching came to verge on the edges of fire.

A hand reached down to her, and Tamtcha halted. Anzund's faint shake of her head was explanation enough. Sleep beckoned to both of them as Tamtcha moved up to gather her lover into her arms again. Anzund nestled into her shoulder, sighing, then turned Tamtcha's face to hers for a last kiss. :I want you to know, my fine protector... I feel very loved.:

Tamtcha smiled, nuzzling back into Anzund's golden hair.

:Very much loved.:

"Because you are."

Chapter Twenty

The sky was moonless, but clear. It was as if a carpet of rich velvet spread above, displaying starry gems in an array of solitaires and clusters. The sight of night on the Barren Ranges never ceased to amaze Tamtcha, and even tonight as she and Kahl stood at the edge of the Ring Bluff with that enemy encampment on the eastern horizon, the majesty of the night touched her. For the barest of moments she forgot the battle that would begin, and with a breath of the sweet spring grasses, she merely remembered that these lands were precious.

A blackness in the east drew her attention, and realities reasserted themselves. She scowled at the thickening tendrils that crept across the stars. The inky void began to smother those small lights with a heartless regard to beauty.

"Can you make out what that is, Kahl?"

He turned from surveying their own camp behind them. The lines of his face grew stony. "His evil mist. The Dirktur sends it scouting for us — and to smother us with fear. In a few hours, it will eclipse every star in the sky."

"And come dawn?"

"He will dispense with the darkness, but it will not be a

sunrise as we know it. This mass will turn white... a blanket waste of Chaos. The light is sends will be harsh and shadowless."

To the north, beyond Kahl's shoulder a somethingness sparkled and then faltered. Tamtcha stepped around her once-foster father. He followed her gaze. The fiery lights burst forth once more, and this time they did not vanish. Sheets of liquid color danced, leaping and dazzling in hues of first blues then greens, then vibrant oranges. Curtains of each prism color came and went — living lights of the Winds reaching for the cherished stars.

"Perhaps the Dirktur will find his mists matched," Tamtcha murmured. Kahl answered with a grim but satisfied smile.

:What are those?:

Tamtcha glanced around as Anzund approached, a dim figure stepping from the night. Her love took her hand and squeezed before Anzund nodded back to that brilliance. :It looks as if the Barriers themselves dance upon the land.:

"Perhaps they do," Tamtcha mused, remembering the place Anzund had shown her in their Dreamings. "We call them the Windlights. They are brighter some nights than others, but seldom have I seen them so commanding. They come from the north, always there where you see them now. They are north of the Ranges... beyond even the Storm Folk's Tundra. The Storm say they mark the Top of the World."

:They're such wondrous lightsongs!:

"Can you tell then if they come to fight the Choir's mist?"

Startled, Anzund asked quickly, :What mist?:

"The blackness — there."

Kahl growled, a deep rumble akin to a weazlbear's ire. "He would chase hope from our hearts even as he does the light from the sky."

The Shamyn's Apprentice glanced above, then moved to study that distant quarry in the basin below. Her gaze grew hard and cold. The demonkind had lit no fires; they had no need of any. It was only their leader and a scant few human followers that required such luxuries, and those were undoubtedly sheltered by larger tents and boasting braziers. So their camp was a sprawling, still mass of black shapes. Even at this distance, the unnatural void was visible — a kind of denser nothing in the midst of the Ranges' night cloak. Without turning, Anzund knew the Chatu's camp would be quiet with faint, small glows of shielded campfires and neatly laid rows of tents. Shadowy figures of protectors would be slipping between fires, tending ponies and weapons — fighting the waiting before retiring for a sleepless rest. The posts would be changing soon, and there would be some increase in the camp's activity as the new scouts exchanged positions with the old.

But in no way, Anzund knew, would that eerie, inhuman — absolute emptiness! — ever lay claim to their camp. What she saw below was lifelessness, complete and total lifelessness.

"I still don't understand what he hopes to rule when this is over," Tamtcha mumbled. "Devastation — rubble like he left in Nyor? What use has he for such ruin? What use is that to anyone?!"

"If he succeeds, death will be his servant, not master, my kowndaughter. He will have an innumerable number of lifetimes to reconstruct the Chaos into whatever he likes."

:As long as his sustenance is fed by bloods and terror,: Anzund amended for her protector. But her grey eyes never left the lower land's camp.

Kahl suddenly glanced at Tamtcha. "May'r comes. Don't leap out of your boots."

Chagrined, Tamtcha nodded. The last time poor May'r had appeared out of Tomorrow — right beside Tamtcha — the protector had nearly tossed a knife through her daughter-to-be.

"Fair eve to you all." May'r placed a hand beneath her heart formally. Tamtcha noticed she had materialized a bit further from them then on earlier occasions.

"Kahl warned me," Tamtcha grinned. May'r blushed but was reassured. She came a bit nearer and Tamtcha noticed her attention fell to Anzund. Gently she tapped her beloved's shoulder and absently turning about, Anzund seemed surprised to find May'r had joined them. Concern swiftly replaced confusion.

"I'm not certain there's anything to be done," May'r began slowly, including both of the other kownbearers with a tentative look. "But there is a despair growing with all our people. I realize, I haven't seen the night before battle, so I've nothing to compare their fears to. Still, they have noticed the rising mist."

Tamtcha grew grim, noting that inkiness had already swallowed the entire eastern horizon.

"They grow uneasy from it, but there is more than that. They struggle with a frustration. They are feeling more and more helpless to defy the strangeness."

Kahl grunted, nodding. At Anzund's quick query, he shrugged. "It's to be expected. They're denied their music and dance."

Anzund looked appalled at the idea, and Tamtcha explained quietly, "The eve before a caravan raid, we play the finger flutes and use our pikes — instead of the log drums — for rhythms. We dance a dance of slow step, a ritual of mourning for those we may lose in the coming battle. Then the rite changes, and the rhythms grow faster — into a defiant challenge against the White Chaoses. It becomes our pledge to the Winds and to ourselves that we will protect the Today we cherish."

Shaking his head sadly, Kahl again gestured to that void of a camp. "So near to them, we dare not tonight. It'll only announce our number and strength. Usually we're further out, and the noise doesn't betray us as we stay upwind."

May'r clear eyes met her mother's steadily. "I would think they already know the strength of our force."

With a wry twist of her lips and a nod, Anzund admitted it.

"Roughly they do," Kahl amended. "But send out the flute notes and that black mist will come honing in like a pony to water. And once the Dirktur knows exactly where each bedpallet is placed, he'll not need to wait for dawn before sending his demons."

The bright curtain of the Windlights called to Anzund. She moved away from their small group, listening to that power of lightsong.

Tamtcha gestured to her with an open palm. The others turned to Anzund, understanding Tamtcha's words would be hers. "There is another way to thwart this black touch. A way of defiance, not silence. May'r is right. The Dirktur knows enough, we will expose nothing."

"If the mists don't find us," Kahl repeated, uncertain.

"The mists will not find us." Tamtcha's voice hardened with resolve as she felt the determination within Anzund grow. "It is time this Dirktur learns what he faces tomorrow. It is time to force him into arrogant foolishness or sheer panic. It is time he discovers the Shamyn's Apprentice is a lightsinger.

"Now go — tell our protectors and healers that it is time to dance."

Kahl and May'r faded away to do as bade. Tamtcha stayed and drew nearer her Honored One. "They will tell Baij and ours of Today as well. The three Plains will dance together tonight."

Anzund nodded. Their gazes both went to the demonkind.

"Are you sure about announcing yourself now? He may simply run."

:Even if he is a coward — which I doubt — given he claimed the staff and Eye of the Storm from the Chaoses — I'll not let him escape by retreating.:

"What will you do?"

:Encircle him. And his black mists will not claim the skies tonight — nor create the whiteness tomorrow. Let him fight us beneath the gold and blue of sunlight!:

Behind them the Chatu began their dance. The eerie luring wail of death's calling rode out upon the Winds. Below a sudden crack of the whitest lightening broke through the demon camp. A billow of black smoke mushroomed into the heavens, and curling — rolling west en masse it came.

Lightening struck again.

"Your staff?!" Tamtcha suddenly realized it must still be in their tent.

:I won't need it, not with the Chatu flute song and the Windlights to wield. Granted, the spell will last only a bit. He will find how to undo it before morning. But it will leave us without the mist and him without the time to retreat... he will learn uncertainty.:

The blackness was nearing, coming with all the force of a thunderhead. But the flute notes rang clear. The rhythmic clacks of pikes and bows rose in a steady guard to join the flutes.

Anzund stepped forward to the cliff's edge.

:Now!:

Her hands threw up a song of soaring, splaying sparks. Fanning — scattering upwards to star and outwards to each horizon, the glittering thickened until it edged the furthest lengths of that mighty bluff -- and then it spilled down and into the east, until a wall of gold dust surrounded the basin and the demon camp within.

The black mist rolled back into itself, then sent lightening bolts against that imprisoning ring. But Anzund's wrists flicked her palms out, and suddenly the Windlights themselves swept up to complete the wall.

In the center, the hateful mist shrank and coiled into a single column.

The Chatu's song changed, and the power in the flute and pike grew challenging. Anzund laughed and tipped her head back in sheer defiance, the Windlights about her rushing through her... and she loosed a final song.

A boom shook the earth. A star shattered in the night above. Fiery streams descended, caging in the demonfolk and Dirktur as those strands of golden light above joined with the Windlights around. Her blonde hair whipped and tore from its braid. Her hands stretched high. Anzund stood within that torrential wall and sang... her face aglow with life and power. And in that moment, she allowed herself to believe — truly believe! — that they would triumph.

>>> <<<

Dawn came swiftly with very little fanfare. The range grasses in the west were tall yet still too supple from the spring rains to clatter much. The warbling grass wrens were apparently elsewhere. Even the stomp and shuffle of the protectors' pony lines below seemed muted. But the sky was a cloudless blue, untainted by fog or smoke; and the kownbearers stood with the Shamyn's Apprentice, feeling the light of the early sun on their faces, and they were satisfied.

In the distance below, the black mire of the Dirktur's demon camp remained unchanged. At the foot of the Ring

Bluff, and only half-exposed amidst the clefts and rubble, Baij's force waited. Behind them, cloaked by the cliff itself were Kahl's greater numbers. Above, May'r's archers lay hidden in the taller grasses and stony crevices.

Anzund eyed her folk anxiously, aware of how vulnerable they were if one only knew behind which spells and rocks to look. She fingered the edge of her lavender headscarf as it tickled her nose; she couldn't quite seem to get the thing wrapped comfortably today. Sweat trickled down between her breasts, and she irritably gritted her teeth against her quaking nerves.

"Waiting is always the hardest," Tamtcha said softly, her words too low for the others to hear.

Anzund glanced at her gratefully, wondering how her beloved had known.

"The last hours are particularly wicked."

She could have smiled, if it weren't so awfully true.

"Why don't they come?!" May'r hissed. She wiped the moisture from her palms on her pale leathers, switching the golden bow back and forth between her hands. Its leather grip was already staining with the dampness.

"Patience," Baij murmured. But Anzund noticed how his thumb was wearing a shiny place into the reins he held. The two ponies behind them were equally alert, although quiet. Kahl shifted his stance a bit and recrossed his arms in the other direction.

"I hadn't thought to ask," May'r voice was calmer this time, still muffled by her headscarf. "But what happens if he doesn't challenge you today?"

Tamtcha's palm opened to indicate Anzund and then spoke herself, so that they all might hear. "He will challenge, if merely to test what powers my staff has against his."

"Yet if he withdrawls before defeated?"

"I'll follow him, unless I can not." Tamtcha didn't like the taste of those last words nor that brittle sharp mindlight in her head.

"In the latter case," Kahl muttered, "we meet again in the morning to continue the fight."

Baij slanted a wry eye to Yesterday's Kownbearer. "With a few midnight raids in between, if yours are up to matching my riders?"

With a trace of his younger arrogance, Kahl answered with a quick nod. "We'll keep up with you, my friend. This morning and later." Then the levity vanished, "As long as our Shamyn's Apprentice stands, we'll return with the Winds' prayer."

Baij too sobered. "Send those of mine back when you can, Kahl. We've too few trained for this frontal assault as it is."

Tamtcha let the words hang in silence. They each knew May'r and Kahl would return even if cut down, so long as Anzund could mark the place to return to and the Barrier Winds had the power to send them. Should something happen and Anzund died... or the Winds be depleted by the Dirktur himself... then those of Yesterday and Tomorrow would remain only as long as their wits and skills kept them in Today. Once struck down then, they would not be able to return to advise, to fight — or to be born.

Anzund prompted her and Tamtcha straightened a bit. "Anzund would remind you, Kahl, that anything slowing your return must be dealt with quickly. Get word to her as soon as possible. And you, May'r, if the Dirktur's spells even begin to injure any of yours in any way at all, don't wait to tell her!"

"I know," May'r nodded. "We all know."

"Especially yours," Kahl asserted with all the brusqueness of a concerned parent. "We want you each born whole."

May'r's grey eyes found Tamtcha's, and her voice was quiet as she amended, "First we must have a Plain to be born into."

You are your mothers' daughter, Tamtcha thought.

Anzund suddenly stepped forward, her lavender and indigo satins strikingly bright among the pale leathers of the others and the dullness of the Bluff. Her staff tipped and its crystal flashed as a sun's ray caught. Beyond, in the heart of that blackness, an answering bolt of whiteness leapt high.

"Essence to Eye," Tamtcha murmured. Anzund did not turn, but with the others she listened to that sing-song chanting tone... the one she knew so well from Nahessa. "The Eye beheld the shaping of Essence, and in the beholding both form and witness were born."

Anzund frowned behind her masking scarf, but said nothing despite the uncomfortable shuffle of her companions. She felt rather than heard Tamtcha return to them, and she wondered vaguely if the Kownbearer even remembered uttering the words. It did not reassure her at this moment to remember how tightly bound the two staffs were — how did one defeat an enemy that was indeed part of oneself? She suspected, it would not be done on the Plain of Today.

The Dirktur's camp began to break apart. At its edge, the inky blanket started to take on the shape of fighters, both mounted and afoot.

"Remember," Tamtcha muttered, "this Dirktur will gain strength with our blood. The demonkind may fall to pike and arrow, but their numbers will be renewed as his spells are. Do not leave the Bluff walls too far behind in a pursuit. It will only gain him advantage, not us.

"It's his death we seek — whether by surprising him on the field with a pike while he battles Anzund from afar... or by forcing him to face her here without his demons about him. It's his end we must see. Nothing else matters."

"Even if we need battle all spring," Kahl swore. "We will take him."

Then the others left Tamtcha and Anzund to watch that Dirktur's approach. Kahl and May'r dissolved into air and Baij with his pony marched for the descending trail back among the crevices, going to join their protectors. Below, the dark mass grew clearer in its figures, but Tamtcha didn't expect those forms to grow any more humanlike. Her throat felt dry. "Do you know what the shamyn meant to say to you?"

So she did hear herself, Anzund thought. :Yie... a cautioning for my task. Take heed of how I slay this Dirktur or both Essence and Eye with be destroyed with him.:

"And yourself as well."

:With all we know of the Plains.: Tamtcha said nothing to her at this. :I did speak with Nahessa before dawn.:

Tamtcha moved nearer, listening. Through the mask of her scarf, her gaze narrowed to a dangerous glint as she searched for that betraying white bolt again.

:These demonkind are all of Today's Plain—:

"The Choir never believed in another. Why would their

demons come from any other?"

:But… they are fitted with spells to kill Yesterday's windsouls. Kahl's folk will have to endure the dying, before their return to us. I only hope May'r's will be spared that.:

Frowning, Tamtcha murmured, "Forgive me the rash words. My temper grows short."

Anzund nodded understandingly. :You were right. Waiting is not easy.:

"So, did the Shamyn's Circle say this foe doesn't know how to use Tomorrow's spells? Or has he simply not guessed our archers are children-to-be?"

:Nahessa didn't know. Keep him busy enough, and he may not have time to figure it out either way.:"

"Yie… at least it will give May'r and hers a short stint of surprise."

:I only hope they use it effectively.:

"She will."

Below, that white bolt shot upwards again. Tamtcha noticed Anzund's staff didn't answer the challenge. Little need to, she thought sourly… on this barren ledge in bright colored satins, the Shamyn's Apprentice was only too visible. The lightening flashed again. "That's him then."

Anzund nodded. :His power signature.:

East and northeast, Tamtcha noted. "Sing to me if he veers much from that course."

Anzund nodded again. Beneath Kahl's and Baij's protections, Tamtcha and Zharin would lead a small band into the mayhem and try either to slay the Dirktur or break his staff before he rose to this cliff. If nothing else, they would force him to weave his spells faster and… hopefully… more ineffectively.

Tamtcha swung up into her saddle. Sundancer pawed the ground, ears forward and nostrils wide. But Tamtcha was less eager than her mount. Anzund's grey eyes turned to hers. The sparkle of lavender in those clear depths spoke of readiness. For a moment, they simply stared at one another… words lost.

Dancer snorted, sidestepping.

:Fair hunt to you, Kownbearer.:

The mindtouch was familiar within her and intimately gentle with its rose and blue; Tamtcha swallowed hard, eyes stinging. "Fair Wind, Lightsinger."

Dancer spun about, and they cantered off for the path.

The sun rose and dust began to lift from the soles of that demon force. The air took on the arid taste of late summer as the enemy's master absorbed the last drop of spring's renewal to bolster his powers. The dismal black and grey figures spread wide, crossing the basin in a swarm.

Tamtcha watched, standing on her saddle upon a stone – a still Dancer amidst the Bluff's shadows. When they passed the appointed place, her arms uncrossed and she lifted a hand in silent command. Baij and his most experienced filled in a front line, barely one-third the length of that descending, and went to meet them.

:He stays to the rear.:

Tamtcha nodded absently at that voice in her head. She signaled again, and half of Kahl's protectors, arrayed in smallish groups, trotted forward from the cliffs. This time, they ranged along the entire line of those approaching. They were armed with javelins for short range tossing as well as pikes, but unlike Baij's protectors, these lack the small, hard leather shields. Without the benefit of the winter's training, the things would have only been dangerously awkward. Instead, Kahl's folks were relying on the ponies' quickness and their pikes — they would circle in wide, strike and wheel out again, only to be replaced by reserves and thus forming near continuous waves of stinging skirmishes.

:Those anticipating Baij assemble in a tighter formation. The Dirktur still lags behind, centered.:

As she'd expected. Tamtcha only hoped the protectors were skilled enough not to be demolished in the initial clash. She hoped, too, that this Dirktur did not suspect the skill of May'r's archers.

She dropped to her saddle, and Zharin quickly reined in beside her, handing her the small shield that fit snugly to her forearm and the Winds Blessed pike. Tamtcha nodded grimly, eyes cast ahead as if she could see their quarry. "Right where we hoped. We'll cut in behind the south edge of those Baij engages and drive through... as planned."

In the pit of her stomach, Tamtcha suddenly felt something was wrong. Everything was looking too predictable. This Dirktur was either too arrogant of his power — and possibly rightly so — or else he had a poor head for strategy. She tried to remind herself that Choir politics and warfare were very different sorts of hunting... but she wasn't sure she believed it.

It began. The shrill keeling of Baij's warriors heralded the attack, ponies breaking into full gallop as May'r's archers loosened their strings. With a heavy whoosh the Dirktur's magics turned the arrows into flaming bolts, but Anzund had anticipated that with counter spells, and the fireballs only hurtled ahead on their course. The demons screamed as the fiery wave descended, and their lines broke. Baij's protectors struck in the chaos.

:Your south-side hole opens.:

"Now!" Tamtcha snapped and Zharin's dozen charged out — the best strike-and-dodge specialists in Today.

They fanned wide in a feign to join Baij then gathered, suddenly becoming a wedge and drove in behind the crazed sword-slaying figures. Pikes snaked out and slashed arms, separating limbs from weapons. Heavy blades rose in answer, chopping pike poles but jarring at the steel rod centers and rattling bones of protectors and demons alike. The sun glistened off silvers as maces swung high — scarves tore away with steel slashes, unsheathing gold stars in the tigereye bands — and magically the stones flashed and blinded.

Their enemies screeched as weapons turned aside. Chatu pikes lanced forward with the weight of pony and protector to drive through three at a time before dragging free again. Ponies shrieked as demon mounts and foot soldiers alike gouged hides with fanged jaws. Protectors sunk knives in black leather skins as teeth sought their own shins.

Hooves descended on the fallen scaly devils as bloodied claws sought to drag protectors from their saddles. Then a fiery hail was loosed again as May'r's archers sent a volley into those ahead of Tamtcha's group. The way cleared for another pony length, and they were moving forward once more.

They trampled, dodged and wheeled. Pikes twirling —

demons screamed as savage met savage and on both pony and ground, red blood turned black from heat and grime.

Tamtcha felt the sun grow suffocating and hot. Her soul hardened and she shrieked, her trilling challenge picked up by first Zharin and then the others. The Winds swept down from the upper bluffs and circled back at their call. The basin suddenly rang with the war cries as the Chatu behind heard and answered. And again the arrows flew with fire.

White bolts of thunder defied their rally. Tamtcha bared her teeth in feral greed, unmasked by the torn headscarf. Her keeling cry rose from the battle din, and Dancer lunged towards that wielder of lightening. Zharin shrieked and followed at their heels.

Pikes lowered and leveled. Ponies leapt the last meager demon bodies of defense, and the black-helmed victim turned in surprise just as the two spearheads took him.

This is wrong! Tamtcha thought again.

The body lifted from the lizard-like mount, doubling over as the pikes pushed him up and out into thin air. Then he was downed and pinioned to the ground.

The forces around them scattered suddenly. The air split with a boom and pellets of streaming fire descended. Demonkind and Chatu ponies bolted, screeching in the chaos. But the small group of protectors gathered about Tamtcha barely noticed. Reins in hand, Zharin stood beside Dancer with that black helmet in hand. Staring at that corpse, Tamtcha felt the raging impotence of failure take her.

There was no sign of that paste-white skin nor ebony hair. They had been misled. This human lackey was merely the Dirktur's pawn.

Repulsed, Zharin tossed away that deceiving helmet and nearly snarled as she uprooted their pikes from the imposter. Then abruptly, they all looked back towards the Bluff and the mayhem.

"Sweet Winds!" Tamtcha breathed in utter horror.

Above the cliff edge was smoldering with patches of fire and smoke. Below, an inferno raged, devouring demons and Chatu together. The great curtains of Windlight that Anzund had once called to challenge now leapt high to protect as they circled the scattered groups of Baij's riders. The maelstrom of terror descended again, and Tamtcha's gaze rose to the sky in disbelief.

A white serpent with black-edged scales and clawed, bat-like wings of onyx, hovered high over the upper plateau. Fangs of ebony — eyes of ebony shimmered in the sunlight... shimmered of hungry hate as it hissed flaming venom at its prey. Straddled on its shoulders sat a dark-robed figure that bandied a white staff. The black crystal at its end winked and spewed jagged bolts of lightening.

"How stupid could I be?!" Tamtcha swore. He, as they, had planned this — separate Anzund from the best of her forces by luring Tamtcha after an imposter, then confront the Shamyn's Apprentice alone. And if he could destroy the whole of her people in the process, the more power he would have to fight her with.

The upper range grasses were blazing with full fury now, and Tamtcha felt her stomach clench at the thought of May'r and her archers roasting in that death trap. But no, they would just retreat to Tomorrow's Plain, wouldn't they?!

The sky creature squealed as it paused so far above that barren ledge where Anzund stood, coiling and arching for another attack. Tamtcha blinked and then squinted. At the very edge of the Bluff... behind the Dirktur's beast, a pale figure rose to its feet. Silhouetted against the leaping flames, a bow lifted.

The sun flashed gold off of the Winds' bow. Her throat closed as Tamtcha recognized that woman of Tomorrow. Helplessly, her gaze flickered between May'r and Anzund. Fire rained down upon the Shamyn's Apprentice, dissolving into black streams of smoke before hitting — but pressing closer by the second. An arrow flew — a pure glint of gold.

The screech was deafening, and the creature reared back, wings flapping as the Winds' arrow pierced its scale armor. Lightening flashed after the attacker, but the Dirktur's staff found no target; May'r had already dissolved from Today.

Then the beast was falling, its massive fanged head pulling it downwards ever faster. Until abruptly, it vanished.

Tamtcha's harsh gaze swept the bluffs. Somewhere — there! A bare pony length from Anzund, he stood. He held the staff before him with both hands, like a guardian's scepter. Tamtcha saw Anzund lift the Crystal of Essence in response.

Each swung and staffs clashed — the Plain of Today shook and Dancer reared.

Lavender-silver and white exploded upon the ledge. In a star burst of power the two figures were eclipsed, and in one horrendous moment, they both disappeared.

Tamtcha brought Dancer down as the ground tremor subsided. She held her breath, scanning that distant cliff in dread. It barely registered that the flames and demons had vanished — that the Windlights were gone. With a heart wrenching fear, she whipped Dancer around and sped for the ridge trail.

Anzund blinked and rounded, tucking and sweeping a leg back as hands came from behind to choke her. They went down in a tumble and separated. She was on her feet and backing away before he moved. But the man made no attempt to rise. Instead he settled on one knee, leaning an elbow heavily on the other as he regained his breath. She thought he must be insane to try any sort of physical attack. He laughed, a self-mocking sound that spawned only stronger suspicions from Anzund. She put a few more wary paces between them, and his inhumanly white face cracked a grotesque smile at her caution.

She stared at him, controlling her revulsion with effort. His brow lifted, mocking her this time. But he was accustomed to the reaction of fools by now. The change in his face merely underlined the change in his power; he now wielded the Eye of the Storm and all could see that merely by seeing him.

Anzund felt her lip curl, sneering. She too remembered where his face sprang from. She had no respect for that corruption and evil.

Both were reflected in his inhuman countenance. His skin had grown whiter than bleached flour... the white of a sun-bleached skull upon the Barren Ranges. His teeth were like his sky creature's scales, white with black edgings. His mouth when he smiled was as tar black as his hair. He had neither eyebrows nor lashes, only shiny ebony marbles where eyes should have been.

He waved at her dismissively, calling attention to the black fingernails and skin folds on his pasty hands. "You aren't even a Kownbearer — not even a warrior! Didn't they bother to grace you with that sacred trinket? Or did they feel one of my slaves' children would only defile a holy tigereye?"

Anzund was aware of the laced pressure of her provider's band beneath her satin sleeve. She was grateful to know there were such gross limitations to his general knowledge; it meant the Shamyn's Circle still withstood his spying scrutiny. Perhaps it also meant he had an equal amount yet to learn about his staff and the Eye.

"Do you know where we are?"

She said nothing, and he gestured to the thin whisper of a line behind him. "That light is everything — existence. The Winds' creations, your dear Chatu would call it."

She still gave him no response. His eyes narrowed in speculation. But then she didn't expect him to truly believe in her ignorance. He knew she was wielder of staff and Essence.

"We're on the Edge of Mortality." He rose, feigning stiffness. He began a slow- gazed perusal of their surroundings. "This greyness — it's sheer nothingness."

Anzund didn't need his lecture. She had half-suspected their clash would send them here... here where neither black-and-white assumptions nor the colorful complexities of reality yet existed. This was the realm of both Essence and Eye. This was the not-yet-place of existence, a point where Essence had not yet shaped form and the Eye had nothing yet to witness. Here both forces floated while beyond in that little line of light, the Winds waited to create the Plains; but first the Eye and Essence must generate existence here or there would be nothing for the Winds to create with.

An odd space of non-space... Anzund thought with sudden weariness. The greyness was all-encompassing and depressing in its emptiness. She wished for at least a little of the blueness in Dreamings... a little of something, even a faint lightsong.

The Dirktur turned back to her at that very moment, and suddenly he grinned. "Ahh — she speaks at last! But to whom, I wonder? There are none here, save us. No power, save that of your soul's essence."

Anzund glanced to either side of herself at his wave. She saw the fluttering edges of the Windlights flanking her. She eyed him with suspicion, wondering if he really understood what he had just said. If he did, then why had he acknowledged her lightsongs as present? Why acknowledge any of her powers as here?

"And you may have a pretty soul, my shamyn child, but you are not stronger than I. Here where your Chatu crones cannot reach you to help you, you're going to have to rely upon yourself... a rather petite self, unfortunately." His smile became a leer, "In the end I shall win. I shall break you with my bare hands, if nothing else. Then I will return — sole proprietor of Eye and Essence. And you... I won't even allow enough Essence of you to remain for you to become a memory!"

A quiet feeling of strength, a calm assurance, began to fill her heart. Anzund realized this man truly did not understand the things he dealt with. He was mistakenly defining her with her human attributes. Whether consciously or unconsciously, he assumed she was Lightsinger and Shamyn's Apprentice... and in his boasting, he also evidenced at least a small doubt about his own understanding of her powers. His assumptions and doubts manifested her identity — and powers — as she was familiar with them. By his mere perception of her, he could have changed her abilities... he was, after all, the Eye.

But then he grasped neither the powers nor limitations of that role. His second mistaken assumption voiced that ignorance: He could not actually harm her with his bare hands... he could not directly do anything to her really, he was the Eye. He was the observer, not the actor.

Whereas she, she was the shaper... the Essence.

He saw the subtle smile lift her lips, and his own faltered. She threw up her arms, and his face reflected amazement — fear at the whooshing answer of the Windlights behind her.

He muttered an incantation of something, but he held doubt.

Her smile grew. She pointed her command, and the Windlights ringed him. He stuttered another phrase, and she laughed, closing her palms to ensnare him, creating a translucent egg shell of lightsong around him. He touched his prison, then pounded it with fists. The singing prisms glittered with silver-laced laughter, and she knew — in this moment, the

Plains were safe from this beast.

Then suddenly the greyness about them seemed to vibrate. She looked towards that distant line of existence curiously, wondering what disturbance could be so far reaching.

His scream brought her back around. Shuddering, writhing upon his knees, his blackened eyes widened in terror at some invisible tormentor.

Tamtcha dropped her reins and stood before the two staffs. Driven into the rock of the ledge, they each stood upright. The white shaft and black crystal of the Dirktur's exuded waves of shimmering heat. The indigoes and amethyst staff of Anzund's stood with lightsongs flickering about its top. Between the two an arch of silver-laced blue hung suspended, not quite touching either the Crystal of Essence or the Eye of the Storm, although it clearly bound the stones together.

Of the Shamyn's Apprentice and the Dirktur, there was no sign. There was not even a footprint in the dust.

Tamtcha stood there, believing in her heart of hearts that it couldn't end with her beloved's death. The wisps of lightsong hovering about the Crystal of Essence held her gaze for the longest moment. It couldn't sing without Anzund being... somewhere. Tamtcha refused to believe it could.

But if that staff attested to Anzund's continued life, then so did the other warn that the Dirktur still lived.

Tamtcha stepped forward. Her task had always been to destroy either that staff or the Dirktur before he shattered everything dear to her.

She reached out slowly, fingers tingling from those odd, steaming waves of heat and energy. Her courage almost failed, and she had to pause to wipe the sweat from her hand. She was not a shaman.

There was no one else.

Tamtcha stepped nearer and took hold of that ivory pole. She felt a flush of energy rush though her, spreading up her arms and consuming her down to the soles of her feet. With a wrenching tug, the thing came away from the ground and the arch binding it to Anzund's staff sizzled out.

The ivory grew warm, humming and beginning to quiver

within her grasp. She clutched it more tightly, turning her face away as the shimmering became a painfully bright glow. But the light intensified, and she had to shut her eyes.

As quickly as it had begun, it was over. Tamtcha ventured to look again, and in surprise opened her grasp and stared at the staff laying across her palms. The shaft was the pliant kind of sapling wood used to build lodges. The black crystal had shrunk to the size of a kownband's stone... and like a kownband, it reflected the burnished star of a tigereye.

A faint aura of gold dust grew around the tigereye. She righted the staff, and a tiny trail of lavender and indigo began to swirl amidst the lightsongs on Anzund's neighboring staff. Tendrils grew from both auras, reaching for one another. When they met, they entwined like thinly braided rope, and gradually the coloring shifted until it was a fine, sparkling coil of blue and rose with just the faintest etchings of gold and topaz.

"Buy the Winds' Blessings...," Tamtcha felt her resolve waiver. A Chatu soulstone? Dare she destroy such a sacred emblem on such a powerful tool?

She wished Kahl had not disappeared with those flames — or that Nahessa were nearer. She needed the knowledges she simply did not have.

Then she would wait until she had them. She reached for Anzund's staff, thinking to keep both Eye and Essence safely guarded until she had acquired answers, but at her touch the world exploded into a prism of light.

The Dirktur sobbed and within his shell collapsed on all fours. Hatred stared at Anzund from that face, but blood ran from his eyes, not tears... and although the rest of him had not changed, those eyes had. They were again the eyes of a mortal man with iris and pupil, white about the sides. He opened his black mouth and snarled a curse. More blood spilled from his lips, a macabre redness against that white, white skin.

The greyness flickered and vanished. Rich ambers and earth browns awakened in whirling patterns. The line of existence thickened, seeming closer. Anzund looked beyond the Dirktur's cage and saw a bewildered figure slowly turning about. She realized then what had happened.

:Stay where you are, Beloved.:

Tamtcha spun to face her, shock melting into hope.

:Don't say anything.: Anzund felt the dangers press forward. Explanations could so easily alter perceptions, and the Plains were too fragile for such carelessness. :I have to finish dealing with him. But now that you're here, it will go quickly. I need you to simply watch... watch and believe in what I can do.:

That crooked, heart-meltingly fond smile answered her, and she couldn't help but respond. She knew there was nothing Tamtcha believed she could fail at. And that quite simply gave Anzund the power to vanish the Dirktur from all existence, forever... because, after all, what the Eye beholds becomes the shape of Essence.

>>> <<<

Tamtcha blinked at the brightness. Above the sun suggested it was still mid-day. The Winds had cooled the aridness, however, and with the banishment of the Dirktur, spring had returned.

:Do you like what I did with your trust?: Anzund murmured, a soft joy of pale greens dancing about her mindvoice. She slipped beneath Tamtcha's arm and turned her confused lover to face the basin. :Do you?:

Tamtcha stared in wonder. Then quite suddenly her eyes filled with tears, and she let them come. She didn't care, because it was indeed beautiful.

Gone were the black-sooted ravages of the fires. Gone were the bloodied carcasses of dead demons and lost friends. Not a sign of broken pike nor lost sword remained. Instead, the valley stretched wide in a rolling blanket of wild flowers and grassy stalks. Grass wrens chattered and their bickering carried high on the Winds. The sky reflected an endless, blue-blueness without that haunting foreboding of the past year's Dreamings.

Anzund guided her around again, and Tamtcha nearly laughed. The Ring Bluff hosted line upon line of pony, protector, archer... healer. From the nether regions, with Tamtcha's immutable belief in her, Anzund had restored each protector and pony of Today... and she had brought those of Tomorrow and Yesterday back to know their victory.

:You approve, then?:

Tamtcha looked down at her, nodding, and then noticed, "The staffs... they're gone?"

:They've been returned to the Winds for safe keeping.:

Their eyes met, Tamtcha searching those grey depths for what she could not find.

:I am still Shamyn's Apprentice. But the other — the Essence is self- contained again. Essence and Eye no longer need either of us.: She found she could not read that gold scrutiny, and she grew worried as she once had after a battle of trollincraigs. :Does it... disappoint you? That I have changed so much?:

Tamtcha lips quirked and then the indulgent smile broke free. "May we live long enough to know how silly our insecurities are...."

:Sassy!: Anzund grabbed her behind the neck with one hand and pulled her down for a kiss.

A roaring cheer broke them apart, bringing their attention back to the Chatu surrounding them. Pikes and javelins, bows and arrow shafts — all clapped together high over heads as Baij led them with a whooping holler of victory and approval. Anzund blushed and buried her face against Tamtcha for a moment. But when she ventured a glance up, she noticed her protector wore an unabashed, delighted — overwhelmed grin, and she decided it couldn't be too bad.

Tamtcha cupped her hand against her chest in heartwish and recognition of everything everyone had given. They cheered all the louder. Her gaze fell to Kahl; he nodded his silent pride of his once-foster daughter. She saw May'r next to him and felt herself crying again. There would be time now, for memories, for cherishing... and for Anzund.

Her perceptions narrowed then, until there was nothing but Anzund. Her fingers curled beneath Anzund's chin, and her Honored One faced her readily. That bemused expression faded into a tender, reassuring smile.

:You are still my First and only Protector.:

Tamtcha kissed her thoroughly, and neither of them noticed this time when the Chatu's jubilant outcry redoubled.

* * *

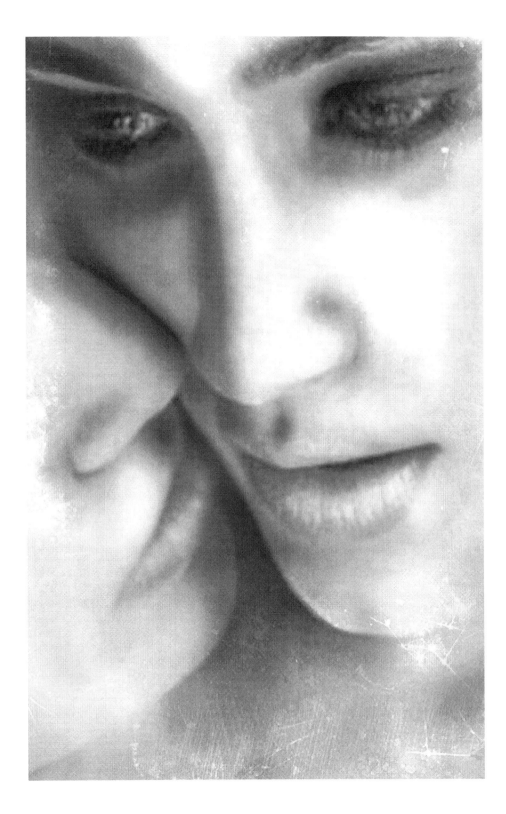

Death, Sweet Suitor Mine

This is an autobiographical short story that Chris Anne wrote and that was published as a stand-alone volume after her death, at her request. This story is the only piece in this collection that was ever previously released to the public and even at the eleventh hour, it was almost pulled.

I do not know if any of Chris Anne's close friends or family have ever read this story. I know only that she didn't want to talk with anyone about it. She wrote it for her and for her readers to understand her. It wasn't the last thing she wrote before she died but it was meant to be a parting gift.

Chris Anne lived with cancer for more than a decade. She knew there would never be a cure, only remissions, and resurgences, time passing, new symptoms, elements of her life changing. What was this like? To live with death every day. To dance with the truth... not dance around it.

For every person, life with cancer is different and no one can tell a universal story of what it does to a person's life on the short term or in the long term, whether they survive it or not. But for Chris Anne, living with death was like this. It was like living with a suitor who was sometimes quite welcome and sometimes not.

Everyone who knew Chris Anne, misses her. We miss her sharp intelligence, her unwavering acceptance, her creative mind that seemed overflowing at any given moment with new and incredible ideas. I feel so very grateful that the one thing we don't have to miss, are her words.

I can't," I murmured. "I made a promise."

Her hand stilled, and I ached. Every muscle I had moaned in betrayal, clenching now... almost bringing me to climax so denied me mere moments before.

I groaned and rolled into her, helpless yet torn.

Devon smiled then. I could feel it in the way her cheek moved against mine. Like a kitten, innocent and unaware, I wanted to deny that pledge... deny that thin voice inside. I wanted to rub my cheek against hers, enfold myself into the silken length of her, and forget.

But I had no innocence to hide within. Beguiled and half-consciously, I had sought this... or at least, I had been guilty of ignoring those flickering flames of warning in the beginning. Or how else had the bonfire leapt to be?

"Please," I begged, even as my mouth pressed against hers. "I can't."

I tried and just barely broke our kiss. But somehow I couldn't abandon her more than that, and I found myself open-mouthed and hungry... biting her shoulder. Her laughter was a low throaty sound. I squeezed my eyes shut, yet still I clung.

"Can't or won't?" Devon challenged. Her tongue teased, slipping into my ear.

I jerked away in a spasm of reality and reflex. I hated anyone near my ears. The vulnerability of it always twisted my stomach into terrified knots.

Devon sighed. She drew back a little, looking down at me with a mixture of fondness and exasperation.

I swallowed. The motion hurt; a pain I deserved. Naked and imprisoned within her arms, it was a battle to grasp at coherent thought... how could I draw another's image in mind?

Carina and me... even after knowing she saw the seduction Devon planned for me, I had promised not to leave.

"She'll understand."

I blinked. Devon's dark eyes turned gentle as she watched me in my confusion. I always forgot how easily she discerned what I thought.

"She will," and her voice was as tender as her hands upon my skin. My arms cooled as she stroked them. The sweaty dew of our loving had already drenched the sheets. "She more than half expects it."

"No," I whispered hoarsely. "She fears you, but she still trusts me."

A crooked smile appeared. There was a sad sort of kindness in it.

The moonlight streamed in through the cracks of the venetian blinds, and Devon glowed plainly within the beauty of those solver strands.

"No," I repeated, "Carina does still trust me."

"But you're not denying she'll understand." Her tone was

pitched low and the words were not spoken as a question, but as a teacher's patient litany.

My body trembled beneath hers.

Her smile deepened, her gaze caressing the line of my brow, the bridge of my nose in a way that spoke of what could come. And I thought of Carina with failing resolve. I knew it was true; Carina would understand... but would she forgive?

"Yes, she will. She'll be angry, but not forever. I promise you." Almost reverently, the back of Devon's hand brushed against my face. Her lips descended slowly — so very slowly — to hover against my own. Her breath felt warm as she added, "My sweet lover... trust me."

I turned away, but her mouth only moved to claim the curving bone of my cheek. This time she wandered upwards, her tongue lingering along the downy edge of my eyelid.

"I have never lied to you." She didn't pause but nibble higher. "When have I ever lied to you?"

"Never," I gasped. Yet shame made me strain away from her... seeking the chilly dampness of the pillowcase in some vain hope of escape.

"And how long have I been here beside you? Waiting?" Her fingers played upon my breast, awakening a helpless fire. "How long?"

I groaned and put my hand over hers to stop the tortuous begging of my body. But she didn't need an answer. We both remembered the day we met so long ago. Only I hadn't recognized her... Hadn't understood her presence in my life until mere weeks ago.

"More than two years we have between us. And I've waited, haven't I? For you. Waited until the degree was finished."

I wanted to cry at that... at the frustration and helplessness of that now fruitless climb. It had taken so long.

I remembered suddenly, I had almost lost Carina in that fight.

"Waited until your book was finished. The sweet hours we all spent as you read, reweaving, polishing that book. Have you forgotten?'

The sob choked in my throat. Carina had welcomed Devon and the quiet interludes of escape from my duller work;

those calm respites Devon had brought had been gifts to both of us. But in those days, neither Carina nor I had recognized the inevitable path Devon was drawing me along.

"Tell me why the waiting should not be done?" Devon breathed softly into my ear, creating tremors of agonizing desire this time. "Why should I wait now, Lover Mine? Why should we—?

My chest hurt, and I gasped for air — for some faint breath of sanity

"Are you suddenly afraid of me?"

"No — of myself."

That stopped her. She took my face between her hands and forced me to look up. Her quizzical frown reminded me; I'd never seen her unsure of anything.

"Are you afraid of how it will be with me? Afraid of us?"

I shook my head, her hands still holding me beneath her study. I realized vaguely that her eyes were more sable-black than brown. The moonlight created sparkles like stars in her gaze. The edges of iris and pupil blurred in that combination of sable and star dust.

Then gradually, the perplexed expression faded, and she began to nod. It was as if she had reached inside me and found an answer, despite the fact that I could not explain my heart's duplicity.

Her mouth grew into a gentler smile, a bare softening at the corners of her lips. But I felt the tension begin to leave me. The desire eased, melting into the night's depths like a sigh into the breeze. Her fingertips combed aside the shaggy hair over my eyes; I felt as if she had just placed a kiss there, although she had not moved.

"Are you still afraid of living, Little One?"

She said it, and I knew it must be true.

"After touching so many lives in so few years, I'd thought you'd learned more."

Awkwardly, I managed some sort of nod, then a shrug. "I find I understand by listening, but..."

Devon nodded again, finishing what I could not say. "Understanding is not quite the same as living."

Then she leaned forward and did kiss my forehead. It was a gesture of farewell. My heart panicked and I found myself reaching for her. She stopped me simply, a palm upon my wrist.

"Now it is my turn to say no." Her smile gentled the solemn tone of her words. Regret mingled with the stars in her eyes. "I find, after all, that I do wish you to be a bit older."

And then suddenly she was gone.

>>> <<<

The morning sun pushed in through the windows. Tears blinded me as the yellow light turned silver along the column of the IV-pole beside my bed. The sounds of the hospital's morning shift began to creep in under the door.

Determinedly, I mastered the tears and grief. I would not cry. There were people to reassure... books to plot.

But she hadn't taken the pain with her, merely added her loss to it. It still hurt to breathe... to simply be awake. I looked at the tubing attached to me; the slow drip of the IV-bag boded ill for the day's length. There were going to be too many hours; too many hours for thinking with too little energy to do anything else. The absolute weariness was overwhelming, and I felt the tears wetting my face. Sharp pain struck in my chest, a despairing reminder that my lungs didn't know how to breath and sob at the same time. It was going to take time before my body learned to function again. In a frighteningly clear moment, I realized what Devon's leaving actually meant. And I knew she was right — living could be so very terrifying.

>>> <<<

I shrugged a bit as I climbed out of the car, hoisting the cumbersome strap of my briefcase into a more secure nest on my shoulder. Door locked, I turned to face the torrent of the rain beyond the roofed edge of the carport and drew on the hood of my canvas jacket. It was spring, and though the neighbors had been grumbling about weather, I still found myself smiling and enjoying the dampness as it scented the air... the rhythms of the splashes upon the pavement. Today it all seemed the sweeter, since my teaching was done for a bit — mid-term grades had been filed and the university quieted with the onset of the semester break. Even the fact that it was the second anniversary of Carina's leaving hadn't been able to change my mood.

It was the sort of day that should begin something special, I thought, then smiled at myself. So often now I caught myself thinking such things about each day. Still... perhaps a new novel?

Sit with a cup of tea, a fire warming the hearth, Grandmother's quilt warming me, and yes... a new adventure might just begin to take shape.

That faint smile lingered on my lips while I began the irascible task of tracking down my apartment keys in the outer pockets of my briefcase. I consciously kept my home and office keys separate now. Each thing with it's own place with it's own time.... I had finally learned the beauty of the immediate. In turn, that appreciation had gifted me with more strength and clarity in dealing with the daily minutia of the university; it left me with more to give the students themselves.

I glanced up at movement in the flowering bush, glimpsing the tail feathers of a small bird I'd startled. Then from the corner of my eye, I caught a shape stepping forward through the rain. I froze, not quite able to reconcile the unexpected with the moment.

From the edge of the sidewalk, Devon approached. Dark hair, unruly and straggly even when drenched... the brown suede of her jacket darkened like cocoa in the downpour. She shrugged awkwardly, pushing her hands into her jeans pockets.

Then suddenly I was smiling for her, and a slow, deep rooted joy began to bloom in my chest. Her dark eyes began to sparkle. A crooked grin appeared. Without a hint of arrogance, the tenderness of her hesitancy melted into the quiet confidence I had known so well.

"We can be just as slow as you like." Her voice was so soft, it barley lifted above the rain's spatter.

"Slow and sweet... like the summer's breezes?" I was still smiling.

"No last minute surprises this time. I promise."

I found I trusted her word. With a single brow lifting, I tilted my head and inquired, "So certain of me?"

"Yes," her low, rich murmur made my soul tingle, "I

am."

Yes, I thought... and knew she had every right to be certain — that I wanted her to be. I nodded towards the stairway to my door.

"A cozy quilt by the fire?"

"With clover honey in the tea."

I nodded, and she went to climb the steps in front of me.

* * *

Made in United States
Troutdale, OR
06/09/2024

20360674R10146